It all happened in a flash. A small car, coming just a trifle too fast up the greasy street, braked to avoid a prowling cat, skidded, swung round at right angles and mounted the pavement. The two men leapt for safety—Scales rather clumsily, tripping and sprawling in the gutter. Drury, who was on the inside, made a quick backward spring, neat as an acrobat's, just not far enough. The bumper caught him behind the knee and flung him shoulder-first through the plate-glass window of a milliner's shop.

When Scales had scrambled to his feet, the car was half-way through the window, and Drury, very white and his face bleeding, was extricating himself from the splintered glass, with his left arm clutched in his right hand.

"Oh, my God!" said Drury. He staggered up against the car, and between his fingers the bright blood spurted like a fountain.

DRURY WILL DIE BEFORE THIS STORY IS DONE, AND JOHN SCALES WILL BE HIS KILLER. SINCE SCALES HASN'T ARRANGED THE ACCIDENT, WHAT INGENIOUS MEANS *HAS* HE USED . . . AND WHY WON'T ANYONE, NOT EVEN SCOTLAND YARD, KNOW HE DID IT?

SIX AGAINST THE YARD

In which

Margery Allingham
Anthony Berkeley
Freeman Wills Crofts
Father Ronald Knox
Dorothy L. Sayers
Russell Thorndike

Commit the Crime of Murder which

Ex-Superintendent Cornish, C.I.D.

is called upon to solve

BERKLEY BOOKS, NEW YORK

This Berkley book contains the complete
text of the original hardcover edition.
It has been completely reset in a typeface
designed for easy reading and was printed
from new film.

SIX AGAINST THE YARD

A Berkley Book / published by arrangement with
Harold Ober Associates, Inc.

PRINTING HISTORY
Selwyn & Blount edition / August 1948
Berkley edition / October 1989

ISBN: 0-425-11778-2

A BERKLEY BOOK® TM 757,375
Berkley Books are published by The Berkley Publishing Group,
200 Madison Avenue, New York, New York 10016.
The name "BERKLEY" and the "B" logo
are trademarks belonging to Berkley Publishing Corporation.

PRINTED IN THE UNITED STATES OF AMERICA

10 9 8 7 6 5 4 3 2 1

CONTENTS

Margery Allingham

IT DIDN'T
WORK OUT

THIS IS A confession. I want to tell the whole truth and to explain how it happened.

In the first place my name is not Margery Allingham. I was born Margaret Hawkins, and later on, when I went on the stage, I changed it to Polly Oliver. I don't suppose you remember the name now, but your fathers might, although I don't know . . . it's no good me pretending.

I was clever and I had looks when I was younger, but I was never what you might call a top-liner, not like Louie. It's really because of her that I'm confessing at all. The fair boy, who looked too young to be a policeman when he took his hat off, didn't suspect me. I don't think anybody did, not even the coroner, and there was a shrewd old man if ever I saw one.

I suppose you would say that I've got clean away with it, but I want to tell about it because of Louie. After all, she was the main cause of it. If it hadn't been for her, poor old girl, I certainly shouldn't have ever brought myself to stretch out my hand and——

But I'm coming to that.

Louie and I were pals, not like girls on the stage are nowadays. I'm not saying anything against them, but they're not the women we used to be. Little bits of rubbish they look to me, as they come in and out of my house. They don't look like actresses. That was one thing about me and Louie. In the old days—I'm talking about thirty or forty years ago—if you saw us a mile off you'd know we were in the profession, with our white boots and our bits of fluff, and the boys running along behind.

We met in burlesque. I was in the chorus, and she had a little part: nothing much, you know, but she used to come on in front of us girls and say, "Here we are, boys!" I can see her now, her figure pinched in and her tights glistening, and her bright yellow curls, which were always real—more than mine were, I don't mind telling you—bobbing up and down as she moved.

Even then she had that spirit—"verve" we called it then, and "pep" they call it now—which made her name for her afterwards. Louie Lester: you've all known it since your cradles, you've all heard your fathers talk about her and most of you have seen her. She went on the halls in nineteen hundred, and she still headed the bill in nineteen-eighteen, at least, up North.

I remember her best in the early days when she was making her name. *Grandpapa Has Done It Again, Jonah Likes a Little Bit of Pink, Forget It and Kiss Me Again*—Lorn wrote all those songs for her and she ought to have married him. You must remember the act? First there'd be the little twiddly bit from the orchestra, then the red curtains'd go up, and there'd be the "Town Hall" set with the piano and the potted palms, and Lorn himself in the early days sitting there playing. The house'd be clapping by this time, and then the silver curtains that she travelled with would part over the archway centreback and out she'd come, all twelve stone of her, silk stockings, petti-coats, white skin, and eyes so blue they made the sap-phires Jorkins gave her look like bits of glass, all twinkling and shaking, and giving off great waves of life like a dynamo going all out.

They used to say she never had a voice, but she had. It

was tuneful, and it filled the hall. She hadn't any fancy notes, but she put the stuff over. And she never tired. They could shout for her again and again and she'd still give them a chorus and lead 'em over the difficult bits like kids at a singing class.

They loved her and she loved them. Her turn was like a reunion.

I haven't described her now—I don't suppose there's any need to—but since you probably remember her when she was stouter and noisier, although she never lost her spirit, I may as well tell you how I saw her, and how I always think of her.

She was tall and fair, with blue eyes and a wide mouth, and a figure that was fine and strong and very human, and she radiated affection. I think myself that was her great gift. You felt she loved you, everybody did; taxi-drivers, people in shops, the orchestra, the house itself, they all sat up and preened themselves when she smiled because it was a personal smile, if you understand me, meant for you and genuine because she liked you. It made her what she was and it kept her there for a long time.

I'm telling you all this because I want you to understand why I did what I did do and where I made my mistake, my terrible mistake.

She met him when she was at the top of her career. There were thousands of men she could have married, men with money, men who could have given her something. Or there was Lorn, if she wanted somebody to take care of. Lorn would have died for her—did die for her, when you come to think of it. She didn't know he had consumption and that theatre up at—but it was pulled down a long time ago and there's no need to rub it in—was a death-trap, notoriously.

Still, that's not the point. As I say, she might have married anybody and she chose Frank. I don't know what he was. Something in the orchestra, in a little one-eyed town whose very name I've forgotten. I remember when she brought him round to my dressing-room—I was still in burlesque and only just out of the chorus. I looked at him and she said: "This is Frank Springer. We're going to be married," and I waited for her to wink at me, but she didn't.

I didn't like him even then, and her money hadn't gone to his head at that time. He was an undersized, flashy little object with so much side you wondered he didn't fall over. He could talk: I gave him that. There was nobody who could talk so well to people they didn't know. The first half-hour you were with him made you think you'd discovered something, but all the other half-hours were a disillusionment.

And she never saw through him. At least I don't suppose that's quite true. But she never saw right through him. It made me wild then, and it still makes me wild when I think of it. To everybody else in this blessed world that man was a four-flushing gasbag, a fellow with such an inferiority complex, as they say now, that his whole life was spent trying to boost himself up to himself, and the more weak and hopeless and inefficient he saw himself the wilder and more irritating his lies became.

I had enough of him on the first evening, and when I got her alone I began to laugh at him, and that was the first time I ever saw her "funny."

She wasn't angry, but a sort of obstinate look came into her face. I can't describe it and I won't try, but it was the one thing I never understood about her. He was the one subject on which we never were frank, and one is frank with pals one's known and worked with.

"You're not really going to marry him, duck?" I said at last. I was quite startled by this time.

"Oh, don't you like him?"

It was all she said, but there was an appeal in it. She had a way of doing that, of saying ordinary things and making you feel they were important.

"Yes, I do in a way," I said cautiously, because I didn't want to hurt her. "But you're not really going to marry him? Is he rich?"

"He hasn't got a brown," she said, and she sounded pleased and somehow complacent.

I was younger then and I hadn't learnt what I have now, so I'm afraid I said what I thought.

She walked out on me and in the morning when I tried to get hold of her she told the old girl to say she was out. That was the first row we ever had, and when I met her again it was after her big hit at the Oxford with *When Father Brings the Flowers Home With the Milk*. We had a drink together and she said she was married.

I said I was sorry for what I'd said about her husband— after all, when a man's a girl's husband it makes him somebody—and she warmed up to me again and I felt things weren't really so bad. I was out of a shop at the time and I saw her at the second house, and afterwards I met him again in the dressing-room.

He was horrible.

Even afterwards, when he was old and I knew him for what he was, I never really loathed him as much as I did at that first meeting after they were married. He took all the credit for her success, talked about her as though he'd made her, and he wore a diamond and chucked his weight about until it made everybody sick. There were a whole crowd of us there, her old friends and several new ones and a lot of smart people. They were nice to him because of her. But he took it all to himself and, although it was a jolly enough gathering, for the first time I saw her in that atmosphere which never deserted her all her life.

It's hard to describe it but it was a sort of pitying-polite atmosphere, almost as though she'd got a hump or a wooden leg, and everyone was too fond of her to let her know that they'd noticed it.

Lorn was sitting in a corner. His illness had got hold of him by then, but we didn't know it. Frank was rude to him and had the impudence to criticise the way he played one of his own songs, but he didn't say anything. He just sat there shivering and sipping his glass of the champagne somebody'd brought in.

He looked so miserable that I went over and joined him, and afterwards, when Louie had fixed up to go out to supper at some titled chap's house and Frank had invited himself and promised that she'd give a show there, announcing he'd accompany her himself, Lorn and I went off and had a meal together.

We went to a Sam Isaacs'—I don't know if it's still there—and had some fish and stout. I had a job to make Lorn eat; he just sat shivering. Neither of us mentioned Louie at first. I knew he was supposed to be in love with her, but then most people were. It became half habit, half affectation with every man who knew her, and I suppose Lorn knew her as well as anybody in the world.

He sat playing with his food, turning it over and over on his plate and looking at it as though he were not at all sure what it was.

"How d'you like him?" I said at last when every other topic had failed.

He put down his knife and fork and looked at me across the little table. Now that I've seen death in a man's eyes I know what it was that shocked me so in his expression.

"Oh, God, Polly!" he said. "Oh, God!"

"You eat your grub," I said, because I was flustered and embarrassed by him. "You mark my words, my lad, the time's coming when it's going to be easy for a respectable woman to get in and out of marriage. She'll get tired of him and pack up."

He looked at me earnestly. "Do you really believe that? Because if you do you're more of a perishing little fool than I thought you were."

"Isn't that what you think?" I said.

Neither of us was in the mood to get touchy with the other.

"No," he said, so quietly that I stared at him. I can see that pale face of his with the great high-bridged mournful nose and the wildish light eyes to this day. "No," he repeated. "She loves him, Polly. She loves that little squirt and she'll go on loving him until she breaks her heart or someone takes him by the back of his scrawny little neck and twists it round and round until his head falls off.''

His voice had risen on the words and one or two of the other people in the room—it was a quiet little place— looked round at us. I felt uncomfortable.

"You be quiet," I said. "Don't say such dreadful things. Frank's not the type to get done in and if he is it's not going to be by you or me."

I remember I choked over the last word, and he laughed and gave me a bit of bread and we cheered up after that. But I think of it now sometimes. It's twenty-five years ago. I didn't believe in the subconscious or fate then, and I don't now, really, but I did choke him and I did kill him.

Lorn took me home that night. I was digging at old Ma Villiers' just off the Streatham High. You certainly wouldn't remember her, but she was a fine old trouper and had been quite a queen of melodrama in her day. We sat round the fire in her kitchen and I can see her now standing on a swaying chair, ferreting about in the cupboard for some cinnamon for Lorn's cold.

After he had gone—and he went slowly, I remember, with heavy steps like an old man—she stood talking to me while I filled my hot-water bottle from the kettle on the stove. She was a great gaunt old woman—they don't all run to fat—with a shock of grey hair and a Shakespearean manner.

"There's death there," she said. "You won't see him again."

I was sharp with her.

"He's all right. He's only got a cold and he's fed up because his girl's married somebody else."

She looked at me sharply with her little black eyes.

" '*A scratch, a scratch, but marry 'tis enough,*' " she said. "You won't see him again."

She was right. I didn't. I never saw Lorn again. I heard about his death long afterwards from some people who were in the same bill as Louie up North when Lorn collapsed. They were nice people, a dancing act, who came into a burlesque show in which I was playing. We were calling them "revues" by that time. I remember the woman, a pretty little dark-haired thing, she was called Lola Darling, telling me with tears in her eyes of the awful row there had been back stage, Louie insisting that Lorn was not fit to go on and Frank bullying her and swearing first at her and then at Lorn, and finally Lorn staggering out to the piano and doing his little bit in the icy draught that would have killed an elephant, let alone a man half dead already. And then Lorn collapsing—dreadfully vivid she was, I dreamt of Lorn in pools of blood for nights afterwards—and being rushed off to hospital and dying there.

"Who's accompanying her now?" I said, and when she told me Frank was doing it himself I felt anxious.

He didn't smash her career at once. Nobody could have done that except Louie herself. But he chipped away at the foundations of it, if you understand what I mean. The rumour went round that the act was temperamental, but that didn't matter while she drew the houses.

I didn't see much of her then. She used to write to me sometimes, but her letters grew guarded. At first they were all about Frank. Frank did this, Frank did that, Frank was so clever, Frank won three thousand pounds at Doncaster on one race. But afterwards I didn't hear so much about Frank. She wrote generalities.

All the time, though, she was at the top of the bill, and when she did come to London her old songs went down just like they used to do, even if some of the new ones weren't so successful.

The rumour went around that Frank was jealous of Lorn's memory, and threw a tantrum every time she revived one of his songs.

He wrote one or two for her himself, but they were terrible, and even her personality couldn't put them over. I believe he gave her hell when that happened, but, of course, nobody knew about it then.

That was the beginning of the secret life she led, the life that turned her into two different people.

Meanwhile I was having my own adventures. My husband—did I say I had a husband?—died and left me the little bit of money he had, bless him. We never got on together but we never worried each other. I banked my money and went on working.

It was war time now and there was a lot of stuff going. I was so hurried I didn't have time to think. We were all so busy making merry in case we died to-morrow that I didn't realise I was getting older, but I was always a sound worker, reliable and steady, and the managers found me little bits so that I could live and save my spot of money.

It was nearing the end of the war that I first saw the new Louie. We hadn't set eyes upon one another for two years, and although there had been rumours about her, her extravagance, her wildness and the sort of crowd she was mixed up with, I was not prepared for the atmosphere I found when I went round to her dressing-room at the Palladium after my own little show at the Winter Garden was done.

I tapped on the door and the dresser opened it half an inch. It was a new woman. Old Gertie had got the sack, I heard afterwards. This new one was a beery old party with a face like a frightened hare. When she saw I wasn't going to hit her she opened the door a fraction or so wider.

"You can't come in," she said. "Miss Lester's resting."

"Resting?" I said. "What's she been doing? Swimming the channel?"

"Polly!" I heard Louie's voice from inside and I pushed the woman aside and went in.

She was lying on a couch, her make-up still on but standing out from her face as though the skin beneath it had shrunk. I hardly recognised her. She was heavier, older, and although still lovely there was an exhaustion, a weakness which was incredible when associated with Louie.

"Oh, Polly," she said, "oh, Polly . . ." and burst into tears.

This was so unlike her that I forgot myself entirely.

"Why, Duck," I said, "why, Duck, what's the matter?"

She wiped her tears away and looked nervously at the woman.

"You clear out, Auntie," I said. "Go and have a drink. I'll look after Miss Lester."

The old rabbit stood her ground.

"Mr. Springer said she wasn't to be left," she said.

"Mr. Springer said . . . !" I gaped at her. "You get out!" I said. "Gawd luv a policeman, what d'you think Miss Lester's going to do? Blow up? You get out. And if you meet Mr. Springer, you tell him I told you to."

"Oh, no, Polly, no." Louie put her hand to me and clutched my arm and I looked down at her hand and saw that her rings were paste. I can't tell you why, but that shocked me more than anything I've ever seen in all my life . . . yes, more than his face when——

But I'm coming to that later.

Finally the old woman went. I'm not so big, and the last part I ever played was a burlesque charwoman, but I usually get what I want when I set my mind to it.

When the door was closed behind her I locked it and turned to Louie.

"Are you ill?" I said.

"No. Only tired."

"How many shows have you done to-day?"

"One."

" 'Strewth!" I said. "What's the matter?"

She began to cry again.

"I don't know, Polly, I don't know. I'm all right when I'm on the stage, but afterwards I'm laid out. I used not to be like this always, did I, Polly? Did I?"

"Of course you didn't," I said. "You ought to go along to see a doctor."

"A doctor?" She laughed. "Frank wouldn't like me to do that."

I tried to point out to her that it wasn't much to do with

Frank, but that made her laugh. She wasn't bitter about him. She was very nice.

I was really frightened for her by this time and I remember sitting down at the foot of the couch and trying to get the trouble out of her.

But you're helpless, you know, you're so helpless when you're only fond of people and haven't any authority.

"How are things going?" I asked her.

She shot me a little sidelong frightened glance.

"All right," she said dully.

"What do you mean?—all right? How are bookings?"

"Oh, good. Good. Frank says they've never been so good. He's my manager now, you know."

"What! Old Tuppy gone?" I was shocked. Tuppy had put Louie on the map years before.

Her mouth twisted. "Tuppy was killed. He would join up—over age, you know. Killed the first day he landed. He's gone. Everybody's gone."

"Except Frank," I said rather pointedly.

She was up in arms at once.

"Frank's over age and his chest's weak. There isn't a doctor on earth who'd pass him."

I tried to be more cheerful.

"Well, if money's all right what are you worrying about? You're not losing your popularity."

She hesitated. "Money isn't too good. We—we have to live extravagantly, you know."

I looked down at her hands and she hid them behind her like a child.

"What do you mean, have to live extravagantly?"

"Oh, publicity," she said vaguely. "Frank—I—I mean, we've had a lot of betting losses too. I've never been in debt before, Polly, and now I'm getting tired. I get too tired to rehearse, and I've got to go on or I don't know where we'll be."

"D'you mean to say you haven't saved anything?" I said.

She shook her head. "Nothing. And now we're getting

old. I can feel it coming on. I'm still successful, but it's not going to last. I don't get the big hits I used to. The songs aren't so good and one can't go on for ever.''

"Look here," I said, "you've worked all your life and your husband's gone through your money and you're tired, my girl. You want a holiday. Give it up for a couple of months. Go down to the country.''

She closed her eyes. "I can't. I can't afford it. I haven't got anything I could sell, even. Besides, Frank wouldn't let me.''

I told her what I thought of Frank. It took me a long time and when I'd done she smiled at me.

"You're wrong," she said. "You've never understood Frank, Polly, and you never will. He just doesn't realise, that's all. He's so strong, so full of himself.''

I remember putting my hands on her shoulders and looking down into her face.

"Louie," I said, "you're sacrificing yourself for that man and he's not worth it. Now I'm going to say something that's going to hurt you, but I'm an old friend and you've got to take it. I've heard all sorts of tales about Frank. What about this little 'bit' on at the Empire?''

I could see the colour fade out of her face under the make-up.

"Oh, they're talking about it, are they?" she said. "Haven't you heard about the others too? You're a bit behindhand, you know, Polly.''

"Gawd!" I said, and I didn't get any further because there was an almighty row outside the door and Louie was on her feet immediately.

"Quick, let him in," she said. "We've had two barnies with the management already.''

He came in and I shall never forget him. You'd think that a mint of money spent on a man would at least make him fatter if it made him nothing else. A wizened little brick-red mannikin he looked, not even too clean.

He glanced round the room, ignoring me.

"Where's Eva? I told her not to leave you.''

"I sent her out," I said. "I wanted to talk to Louie."

He swung round and peered at me and she tugged my sleeve warningly.

"Miss Oliver, I did not want my wife disturbed."

Even his accent was wearing thin and, having decided that he had finished with me, I suppose, he returned to her.

"We're going on to a night-club," he said, "and if you're asked to sing, damn well sing, because it'll probably be your last chance with the shows you're putting up here."

"My God!" I said, and I began to tell him exactly where he got off.

He stopped me.

I've been on the stage all my life and I've never heard language like it. I could hear footsteps in the corridor outside and I can see Louie's face as she turned to him imploringly to this day.

"You're drunk," I said at last when I could get a word in.

But he wasn't. If he had been I could have forgiven him. He wasn't drunk. He didn't need drink. He was like it naturally.

"Louie, for God's sake leave him," I said.

That did it. The balloon went up. I've never had a row like it and I've been in a few. I remember turning to Louie in the middle of it.

"He's ruining you, old girl. And you've ruined him. He ought never to have had more than three pounds a week in his life. You've given him so much corn he's blown his head off."

Of course it didn't do any good. I might have known. She stuck to him and stood by him even then while a crowd of his little girl-friends were waiting for him at the stage door in his own car, anxious to get every little bit they could out of him. Even then she stood for him, poor old girl.

He threw me out—physically. Took me by the shoulders

and pitched me into the corridor. I was wild. I was beside myself.

"I'll kill you for this," I said.

But when it came to it and I did kill him I wasn't in that mood at all.

They came to live in my house at the end of the 'twenties. We all get old and I admit that the discovery came to me as a bit of a shock, but it didn't throw me off my balance. It was the same sort of feeling I had when I realised that I couldn't wear a ballet skirt any longer. Something had to be done about it. It was a pity, but it couldn't be helped.

I left the stage and bought my house with most of my little bit of money. It's not a grand house, but it's just the place for me and a couple of little girls to run when the boarders do most of their own work.

I won't tell you the exact address, but it's up Maida Vale way, nearly to Kilburn, and it stands in a row with a lot of other houses which used to be very fashionable and are still respectable, in spite of the efforts of some people whom I have to call neighbours.

There are three floors, a basement and an attic. I live in the basement. There's a little room for me and a kitchen and a tiny spare room that used to be a pantry where I can put up an old pal who can't afford to pay me what they'd like to.

Louie and Frank started on the first floor. That was at the beginning of the time. Then they moved upstairs, but at the time I'm talking of they were in the attic. There were two rooms, with a little gas-stove in one of them and a sink out in the passage. The windows of the rooms looked out over the parapet, which is one of the features of all the houses in our street. It's a big yellow stucco parapet that finishes the roof off and makes the houses look like great slabs of margarine on a Sainsbury counter.

I don't think I ever really got to know Frank until I had him in the house. Louie I seemed to know less. Every now and again I'd recognise the dear old girl she really was and

I'd see a spark of the old spirit, the old friendliness that had made me love her all my life. But for the most part she was on guard against me. She wouldn't let me get near her. She was always on the defensive, always frightened.

Frank was mad. I came to that conclusion when he gave the Peeler Ventriloquist Act's parrot a great lump of bacon and killed it, and Louie and I were at our wits' end covering the business up.

It's difficult to explain why I should have found that so enlightening, but it wasn't done through ignorance and it wasn't done as a joke, and it wasn't even done out of maliciousness, because he had nothing against the Peeler pair except that they were living in the rooms he used to have. But it was done out of a desire to be powerful, if you see what I mean, and after that I knew he was dangerous.

I find myself skipping the story of Louie and Frank in between that time we had a row at the Palladium and the time they finally gravitated to my attic. It's because it's an old story and a tragic story, the same old miserable story that any one-time star who hasn't saved can tell you.

There were more rows, less good performances, changes in the public taste, hard times and worst of all, a dreadful moment when her old spirit came back and she gave 'em the affection that she used to give 'em, gasping and exhausted and fighting as she was, and they didn't want it any more. And there were empty seats and perhaps even a catcall or so from the gods.

There were other things too: unpleasant interviews with managers who didn't even know the names of predecessors who'd been more than half in love with her.

And all the time there was Frank, making it worse. He'd always done silly things, but being wild with a lot of money is funny and being wild with no money is criminal.

He was never in jail. She kept him out of that somehow. Now and again she got a little engagement. At those times I had my hands full with him. If he could get down to the theatre he'd make a scene. He couldn't help it; he just wanted to be in the picture, like a silly hysterical woman.

He was never drunk, or at least only very rarely and then only when it suited his purpose and he fancied himself doing the Garrick act. Then he'd knock her about. It looks incredible now I've written it down. You remember Louie Lester: can you see any man knocking her about? But he did. I've had the doctor in to clean up a black eye before now.

As the years went on it got worse—worse for me, I mean. She'd always had hell's delight with him, I imagine. But he became an old man of the sea. They couldn't pay me very much at first and they paid me less and less until they paid me nothing at all. Time and again I'd lose my temper and threaten to throw him out, and then he'd laugh at me.

"If I go Louie goes," he'd say. "Can you see her, Polly, sitting under the Adelphi Arches?"

I couldn't, but I could see *him* sitting there and her singing in the street until she could bring him something, like a poor old mother wagtail with an obscene, bald red cuckoo tucked up in her nest.

So they stayed. Times had been difficult in the theatrical profession. They still are. People have still got to live but they don't live so well, and there are too many real business people in the boarding-house line to make it all jam for old women like me, who don't know how to count every halfpenny and haven't learnt how to be mean.

He began to affect my business. I haven't brought myself to tell you his worst fault; I don't know how to describe it without making him sound a lunatic, which he wasn't. If he'd been certifiable I'd have had him done long ago, whatever Louie said.

He used to swank. But it wasn't only that; lots of people swank, especially old pros. But he did it with a sort of frenzy. A man couldn't open his mouth and mention anything clever or remarkable that he or anyone else had done without my lord piping up with a tale of how he'd done the same thing much better.

There wasn't an actress you could mention he hadn't either slept with or taught her her job. There wasn't a manager who hadn't borrowed money from him. All of it lies, silly lies, lies everybody saw through. He used to get on people's nerves and I found I was getting my house full of foreigners who couldn't understand him.

When he couldn't get satisfaction that way he'd do tricks, make out he could walk tight ropes and jump on to the ledges of tables. I used to think he'd kill himself and hope he would.

Louie never deserted him. She used to get cross and I'd hear her pleading with him and sometimes snapping at him. But she'd never do anything definite. She'd never frighten him. She'd never turn him out of the house, even for half an hour.

He lost her all her old pals, some of them useful. There were folks who'd retired and gone down to live in the country who'd have been glad to put her up for a week or so, but they couldn't stomach Frank and you couldn't blame them.

She kept her health wonderfully. You only get a vital personality like that when there's an iron constitution behind it, and it's a miracle to me what a real constitution will stand. He'd exhaust her, beat her, jag her nerves to ribbons, and she'd come up again, a ghost of herself but still ready for punishment.

I gave up trying to plead with her after the first year. She was never angry, only obstinate. She'd never leave him.

They'd been in the attic over a year and things were terrible. It was two years since Louie had had a show and then it was in some dirty little unheard-of hall on the south coast. Frank had gone down there and after the management had had a dose of him, if she'd filled every seat in the house it wouldn't have got her a return booking. And she hadn't filled every seat by a long chalk.

Things were bad with me too. I'd mortgaged the place for more than it was worth and got rid of one of my little girls. Money wasn't coming in. I didn't see what I was going to do.

Then one day, just when it looked as though we'd all be in the street, young Harry Ferris came round to see me. Just walked into the kitchen without ringing the bell, and although I hadn't seen him since he was at school I recognised him; he was so like his Dad. It was all I could do to prevent myself from crying all over him, and that's not the way to treat any manager even if you're sixteen, much less sixty.

He was a nice boy, much quieter and more the gentleman than his father, and he called me Miss Oliver. But he was none the worse for that and he sat down at the kitchen table and talked to me. I soon saw what he was after.

They were trying to revive the old music hall at the New Imperial and he wanted Louie.

"There's a chance for her, Miss Oliver," he said. "A real chance. She could sing all those old songs of—Lord's, was it?"

"Lorn," I said, and I thought of him, the first time he'd come into my mind for years. Poor Lorn! He was just one of the good things Louie threw away.

"Lorn, was it?" said my visitor. "Oh, well . . . anyway you know the songs. I'm not promising anything, but if she did go over big—and she might; there's a great revival in this old hearty stuff just now—well, there'd be a good long run. There's only one thing I'm afraid of, though."

He hesitated and I knew why he'd come to me and not gone straight to Louie; and I saw Frank for what he was for the first time in my life. He wasn't a man at all; he was a vice, a vice of Louie's.

"It's her husband," the boy said, and if he'd said "it's her drinking," he couldn't have said it any other way.

"Now look here," he hurried on, "we're going to start in Manchester, and I want her up in Manchester for a trial fortnight, and I want her there *alone*. Can you manage it?''

''I'll try,'' I said.

''And when she comes to London I want that man kept away,'' he continued. ''It's a great chance, Miss Oliver. Do what you can, won't you?''

''Of course I will,'' I said, and because I was so happy and because he looked like a rescuing angel I forgot he wasn't his father and I kissed him.

He looked very uncomfortable and went off upstairs.

Louie came down to me about an hour later. She was bubbling with excitement as she told me the whole story all over again.

''I can do it, you know, Polly,'' she said. ''I can do it! I know I can. These new kids to-day aren't the war-tired lot who wanted to be sung to sleep. They can stand a bit of noise, a bit of the old stuff. I'm going to do it. Oh, Duck!'' she said, and threw her arms around me. ''Oh, Duck, it's going to be all right!''

We both had a bit of a cry, I remember.

We started talking about the arrangements, how to raise her fare and what to do about her clothes and so on, and then I said:

''I'll look after Frank.''

She looked at me and I saw her openness disappear. It was as though a shutter had been drawn down inside her eyes. She looked at me warily.

''Frank'll come with me,'' she said. ''He doesn't want to be left at home. You can understand it. I shan't mention it to Mr. Ferris—you know how difficult these new managers are—but Frank can come up and stay at different digs. He'll keep quiet, Polly, he'll keep quiet.''

''Now look here, my girl,'' I said. . . .

I talked to her for two hours by the clock and had lunch late for everybody and in the end she agreed with me. She *had* to see it.

''He'll be difficult,'' she said. ''You know what he is, Polly.''

"Yes, I do," I said, "and that's why it's suicide to take him. If I had my way I'd keep him under lock and key the whole engagement."

She nodded gravely. "Yes," she said. "But we couldn't do that. He'd get out. You don't understand him."

"You put your foot down," I said.

There were tears on her cheeks when she gave me her promise.

Half an hour later he'd got round her again.

There were fourteen days before she had to go to Manchester and we had time to get busy. She had to rehearse and we had to get her clothes. I think we both realised how much depended on it. It was the last chance, you see; the last life-line.

I made up my mind I'd see to Frank. I tried arguing with him. I tried pleading. In the end I tried to bribe him. It wasn't until I thought of frightening him that I got him to listen to me at all, and then I saw how it was going to be. He'd agree with me, they'd both agree with me, they'd both promise, and then I'd find him brushing up his best suit and taking some of the money we'd scraped together for her stage clothes to buy himself a couple of fancy shirts, old and horrible though he was.

I saw him beating me and I got the idea of him as a vice more clearly in my head. I had a father once who used to drink, and all that business came back to me as I struggled with him and I struggled with Louie. There was the same cunning, the same promising and going behind your back, and the same utter hopelessness of it all.

Once when she was out he came down and sat on my kitchen table and laughed at me.

"You've tried to separate us all your life, haven't you, Polly? You're not going to do it, d'you hear. I made her. I put her where she was and she'll never do anything without me. We shall be together at the end. She's been a bitch to me, Polly, but I've stuck her . . . and I'm going to stick to her. And if we go down together, well——" he nodded his little round head, "—well, we go down together, see?"

"Yes, you're a millstone all right," I said.

He looked surprised.

"A millstone? I'm her lifebelt."

And I could see by the way he said it that he'd deceived himself and he believed it.

It was then, as I lifted the saucepan off the fire and put it on the draining board, that I began to make up my mind how I was going to kill him. It was a question of who was going under, you see; him, or all of us together.

It's not easy to kill someone in your own house if you don't want anybody to know. I didn't see how I was going to do it, and the need was so great it became a nightmare to me, growing more and more desperate as the days approached and I saw him and her, too, making little sly preparations to get him to Manchester.

If he'd only let her have her chance without him! Just a start. But he wouldn't, and I had to hurry.

I'd let my second floor, which is very nearly self-contained, as all my places are, to Ma Pollini and her family, who had booked up a seven-week engagement on the Stuart Circuit. She was a monstrous old girl who looked like a bull. She used to be in the act herself and still kept them all together, Pa and the three boys and their wives and the two kids. I never knew a woman who was so clean. I wonder she didn't have the paper off the wall. She spoke English all right but not too well and you had to explain things to her very carefully, but there wasn't much her little black eyes missed and I knew I'd got to be careful with her.

Young Ferris used to let Louie go and rehearse up at some practice rooms he had over the theatre. There were pianos there and a clever accompanist, so she was out a great deal and it was good to see her coming back bright and hopeful and to feel her pat my shoulder and say: "It's going to be all right, Duck. Oh, it's going to be all right."

I thought "Yes, by God it is, if I can get rid of this horror for you."

I'd begun to see him like that, like a cancer or a monstrous deformity that was dragging her to death before my eyes and taking me with her—because I knew I'd never let her down however much I argued with myself.

While she was out I used to go up and clean her rooms in the attic and although I got used to him talking I did wonder why she hadn't gone out of her mind. Idiotic lies—dozens of them! Continuous tales of his importance and his cleverness which didn't even sound true. Nothing was too big for him to have done, nothing too small. I happened to mention an act I'd seen that was new to London, a fellow flinging himself down from the flies without a wire or a net or anything, and immediately he caught me up.

"That! . . ." he said. "God, that was an old trick when I was a boy. I could do it . . . have done it a hundred times. Though I'm an old man I could do it now."

I didn't say anything at the time but it gave me the first real helpful idea I'd had.

I went about it very slowly. It began when I started shaking the tablecloth out of the front attic window, that is to say out of their living-room window. I had to fling it wide because it had to miss the parapet, and the crumbs—I saw there were plenty of them—used to float down on to the little balcony outside Ma Pollini's sitting-room. I knew it would annoy her, and it did. We had quite a set-to about it on the stairs and the whole house knew about it. I was apologetic because I didn't want to lose her just then, but the next morning I did it again. There was another row and the third morning I shook the crumbs into a dust-pan as any sensible woman would.

But the fourth morning—however, I'm coming to that.

I am not usually a chatty woman. In my experience the less you say the less people can repeat. And if I'd been the most talkative person in the world I wouldn't have talked to him. But I spent a lot of time with him during those four days and I did my share of talking. I talked about the Pollinis.

"He's a clever man," I said. "That act's come on."

Frank rose to it as I thought he would. I knew he wasn't too fond of Pollini. He'd tried to tap him without much success. No one, not even Frank, could tap a man who looked at you like a surprised bison and shambled off muttering "Don' understand. Git th'hell outa here."

"Pollini?" said Frank. He was sitting in his shirt sleeves, without a collar, on the back of the dilapidated old chesterfield that Louie slept on when they had a row. "I taught Pollini all he knows and he's too much of a stiff to say how d'you do to me these days."

That was the sort of statement he used to make. It had no relation to the truth at all and no purpose as far as I could see, because not even Frank could expect *me* to believe it.

I rambled on. I told him I'd seen young Latte Pollini teaching the kids.

"Hand-springs!" I said. "You've never seen such neat ones."

I won't tell you what he called me. There's no point in writing things like that down.

"Look at this," he said, and he stood there poised at the top of the sofa looking like an organ-grinder's monkey, the white stubble sticking out on his red face.

"You be careful. You'll hurt yourself," I said over my shoulder.

"Look!" he commanded. "Look!"

I straightened my back and stood there, the dust-pan in my hand.

"I'm looking," I said.

Well, he didn't do it. I didn't think he would. That's what I was afraid of. He always took wonderful care of himself. But I went on.

Louie came in when he was telling me how he once walked a tight-rope and threatening to show me if I'd get him one. I had to leave it for that day.

The next day I started again, still on the Pollinis. At first I thought I'd frightened him. He sat there, morose and angry, while I did the room.

It was then I found out about the shirts. I told him what I thought of him and I realised more and more how necessary it was for me to hurry if she was going to have her chance at all.

He began boasting to me. "This time next week we shall be at Manchester. I shall tell them what she used to be like. She's not much to look at now but I'll put her over."

My heart was in my mouth and I very nearly picked up the poker and did him in there and then, and it might have been just as well in a way.

However, I didn't. I went on about the Pollinis and I got him interested. He even did a simple somersault for me and when he pretended that he'd hurt himself I got him a drink, and another.

It was an extraordinary thing, but I only discovered then after all these years that he couldn't drink. A couple made him silly. I left him sleeping.

That was the day I had my second row with Ma Pollini about the crumbs.

The next day I only gave him one drink and I brought it up with me. I'd told my little girl that I was doing it for his health and she didn't think anything of it. People were always having little drops for their health in my house.

Everything played into my hands. He'd had words with Latte on the staircase the evening before and didn't want to hear about the Pollinis' prowess. But I kept on. I let him have it.

"Do a handspring if you're so clever," I said. "A simple handspring."

He saw I was laughing at him and came and thrust his face into mine.

"I can't do it here," he said. "There's not room."

"There's no room big enough for you in the whole world, you old liar," I said.

That rattled him. He opened the door so that he could get on to the passage and took a run, stumbled, actually succeeded in turning some sort of cartwheel, and pitched downstairs, finishing up on the half-landing between me and Ma Pollini.

She came out and I explained to her what had happened. And she laughed. You should have seen her laugh! She'd have made a fortune on the halls just doing it. Tears poured out of her eyes and ran down the sides of her great coarse nose and she shook all over. What with the noise she made and the sound of him swearing the whole house was roused and everybody knew that old Springer had been swanking again and had nearly broken his neck doing it.

Louie heard about it when she came in, and it made her cry.

The fourth morning I watched Louie out of the house. I've never felt like it before or since. Everything seemed to be in bright colours and Louie's old black satin coat shone like a black beetle as she went out under the porch and down the little stone yard that we call a garden and out into the road.

I was trembling and I don't know if I looked funny, but anyway there was no one to see me except my little girl, and she's so busy, poor kid, she doesn't have time to keep her mind on two things together, even if it were capable of it.

I went slowly up the stairs and started making the bed. There was Louie's suitcase half packed, and in a cupboard, where they thought I wouldn't see it, there was his. It's still there, for all I know. All packed up neatly, labelled and ready.

He came out when I was in the bedroom and I knew by the way he fidgeted and talked about his health that he was wondering if I'd brought him up his drink. I sent him down for it.

I'd forgotten it; that's what frightened me. I had meant

to bring it and it had gone clean out of my mind. I wondered what else I'd forgotten.

He went off, padding down the stairs in his stockinged feet, and came back very pleased with himself. I wondered if he hadn't taken an extra dram. He said something uncomplimentary about my little girl and I guessed she'd given him something to go on with.

I started talking about the Pollinis and, as I hoped, the memory of old Ma Pollini laughing at him made him furious. He told me the Pollinis were a lot of stiffs. Wops and stiffs, he called them. He said they hadn't got a trick between them that any man couldn't do if he had his wits about him, and told me what he could do as a child.

I was getting him where I wanted him. I went into the other room where the gas stove was and opened the window when I'd taken the cloth off the table. Then I went back to the bedroom and shook it out of there, so that the crumbs would miss Ma Pollini's balcony.

My heart was beating noisily and I was so long about it that I thought he'd notice something. Finally I did what I meant to do and the cloth slipped out of my hand and landed on the edge of the parapet.

It was very neatly thought out, because, as I forgot to tell you, the window in the bedroom was stuck. It wouldn't open more than six inches at the top. I had to stand up on the sill, push the cloth through and shake it with one hand.

I went back to the other room, where he was sitting up on the end of the sofa again.

"What are you looking at me like that for, Polly?" he said.

I pulled myself together. I couldn't tell him that I saw him in bright colours, just like I'd seen Louie go out of the gate. I saw him in crude colours, like the printing in a twopenny comic. His shirt was bright blue and his head was smudged red.

"I want a broom," I said. "I've dropped the tablecloth out of the window and it's stuck on the parapet. Now if you were a Pollini . . ."

He didn't hear me, or didn't seem to, and I was afraid I'd been too quick. But he was interested, as he always was in silly little incidental things that happened. He went to the other window and looked out. He could see the cloth about fifteen feet along.

"How are you going to get it?" he said.

"I'm going to get a broom and fish it up through the window in the other room," I said. "Or get a Pollini kid to come and walk along the parapet and bring it in for me."

"Let me try with a broom," he said.

I looked about for a broom, though it was the last thing I wanted.

"You'll break my window," I said.

He grinned at me. "I'll buy you fifty windows when I come back from Manchester."

I leant out of the window. The parapet sticks up about a foot over the glass and the windows are built out of the roof, dormer fashion.

"I'll get a broom," I said. My courage was going. I thought I'd have to try some other way. It wasn't working out as I thought it was going to.

I suppose I must have been silent for nearly three minutes, for then he said quite suddenly:

"I suppose one of your Pollini pals would just trot along there and pick it up?"

"I believe even old Ma Pollini could," I said.

That did it. He swept me out of the way.

"I'll do it," he said. "I'll get your damned tablecloth. I can do anything a Pollini can."

He scrambled up on the sill and I saw that he was waiting for me to pull him back. I did. That was the extraordinary thing: I did.

"Don't you dare," I said. "You'll break your neck. You haven't got the courage."

He thrust his little red face into mine. "I'll show you," he said.

I watched him out upon the sill and saw him climb

shakily on to the parapet, which was nearly a foot wide, holding his arms out like a tight-rope walker.

"Don't you dare," I said. "Don't you dare."

Now I'd got him there I panicked. I lost my head. I screamed. I ran to the top of the stairs.

"Bring a broom!" I shouted to nobody in particular and rushed back again.

There was no sign of him, only the big bare room with the stove and the window open at the bottom, and far away the tops of the trees.

I ran over to the window and looked out. He was coming towards me, holding the cloth in his arms. I screamed. I screamed and screamed.

"Be careful!" I said. "Be careful!"

He came to the window and stood there swaying, holding the cloth, his little bulk blotting out most of the light. I saw his short trousers and his shoeless feet in their grey army socks standing on the slippery stucco. He put down his hand to catch the top of the window and at that moment I leant out and caught him round the ankles.

I can hear my own voice now shouting hoarsely:

"Be careful! Be careful!"

I heard him shout and I realised that I could make up my mind there and then.

I pushed.

He threw his weight against the top of the window and a shower of glass fell in over me. I was still pushing, pushing with my head, my arms round his ankles.

I felt him go. I heard his scream. Just for a moment I saw his body swing past me and then there was silence until far below in the little stone yard that we call a garden there was another sound, a sound I can't get out of my mind.

I stepped back from the window and from that moment my mind was clear. There was a noise on the stairs and I ran towards it, screaming, but intentionally this time, knowing what I was doing.

It was Ma Pollini. I tried to tell her but she'd only talk

in Italian and finally I pushed her out of the way and hurried on down the stairs.

Everybody in the house was running out into the street and I remember coming out under the porch and standing there in the bright sunlight.

I didn't see him. There was a crowd round him and one of the Denver boys, who had the ground floor rooms, came and put his arms round me.

"Don't look, Ma," he said, "don't look."

I told the young policeman exactly what happened right up to the moment when I caught Frank by the feet. Then I said I was so frightened that I just hung there until he overbalanced and went out, jerking his ankles out of my arms.

He was very kind to me, I remember.

Then the other men came and I told them the same thing and they said there'd have to be an inquest. And all the time he was lying out there in the yard, with a sheet off the Denver boys' bed over him.

They'd just finished with me when Louie came back. The other Denver boy had told her over the 'phone what had happened.

I shall never forget her as she sat in my kitchen with the police there and listened while I told my story yet another time. She didn't break down and when I saw the calm in her face, the extraordinary repose and dignity, I felt it was worth it.

She never reproached me. Instead she came over and kissed me and said:

"Don't worry, Polly. I know you did what you could."

Then the first floor people took her in and wouldn't let her go upstairs.

The police were very careful but they were never unkind, they never bullied. I thought how young they were, even the oldest of them. I remember the Inspector particularly. Such a boy he looked when he took his cap off.

They couldn't understand how he got out on the parapet, but when I told my story there were lots of people to back me up: Ma Pollini and the Denver boys who had been in bed when he fell downstairs the day before. They all knew him for what he was, and told stories about how he'd show off and how he'd lie and the idiotic things he'd do, and gradually the police got him straight in their minds.

They chose two or three of the boarders for witnesses at the inquest and I had to go too. There was only one awkward moment and that came from the Inspector.

"You know, you killed him, Ma," he said just as he was going.

I suppose I gaped at him because he dropped a hand on my shoulder.

"Let that be a warning to you not to try to drag a man in through a top-floor window by his feet," he said.

I expect you read a report of the inquest. It took up quite a bit in the paper. The Coroner put me through it, but I stuck to my story: I was frightened and I held him round the feet. It was a silly thing to do, but they were all I could get hold of.

Finally they were satisfied. The jury brought in Death by Misadventure and I went home.

A lot of my boarders had come to the inquest with me. Louie was there too, of course, and she gave her evidence very quietly and calmly and I thought she looked years younger, poor old girl.

She went to bed early that night. She didn't want to talk to me and I didn't want to talk to her. I knew it had been a shock and I wanted her to get over it and wake up and find out what it was like to be cured, what it was like to have her chance all over again without the dead weight that had been dragging her down half her life.

I got so used to telling my story that I believed it. It was such a simple story, so easy to remember, so like what really happened.

It became so real to me in the next two or three days that now I have to strain my memory, as it were, to get at the truth.

People were very kind. We had to borrow for the funeral, but it was worth it and as I stood beside his grave I hoped he'd lie quiet and have more rest himself than ever he gave Louie or me.

That would have been the end of the story. I should never have tried to remember the truth and I should never have set it down if it had not been for the one thing that beat me, the one thing that had always beaten me, the one vital fact that I never recognised until now.

This is the day that Louie ought to have gone to Manchester. There are a lot of bills up there now advertising her triumphant return. But she'll never come through the silver curtains and blow a kiss to the orchestra and sing *Jonah Likes a Little Bit of Pink* in Manchester or anywhere else.

This morning my little girl tapped on my door when she came at six o'clock to tell me there was a smell of gas in the house. I didn't go up. Somehow I knew what had happened.

Latte Pollini found Louie lying with her head in the gas oven for all the world as if she'd gone to sleep.

She loved him, you see. I never knew that, or perhaps I never knew what it meant. Poor dear loving old girl.

WOULD THE
MURDERESS TELL?

WHEN I FINISHED reading "It Didn't Work Out," I jumped to my feet with one thought—and one thought only—in my mind: to get to Maida Vale as quickly as possible and arrest Margery Allingham, alias Margaret Hawkins, alias Polly Oliver, on a charge of wilful murder.

Then I remembered:

(a) That the address had not been given, and that it might take some little time to trace it.

(b) That I was no longer at Scotland Yard.

(c) That a confession alone cannot be accepted as proof of guilt.

(d) That it was only a story, anyway.

It is the highest compliment that I can pay to Miss Allingham's skill in the creation of character and atmosphere to say that these eminently practical considerations only occurred to me as I was reaching for my hat—and that they occurred to me in that order.

But was the murder of Frank Springer really a perfect crime?

Frankly, I don't know. Margaret Hawkins might have brought it off in the way that she describes. On the face of it, there was nothing to suggest foul play, and there was the evidence of Ma Pollini and other people which, at least, indirectly, backed up Hawkins' story. But the police, without being definitely suspicious, would, I think, have made a rather more thorough investigation than they appear to have done. And they might have found fingerprints which suggested that the landlady's account of the tragedy was incorrect.

They would certainly have discovered that Hawkins did not like Springer, and her sudden change of attitude, followed by the "accident," would have put them on the right track.

It is possible, also, that someone witnessed the struggle, or some part of it. Were there no houses overlooking the one in which the murder took place? If there were—and remember, the place is "up Maida Vale way, nearly to Kilburn," the murderess was taking a big chance. And even if luck were with her, that takes the killing out of the "perfect murder" class. The perfect murder mustn't depend on luck.

Yet even when we make all these allowances, the crime remains diabolically ingenious. It might, in favourable circumstances, have been completely successful.

I think, however, that Margery Allingham has forgotten one important factor—Louie Lester. She, at least, knew that her husband and Hawkins didn't get on, and she loved her husband, worthless as he may have been.

She needn't suspect the truth. It would be quite sufficient that she couldn't understand what had happened, that she couldn't fit it in with what she knew of Hawkins and her attitude towards Springer, and that she should communicate her half-formed doubts to a police officer. The police would see the possibilities which she hardly dared put into words—which she hardly dared, perhaps, to acknowledge even to herself—and would follow up the new trail.

Margaret Hawkins wrote her account of the crime on "the day that Louie ought to have gone to Manchester," the day when she was found "lying with her head in the gas oven for all the world as if she'd gone to sleep."

Artistically, the story ends there, just as Miss Allingham does end it. But there's a difference between art and life. Things are never so easy—or at least, they are seldom so easy—either for the criminal or for the detective in life. Art falls into a pattern, but life sprawls out beyond the pattern.

So I don't believe that, assuming this incident were reality, not fiction, it would, in fact, be closed.

Hawkins would find the police back in her boarding-house, not merely because Louie had committed suicide, but because, before turning on the gas, she had written— and dispatched—a letter to the police which suggested that Springer's death was due, not to accident, but to murder.

Louie might not have signed the letter. Perhaps she was ashamed of her own suspicions. But all anonymous letters of this kind are considered and investigated. Hundreds of them may lead nowhere, but it is worth while checking up on them all for the sake of the one or two which do contain valuable information. And if it were discovered, as it probably would be discovered, that the anonymous letter was in Louie's handwriting, it would at once become very important indeed.

The situation is now completely changed. Hawkins was able to produce a convincing story before, to reply to awkward questions, because she wasn't really suspected, because she was confident that she was getting away with it, because she had a comforting sense of superiority over the police officers whom she was fooling so nicely. Every-thing was going according to plan. Now, however, the plan had broken down. She is confronting police officers who are no longer inclined to accept her word, who have become sceptical and suspicious.

And she knows what these officers will be able to find out, now that they are on the track, about her hatred of Springer. She knows, too, that somewhere in the house, and certain to be found in the event of a search, is the story of the crime which she has just written. Above all, she has been unnerved by Louie's death.

Her replies to questions will be lame and halting. She will contradict herself. In the end, whether her written account is found or not, she will probably confess.

That is at least a possible outcome of the situation Miss Allingham has outlined for us. I would even say that it is its probable outcome. You remember how badly the murderess was shaken when the inspector said to her: "You know, you killed him, Ma." And the very fact that she wrote down the story of her crime suggests a considerable degree of emotional tension, a profound need to unburden herself in some way. In short, on this morning of her friend's death, she is in a psychological condition in which it would be easy to blurt out a full confession, and it probably requires a real effort of will to keep back the words. The work of a detective would be much simpler than it is if he found every suspect he had to interview in just this mental state.

Yet, I repeat, I'm not sure. Louie Lester might not have written that letter, and there might be no interrogation by the police at this time, beyond questions relative to the suicide. And even if suspicions had been aroused, Hawkins might still have sufficient strength of will—and cunning—not to give herself away. Especially at this stage, when evidence that might have been secured earlier had doubtless disappeared completely, it would be a matter of extreme difficulty to prove Hawkins' guilt to the satisfaction of a jury so long as she herself kept silence.

There is, however, yet another possibility. The manner in which the crime is committed; the motive, which must seem hopelessly inadequate to any ordinary person; the callous, self-satisfied way in which the murderess writes of her deed, as if it were meritorious, all suggest someone who is not altogether sane, who is hovering on the borderline of madness.

The shock of Louie's suicide, in these circumstances, might well send her mind toppling over the verge, with the result that she would spend the rest of her life in an institution.

I certainly cannot see Margaret Hawkins living happily and prosperously for the rest of her life, and taking her secret to the grave with her.

I can, however, see her waking up, screaming, night after night, from dreams of Louie and Springer. I can see her gradually coming to believe that she was haunted by the ghost of her dead friend, until life transformed itself into a vast nightmare, and she was forced to seek peace in the confession and expiation of her crime.

In suggesting these possibilities, I may be taking a more favourable view of her character than is justified. Let us assume that she is tougher and more resilient, and that remorse does not make her life a hell. Her secret may still be uncovered.

The person who has committed murder and done it without being detected, usually suffers from the delusion that the method which has proved safe once, will be equally safe on another occasion.

Smith, for instance, thought that he had discovered an infallible technique for doing away with unwanted women. Chapman cherished the same belief. They both killed once too often—and then the whole ghastly story of their multiple murders was laid bare.

Is there any reason to suppose that Hawkins, having disposed of Springer, will stop short at that? Her narrative shows that she thinks it an easy matter to commit murder, and is no longer afraid of the police. Her first crime proves that she is prepared to kill from motives that must appear flimsy to any normal person. I think it is highly probable that, in a year or two, a situation will again arise in which she will be able to convince herself once more that murder is a reasonable and laudable act. And next time she will be more confident, and perhaps more careless.

Whether she is careless or not, if she chooses to repeat herself and to stage another apparent accident, the chances of detection are at least fifty per cent greater than on the first occasion. Every policeman knows that coincidences do occur, but he also knows that coincidences of this kind may repay close investigation.

Whatever happens in the present case, therefore—and there may, even now, be an unpleasant surprise in store for Hawkins—I should not be at all astonished if, in the end, she stood in the dock on a murder charge and were made to pay the penalty of her crimes.

I can imagine the reader saying: "But the character whom Margery Allingham has depicted is not at all so bad as you have painted her. True, she has committed murder, but she has done so from no sordid motive. She killed a man who was an utter waster because she wanted to save her friend. Really, I think you are being a little unfair. You are taking altogether the wrong view. There can be no comparison between Margaret Hawkins, who is quite a sympathetic character, and the criminals whom you have mentioned."

There are certain sentimental people who always feel sorry for the convicted murderer—so much so that they have no pity to spare for his, or her, victim. There are others who, while horrified by certain murders, find excuses for others. But there is no excuse—there can be no excuse for murder. Human life is sacred, unless it has been forfeited to the law and is taken, after due legal process, for the protection of society. But no private individual can be allowed to assume the functions of judge and executioner. That way lies anarchy.

Also, what authority does the reader have for concluding that Springer deserved to die, or that Margaret Hawkins' motive for killing him was so purely disinterested? Only Hawkins' own narrative. And it is my experience that criminals always try to put the best face possible upon their crimes. Investigation might reveal facts which would show both Hawkins and Springer in a different light. Even on her own account of these happenings, Hawkins is both callous and cunning. There may be something more sinister still in the background which has been suppressed.

I take off my hat to Miss Allingham for having written a very clever story, and devised a particularly ingenious method of murder. But I'm glad, for her sake, that it is only a story.

Father Ronald Knox

THE FALLEN IDOL

IT WAS HIGH holiday in the streets of San Taddeo; shops, factories, even restaurants were empty, and few citizens had the courage to absent themselves from the great square, in which the bronze statue of Enrique Gamba was to be unveiled. For was not Enrique Gamba the Inspirer of the Magnolian Commonwealth; and was not any slight put upon him apt to be regarded in the light of unpatriotic activity? That meant prison for certain; and the Magnolian prisons, although herds of apparently harmless people had entered them of late, never showed any large returns of discharged inmates—nor, on the other hand, did they find it necessary to increase their accommodation. Anxious relatives would receive, instead, a tactful intimation that So-and-so had unfortunately succumbed to the rigours of the climate, or that he had been shot by the warders in an attempt to escape. Everybody knew what that meant. There was rejoicing, therefore, in the streets of San Taddeo, and many were the huzza's raised, and caps thrown into the air, especially among those citizens who stood nearest to the police, and had reason to suppose that the police were looking.

The statue of Enrique Gamba was not to be unveiled by

Enrique Gamba himself. Not that he suffered from the kind of modesty which would have made it hard for him to deliver an oration in his own honour; indeed, it had been understood until yesterday that he was to be the principal speaker. But yesterday afternoon word had gone round that the Inspirer was suffering from a slight cold in the throat; he would not be present at the unveiling, which took place at nine o'clock in the evening, but would content himself with taking the salute of the troops on their way back, and, immediately afterwards, broadcasting a few words to the nation. These autumn evenings were chilly, and the doctors insisted that he should not leave his house. Broadcasting, it hardly needs to be explained, involved no necessity of leaving the house. There was a specially designed microphone in a soundproof room in his suite from which, after pressing a button to silence all the programmes from all stations, he could gate-crash the hearing of every listener in Magnolia. His second in command, General Almeda, was provided with a similar convenience, for he made almost as many speeches as the Inspirer himself. No other such contrivance, it was said, existed in the world.

Naturally it was General Almeda who stepped into the breach on the present occasion, and unveiled the statue. And who had a better right? For had not General Almeda, while the sittings were in progress, tempestuously wooed and won the sculptress? A girl fresh from the University had been charged with perpetuating, for all time, in unaging bronze, the features of the Inspirer: that hawklike nose, that resolute chin, those rugged eyebrows. It was as the Señora Almeda that she was present to-day; and you may be sure that it thrilled her to listen to the man she was in love with—for she was really in love with him, not with his power or with his uniform—praising her own art, while she praised the man who had united beyond all precedent the people of Magnolia, abolished the national debt, and exchanged a flood of telegrams with the League of Nations.

Almeda himself was a genuine soldier; although he was a giant of a man, he did not look the part of national hero

quite so well as Gamba. In the recent *coup d'état*—I beg
its pardon, the recent Liberation—he had appeared for a
time to be playing a lone hand, with the army at his back;
then, quite unexpectedly, he had joined hands with the
rising movement of Gamba, which had all the publicity
and all the gunmen at its disposal. This coalition shattered
the constitutional parties, and left Gamba supreme ruler of
Magnolia, with Almeda as his right-hand man. Naturally
enough there were wiseacres who whispered (you never
spoke above a whisper in San Taddeo, if you could help it)
that Almeda was not best pleased with a position which
forced him to play second fiddle. But no outward sign of
disagreement showed itself between the two men; and
certainly it would have been impossible to speak of Gamba's
achievements in more glowing terms than Almeda used,
on that long-remembered evening of October.

I do not propose to weary the reader with a full account
of the speech. If he is in the habit of "trying to get foreign
stations," he will before now have intercepted a torrent of
Magnolian eloquence, from Gamba, from Almeda, or from
the irrepressible Dr. Lunaro, very much in the same vein.
Whenever Magnolian statesmen find themselves in front of
a microphone they tell us how badly their country was
governed before the Liberation, what peace and what bless-
ings it has enjoyed ever since, and how little reliance can
be put in the tendentious despatches sent from San Taddeo
by correspondents of foreign newspapers—by what they
mean, principally, the *Daily Shout*.

The Magnolians, however, are a simple people; they are
really rather glad to have a government of any kind, and a
relentless propaganda has hypnotised them into an attitude
of ferocious nationalism, which deceives nobody except
themselves into admiration of their rulers. On the present
occasion they applauded the usual rhetoric with the usual
vociferousness, whooped, and sang patriotic hymns, when
the sheet was let down and the bronze effigy stood unveiled before them—the Inspirer, standing at the salute in
answer to all the thousands of salutes that would greet him

from all the thousands of patriotic folk who would pass by. Then they gave three more cheers for General Almeda as he drove off in his car to join Gamba in his house, and streamed away to let off fireworks and drink healths, while the regiment of soldiers that had been in attendance marched back, along the main street, to their barracks.

What gave an extra fillip to these patriotic sentiments was a rumour which had lately gone round; a dastardly attempt was being made by the enemies of the State to burn down Enrique Gamba's house, and Enrique Gamba with it. Did I say "enemies"? So cowed were the spirits of all who disagreed with the Government that only one enemy survived worth the name; and he was no more than a name, scribbled up on walls and subscribed under threatening letters, "The Avenger." Nobody knew who he was, or what party he had belonged to; but his activities were a useful stick to beat all the old political parties with—not to mention the clergy. "Gamba to be burnt out on Thursday evening" had been scrawled up in chalk on an empty hoarding, and promptly rubbed out by the police: then the Government's semi-official paper had reported the threat, and next day—that was only yesterday—the Government's official paper had semi-officially semi-denied it. That sort of thing was useful: it gave the people something to shout about, instead of wondering why bread was still dear.

General Almeda's car drew up outside the Inspirer's house. It had, till the other day, been the Archbishop's house, but Gamba had thoughtfully confiscated it at the exact moment when the Concordat was going to be signed. The Archbishop, not liking to make his own grievance an obstacle to peace, submitted under protest; the only stipulation he made was that the body of St. Thaddaeus the Magnificent, with the altar-tomb which enclosed it, should be removed from the private chapel and lodged in the Cathedral. Gamba did not take much interest in anybody as long as he was dead. He let the Archbishop have his altar, and commissioned Señora Almeda to carve him a new altar in its place, on the model of the old one. It was necessary for him, you see, to be a patron of the arts, and the chapel of the Archbishop's was full of valuable, sometimes interesting stuff. He left it as it was, although Mass was never said there, and it served no useful purpose. The rest of the house suited him admirably, when he had sent a gang of masons through it to make sure there were no secret passages. (With archbishops, you never knew.) He himself lived on the top floor, in a suite of rooms which was cut off from the rest of the building, except for a single staircase with a stout oak door at the bottom of it. Outside this door sentries were posted, day and night; not soldiers, but gunmen of his own following, who had been raised to a kind of brevet military rank.

The commander of these, Captain Varcos, saluted the General and shook hands with Dr. Lunaro, who had accompanied him in his car. "The Inspirer, as you know, has given orders that he was not to be disturbed," he said. "You, General, were to be shown up, because you also, I think, are taking the salute from the balcony. There was nothing said about Dr. Lunaro, but——"

"That is all right," said the doctor, "I will wait down here and smoke a cheroot with you, Captain. I do not wear uniforms and take salutes; I am growing stout already, and these things do not become my appearance. You will not be long, General?"

"Just while the troops march past; that will only be a quarter of an hour or less. And then the Inspirer will be broadcasting, but only for one or two minutes, I expect. I will be down as soon as that is over. You heard the unveiling speech, Captain?"

"All of us. But it is a bad instrument, this; I wish we had a set like the one the Inspirer has upstairs. Then we should miss nothing. Au revoir, General."

However this age compares with its predecessors, it is certain that we have developed a higher standard of theatrical effect. Those who admire the beastly habit of floodlighting ancient buildings will do well to pay a visit to Magnolia; a country, in earlier times, of superb architectural achievement; a country, to-day, of quite execrable taste. As the regiment advanced down the main street of San Taddeo, nothing was visible of the old archiepiscopal residence except the ground floor, where the shaded street lamps caught it. But, as the "Eyes right" was given, a sudden glare of flashlights played over the whole towering façade; threw into relief the intricate mouldings, the deep embrasures; concentrated its effect on an upper balcony, where the familiar figures of Gamba and the General stood at the salute. This balcony opened out of the old chapel; and the archbishops used it formerly when, on state occasions, they gave Benediction to the crowd beneath. Now it was a framework for political puppet-shows, of the kind that is needed to keep the Gambas of the world in power. For ten minutes or so, while the troops were passing, this familiar tableau was presented to the public view; then, abruptly, the flares were extinguished, and the Street of April the First (named, of course, after the date of the Liberation) resumed its normal appearance.

It is our modern habit to gratify the senses one at a time. San Taddeo, after being allowed for ten minutes to contemplate the Inspirer's features in perfect silence, was allowed for ten minutes to listen to the Inspirer's voice without seeing him. The speech came through well enough; the utterance, always a trifle raucous, was not much altered by traces of catarrh. Dr. Lunaro, smoking his cheroot with Captain Varcos on the top floor but one of Gamba's won residence, vetoed the idea of tuning-in. He was a privileged person; and it is likely that Varcos and his sentries welcomed the rare opportunity of not listening when the Inspirer was at the microphone. Lunaro was just grinding out the stub of his cheroot when the oak door opened from within and Almeda appeared, calling out as he did so, "Good night, my Inspirer!"

"Good night, my friends!" The oak door shut, and the idol of a nation's worship was left to isolated glory.

Captain Varcos is not the sort of man I should care to meet on a dark night, supposing him to have any reason for dissatisfaction with my conduct. But there is no doubt that he waited on Gamba as a dog waits on its master; and those who knew the routine of that household were sometimes heard to speculate whether he ever got any sleep. He had been on duty that day since eight in the morning; but that exchange of good nights was not, to him, a signal for bed. He threw a cloak over his shoulders and went down into the street, to make sure that the sentries at the main door were duly at their posts. Then, passing up a little side alley, he made his way to the back of the house, where it abutted on a side street, faced by ugly office buildings. There was no entrance to the house from this direction; the back door had been bricked up, and the ground floor windows were separated from the street by a deep area, behind railings. As if such precautions had been insufficient, three sentries were on guard here too; their only business was to keep a watch on the windows of the upper storey—assassins, before now, have climbed up drainpipes. A light showed in the two windows of the room which Gamba used as his study.

"The Inspirer works early and late," said Varcos. "Keep your eyes on that light, my friends; it is the star of Magnolia's fortunes." And he went back to his post on the upstairs landing.

It must have been about ten minutes later that his meditations were interrupted by confused cries from the street; then a policeman came rushing upstairs, with a little mob of citizens following, irrepressible, at his heels. "Fire!" he cried. "Up there, in the Inspirer's suite! The keys!" "Keys?" replied Varcos, with a string of oaths, "there is no key. We must rush the door—or rather, you, Felipe, run for an axe; we will try rushing the door in the meanwhile. Now, citizens, your shoulders, all together! Here, boy, you are not strong enough for this; run downstairs and telephone for the fire brigade. It has been summoned already? Then telephone for His Excellency General Almeda; he will be back at his house by now. Citizens, your shoulders!"

After three united efforts the upper hinge of the door gave; and, as it fell in, half a dozen men ran upstairs with the same impetus, not heeding the protests of the police official. A cordon had, however, been drawn by now across the main entrance to the building, so that the remainder of the crowd had to content themselves with watching from the street. It was evident that the fire had broken out in or near the chapel; the flames were already wreathed about the balcony from which the soldiers' salute had been returned, scarce half an hour earlier. By the time Almeda arrived in his car the mob in the street was so packed that it was almost impossible to pass. He turned up a side street, and parked his car at the back, where the sentries had stood, but stood no longer—they had been swept away in the general eagerness to help in fighting the flames. From the back, down the alley already mentioned, Almeda returned to the main street, and fought his way through the crowd, shouting his own name to secure himself a passage.

Half-way up the stairs he was met by Varcos himself, and asked eagerly whether they had got the fire under. "The fire—that is out," replied Varcos. "But the Inspirer —we have searched high and low without finding him. I'm going to the back, to see if he can have been cut off somewhere, trying to escape. For God's sake, General, imprison all the fellows who broke in with us; trust nobody except the guards. If there has been foul play"—and he shook his hands in the air, with clenched teeth, as if to invoke some kind of infernal retribution.

Almeda gave a hasty order to the police at the door; every man who had been upstairs, except the firemen and the guards, was to be sent off at once in a prison van, to await interrogation. Then he took the stairs at a run, to find that, after all, the fire had done comparatively little damage. It must have broken out in the chapel, which was now blackened and gutted—everywhere the smell of blistered paint, and the gutterings of candles. The deputy altar his wife had carved, that had been set up only yesterday, was charred almost beyond recognition; plaster statues and plaster mouldings had cracked and splintered all over the floor; windows had fallen in, and carpets had burned to an ash. But the rest of the suite, although thick wreaths of smoke still hung about it, had remained untouched. The lights had fused, and the firemen were working by the glare of their own torches.

Nobody ever believes a place has been searched until he has searched it himself. General Almeda went from room to room, from cupboard to cupboard, as if he still hoped to find some trace of the missing man. He was so engaged when one of the sentries plucked him by the sleeve and told him, almost in a whisper, that Captain Varcos wanted to see him downstairs, at once; it was a matter of life and death.

He was ushered into a waiting-room, where Varcos and Dr. Lunaro sat in conclave, their brows heavy with disconcerting news. Lunaro was just saying, "That much, anyhow, they must be told"; and he added, almost before Almeda had had time to ask how much, "that the Inspirer is no more. That he has fallen from a window to his death."

"And they must not know, Doctor? Or not yet, at least?"

"That he had a bullet-wound through the back of his head."

"Who found him?"

"I," said Varcos. "The moment after I left you. I found the street at the back of the house empty; the dogs had joined with the crowd rushing in, and left their posts. I went close, to shine my torch against the back of the house, and immediately I noticed something dark lying in the area, beyond the railings, you know. I told one of my men to get a ladder, and we went down and found him."

"He was dead, of course?"

"My dear General, a man does not survive a fall from that height, bullet or no bullet. We covered him up, and brought him in to a room on the ground floor, which we have locked for the present."

"Who knows, as yet?"

"Only the sentry—one of the three who should have been on guard. He can be shot, if necessary, for deserting his post." Varcos shrugged his shoulders, as if to imply that shooting was, perhaps, not so good as formerly, since the deliverer of his country lay there clay-cold.

"I can answer for the Army," said Almeda, uttering, with almost brutal abruptness, the thought which was in all their minds. "What about the Free Youth?" That was the movement which had brought Gamba into power; and since he was dead, Varcos must be presumed to be at the head of it.

"The Free Youth," replied Varcos evasively, "will take action in conformity with the situation. But they will want to know who was responsible for to-night's work. They will want to see what the Avenger looks like, General." Almeda flushed, for he had sworn several times, ineffectively, to hunt out this lingering enemy of the State.

"Be reasonable, Captain," urged Lunaro. "It is the police who have failed; it is the police who must find him. Meanwhile, it will do no good for us to quarrel. The Party had better meet—that is what I was saying—before anything is given out in public. At what hour, General?"

"At eleven. I must have the full police report first, and go through it with Weinberg. He should be here by now— why is he not here?" Colonel Weinberg was the Chief of Police.

"He is waiting outside," explained Varcos. "I will make my own report to him as soon as he is at liberty; you, gentlemen, will hardly be interested in the details at present, since you have so much else to consider. Shall I make my report to the meeting of the Party also?"

"That will be best," agreed Almeda. The Junta which ruled in Magnolia was a very small body; and Varcos, although a trusted servant of Gamba's, did not belong to it. "At eleven, then, Captain?"

"At eleven to-morrow. And you will see Colonel Weinberg now?"

"It will be better if you ask him to come round to my house early to-morrow. It is urgent that I should make an announcement by wireless, for there will be all sorts of rumours flying about the city. For the present, then, I announce the disastrous news, explain that the Inspirer is thought to have met his death accidentally in trying to escape from the burning premises, pay the shortest of tributes to his memory, appeal for quiet behaviour and calm judgment—is there anything else, Doctor?"

"Nothing, General. Unless you care to anticipate rumour by adding that if the police find any reason to suspect foul play the Government will know where to fix the blame. That kind of announcement does no harm; and it causes panic among the enemies of the State."

"True; I will make that allusion; it is excellently thought of. Pray heaven we may know! I will hold the troops in readiness, in case of any disturbance; and you, Doctor, will attend to the Press reports; that is understood? Gentlemen, there will be little rest for any of us; but I wish you good night!"

Dispassionate critics are agreed that General Almeda's broadcast, which he made from his own house as soon as he reached it, was a considerable improvement on most of his utterances. He spoke very simply, in tones of dignified emotion; and there was little or nothing of the fire-eating stuff which he was accustomed to talk. He announced that he would make himself responsible for keeping order in the country until the will of the people should have been expressed as to the future government of it, and warned his hearers that, until the Party had made its decision on the morrow, all public expressions of opinion would be regarded as unpatriotic activities. Then he switched off the microphone, and the city of San Taddeo industriously assumed an appearance of complete calm.

Colonel Weinberg, the Chief of Police, was one of the few officials who had been left over from the old *régime*.

His reputation for detecting plots and laying criminals by the heels was really remarkable; and although his political sympathies were doubtful, Chief of Police he was still called—there was a Prefect of the City who dealt with rioting, and a Prefect of National Discipline who had charge of the prisons, so that his power was shorn while his usefulness remained unimpaired. He was a small, grizzled man, with an eye that fixed you only to disconcert you with a twinkle, and a sardonic habit of speech. When he came round to Almeda's house next morning he carried a vast jacket of official papers with him, the result of the researches he had made during the midnight hours. So brisk was he, so fully master of the situation, that you would never take him for a man robbed of his night's sleep.

"I begin with the time-factor," he announced, when Almeda had asked him for a full preliminary statement. "The lamented Inspirer of the People finished broadcasting at the hour of seventeen minutes past ten; at least, that was when he switched off his microphone, and it became possible for the studio orchestra to continue their interrupted programme. And you, General, must have left him almost as soon as he had finished?"

"Yes; I don't suppose we talked for more than a minute and a half before I took my leave. He seemed tired, and I wanted him to have all the rest possible."

"He was going to bed?"

"No, he said he had a little work to do."

"To be sure; that is why the light burned in his study. It was at 10.44 that the policeman on duty in the Street of April the First looked up at the outside of the suite, and saw smoke and sparks coming out by the balcony window. There was some delay, as Your Excellency knows, about breaking down the door, and it is not certain at what precise moment Captain Varcos and the others ascended the stairs. But the hoses began to play on the front of the house, it seems, a few minutes afterwards; and we have the time of that—10.57. The body was found a quarter of an hour later. The abominable incident therefore took place between about 10.20 and about 11.15; that is all the time margin at our disposal.''

"One moment, Colonel; that light which Varcos saw burning in the study—did it go out before the alarm of fire? The sentries, if so, must have noticed it.''

"It went out, apparently, when the lights fused. It was then that the sentries lost their heads, and ran round to the front. These irregulars, General—I always said it—should never have been trusted with such an employment. Now, as to the persons who ascended the stairs. Captain Varcos was first, with two of his men, Ladero and Munoz—both of them highly trusted. The policeman says that he fell on his face when the door finally gave, and ran upstairs in pursuit of the four men who had got ahead of him. At the top of the stairs, however, finding that there were other unauthorized persons coming up, he very properly devoted himself to barring the way, and succeeded in turning them all back. The names and addresses of these persons were taken at the main door; but they are not in custody.''

"You mean the people whom the policeman turned back?''

"Precisely. The four who got past him are in custody. One, Luiz Banos, is a volunteer member of the fire brigade; his statement is that he was passing at the time, and thought he could do more good by rushing in at once, instead of reporting himself at the station. His political views are unknown. The second was a priest, Domingo Sanchez, who tells us that he saw the fire from the street, and ran up with the sole idea of rescuing some saint's relic or other, which remained in the chapel. He was a Carmelite before the Order was disbanded, and is reported to have said in a Sunday school, last February, that the Pope was a more important person than Don Gamba. The third is an old friend of ours, Gomez—the man who edited an Anarchist paper before the Liberation, and has been in custody since, more than once. He says that he lives in an attic on the opposite side of the Street of April the First; that he ran out when he heard the noise, and went to the rescue (as he calls it) because he thought it was his duty as a citizen. The fourth, James Marryatt, is correspondent, as Your Excellency knows, of the London *Daily Shout,* and he acted as he did because he thought it was his duty to his paper. It is, I apprehend, the only sort of duty that young man recognises. The previous movements of all these persons have been checked, and found to be in accordance with their own statements.''

''It is more important to know what were their movements at the time.''

''I was coming to that, General. The policeman, by all accounts, did not go further than the top of the stairs, and then spent his time shepherding the intruders out of the building. Captain Varcos directed the two guards, Ladero and Munoz, to do what they could with the fire, while he himself went to look for the Inspirer. It is not clear whether they obeyed his orders, because accounts differ about the number of people who were in the chapel, trying to put out the fire. Varcos says he did not meet either of them again, while he was searching the house. There are no rooms of any size in the suite except the dining-room, study, bedroom, and conference-room. But there is a quantity of cupboards; and Varcos says he wasted time looking in all of these.''

''What made him do that?''

''He was not certain which were the practicable doors. Also, he says, he had begun to fear foul play; with the fire isolated in the chapel, it was hard to explain why Don Gamba had not come running downstairs to meet them. The lights were out, and Varcos' torch was not too good. It took him about ten minutes or a quarter of an hour to search the rooms. He could find no trace of Don Gamba; he saw no one, except two of the intruders who had broken in with him.''

''Ah! You have their movements checked?''

''The fireman was squirting the ceiling with an extinguisher he had found on the landing. Gomez was trying to beat out the flames with his umbrella. They corroborate each other's accounts. On their own admission, Sanchez and Marryatt followed the Captain in his search of the house. If they are to be trusted, the priest wanted to give Don Gamba absolution; the journalist wanted to ask him for an interview. They are, you see, optimists by profession.''

''And does anybody claim that he heard a shot fired, in all this time?''

''Nobody. But it is to be remembered that there was a prodigious amount of cracking and banging in the chapel, so that those inside it would hardly notice a pistol report. As for the others—'' Weinberg shrugged his shoulders.

Almeda sat drumming his fingers on the table. Neither man liked to ask the other, outright, what Varcos had been doing, that he should have heard no shot fired. At last Almeda said, ''It is certain that the wound was inflicted *before* the body was thrown from the window?''

''Captain Varcos will tell you that when he and the sentry Ladero found the body in the area, the scarf of Don Gamba's uniform was tied round the head. There was blood on the scarf, but no hole through it.''

''Yes. . . . And Varcos found no signs of any struggle in the course of his search? None have been found since?''

''None, General. I know what you mean—Don Gamba was not a man who would easily be overpowered or taken by surprise.''

''He might have been knocked out by the fumes, though. They were fairly strong, even when I reached the place.''

''That is true. Now, as to weapons—the sentries, of course, wore pistols, like the Captain. No weapon was found on any of the four intruders when they were searched. And no weapon was found lying about—no search of the neighbourhood has been conducted, for fear of arousing public curiosity.''

''Did you ask Varcos whether he inspected his own men's pistols, afterwards?''

''I asked him. He said it did not occur to him till it was too late to be of any use, after his interview with you. He did so, however, as a matter of form—naturally, everything was by that time in order.''

''You talk, Colonel, as if you suspected the sentries.''

''It is my rule to suspect everybody and nobody. It is a bad fisherman who leaves one hole in his net. As you see, everything is in a tangle, and when that is so it is more important than ever to keep the mind open. And, General, that is not all.''

''You have found some anomalies?'' The General smiled, for it was a well-known foible of Weinberg's, when he investigated a crime, to discover what he called ''anomalies''—tiny improbabilities to which the ordinary investigator would have attached no importance. ''Ah, come, that is interesting. What troubles you?''

''Several things. And first, General, why have we not found the cap that goes with Don Gamba's uniform? He was wearing it, I suppose, when you took the salute; you did not see him put it down anywhere?''

''He didn't wear it on the balcony, in spite of the cold. He preferred to stand bare-headed, even in his uniform. He may have put it down in the chapel.''

''That is true; but I pay attention to everything that worries me, in a case like this. Here is another point: Captain Varcos tells me that when he went into the study, he found the great safe which stands in the corner locked as usual, and no drawers were open except one, which contained blank notepaper. Now, assuming that Don Gamba survived the first outbreak of the fire, must there not have been things in that safe, those drawers, which he would have been eager to rescue—perhaps, if one may say it, to conceal?''

''There must,'' agreed the General; and he became thoughtful for a moment as he reflected what tell-tale matter must still be locked up in those hiding-places. ''It looks, you mean, as if the Inspirer must have been overpowered at once by the fumes; that is strange, certainly.''

''Don Gamba was not in the chapel much,'' the Colonel permitted himself to say, with the ghost of a smile. ''Indeed, the light suggests that he was in his study. He hears strange crackling noises, as if somebody were in the chapel opposite. He springs up from his desk, puts his hand to his revolver, goes to the door and opens it gently. A little wreath of smoke is coming out through the door of the chapel—he knows at once what that means. He looks in, perhaps, but cautiously, as you or I would. What then? Does he telephone? Does he run downstairs to summon the guard? Does he go back to his study to collect what is important? No; apparently he remains dumb-stricken in the passage until he is half suffocated; then rushes into one of the other rooms, and falls down in a stupor. General, is that what we expected? Did anybody ever know Don Gamba to lose his presence of mind?''

''And I suppose it is no use, Colonel, to ask what you are hinting at?''

''I am hinting at nothing. I find no hints—only puzzles. Excuse me, General,'' he added, as a servant came and whispered deferentially in his ear, ''they are ringing me up from headquarters; may I go and attend to it?''

He was back in a moment, smiling deliberately as men will who have a piece of unpleasant news to laugh off. ''It is best that I should tell you at once, General—the Avenger has been at his scribbling again; this time on the blank wall of a brewery.''

''And the message?''

''The message is, *Almeda next*. But you have despised threats before, General.''

There was a slight pause; then Almeda, squaring his shoulders as if to exorcise an imaginary terror, resumed the previous conversation. ''You were telling me about the *anomalies;* were there any more?''

''Yes, but less definite ones. I mean, for example, the whole business about the body.''

''Oh—was the surgeon's report suggestive, then? I confess it looked to me plain sailing; but, then, I am not an expert.''

''As to the death, yes; he was shot in the back of the

head, at fairly close range, two yards or so. And he broke the right bones in falling from that sort of height; that is all correct. And the body was still warm when Varcos found it, and the surgeon gives the time of death (for what his judgment is worth) as somewhere about eleven. We have confirmatory evidence of this: Don Gamba's wrist-watch stopped at precisely 10.54—either when his body fell from the window or, more probably, when he dropped wounded.''

''Wrist-watches can be faked,'' suggested the General.

''Yes, the murder might have been done earlier; but, as it happens, not later. The minute-hand was bent by the fall, in such a way that you cannot move it without moving the hour hand as well, when the two hands meet. And they meet just before 10.55. So that is all right; we know that the shooting must have been done almost immediately after the door was broken in, or conceivably, of course, at some time earlier—though not earlier than 9.50.''

''What is the anomaly, then, about the way the body was found?''

''I ask myself—why was it thrown out of the window at all? The wound was sufficient to kill; anyone could see that. Why did not the murderer leave the body where it lay, and devote his attention to being somewhere else, instead of dragging his victim's body to the window, at the risk of leaving traces, and then throwing it out, at the risk of being seen and recognised from below? He may have ascertained that the sentries had left their post, but anyone might have driven up in a car by that street to avoid the crowd, as you yourself did soon afterwards. Why was there no blood on any of the floors, if it comes to that? Unless, indeed, the murder took place in the chapel. And then, of course, there is the incredible daring of the whole thing—to shoot a man, and such a man, at a time when half a dozen independent witnesses were running about the suite.''

''So that you would find less anomalies if the murder was done before, not after, the door was broken in?''

''Naturally I have asked myself whether it was possible

that there should have been a man concealed in the suite all the time, who was responsible both for arson and for murder, before the door was broken in. But again, why did he throw the body from the window? Why not take it into the chapel, and leave it among the flames, so that perhaps the bullet-wound would have remained undiscovered? And how did the murderer get away, or how did he expect to get away, with firemen watching from the street, and sentries rushing up the stairs? No, that idea is full of anomalies too; but I do not banish it from my thoughts."

"There's one extra anomaly—how did the murderer get in, with sentries keeping watch all day and all night on the landing, outside the only door that led to the Inspirer's suite?"

"Well—let us be frank with one another, General, and admit that we know what was common knowledge in Don Gamba's entourage. I mean, that he had his private life like other people, and that when he wished to admit anybody who preferred not be be recognised, he gave a special signal at which the sentries had to unlock the door on the landing, and withdraw to their quarters. That meant that the visitor could walk up unseen from the main entrance; or, with a pass-key, from the little private door which looks as if it did not belong to the house at all. From the inside of that door, too, the signal could be given. You yourself, General, must have come in that way before now, when it was important for you to see Don Gamba, and at the same time avoid gossip."

"That is true. And of course it meant that for five minutes or so anybody who knew the state of things could go up to the suite unobserved—or come down from it. But the sentries would be able to tell you—was the signal actually given them on the day of the murder?"

"Yes, twice—once about eight, and once about nine. Captain Varcos says his first idea was that you yourself might be paying an incognito visit; but this notion, of course, had to be abandoned when he found that the visitor left at nine, the hour of the unveiling ceremony."

"You are assuming that somebody came in at eight and went out at nine? Not the other way about?"

"Captain Varcos distinctly heard footsteps going down the stairs at nine. Rain fell soon after half-past eight, and there were no traces of wet shoes on the threshold of the private door when I examined it. Suppose, however, that two people came up, and only one went away. What became of the other one, after he had finished with arson and murder? There were no bones found, you see, where the fire took place. But, yes, it all adds to the mystery, this preference of Don Gamba's for living in a suite all by himself. You are wiser, General."

"Who, I? And yet, if the Avenger had seen fit to start with me yesterday evening, he might have found me unprotected; my wife is away on a visit, and I had sent all the servants out to see the fireworks. And there are no sentries, as you see, outside my door. Bah! It is no good trying to avoid the stroke of Fate, when it is due to fall. Almeda next—very well, then, Almeda next."

"You must think of the country. Take no risks of that kind, I beg, in the next day or two."

"Until you have laid the Avenger by the heels? Well, Colonel, good luck to your quest. In the meanwhile, there is one important point to be settled: are we to tell the people what has happened? I have to meet the council of the Party in a few minutes' time, and that is one of the principal questions we shall be discussing. If it will facilitate the work of the police, to have the story of that bullet-wound kept dark for the present, I am sure the council would be anxious to fall in with your views."

"On the contrary, it is my strong wish that the whole facts should be made public. At the same time, a reward should be offered to anyone who will come forward with information which might throw light on the affair; and possibly, if the council sees fit, an indemnity for anyone concerned in any minor way with the business who will tell us all he knows. Who scrawls up, for example, the Avenger's manifestos? Not himself, I wager. We shall have to plough through a good deal of trash sent in by lunatics, but there is always the chance that something valuable might result.''

With the proceedings of the council, in so far as they were of political interest, we are not here concerned. It must suffice to say, that General Almeda was confirmed, at least temporarily, in his position; and that the Assembly of the People was to be instructed to vote accordingly. A proclamation was drafted about Gamba's murder, which Dr. Lunaro would broadcast that afternoon. Any citizen who gave information tending to clear up the mystery of last night's events was to receive a reward, the equivalent of fifty English sovereigns. A reward equivalent to five hundred pounds was offered for information which should lead directly to the murderer's discovery; and a free pardon was offered besides, if the person coming forward were himself implicated, not as a principal, in whatever conspiracy might have led to the murder.

This proclamation had a curious result. Weinberg had to receive in audience next morning a little wizened man, short in the legs and long in the arms, who was plainly a workman, and ill-paid at that. His manner was guilty of servility: for was he not a poor man talking to the police? But he was obviously full of self-congratulation and self-importance; he had a clue.

''I work as a steeple-jack, Excellency,'' he began. ''I have cleaned sometimes the great cross on the top of the Cathedral, high up among the little birds. I do not work regularly, more's the pity; but when there is anything to be fetched down from a height, or to be set straight out of other people's reach, then folk remember Pedro Zimarra, and they say, 'Come, he will climb up for us.' So it was, you see, last night, when the great flag over the Town Hall would not come down, because the ropes were in a tangle, but high, high up! So they sent for Pedro Zimarra; they always do.''

''At what hour?'' asked Weinberg. He always let the other man take his time over an interview, even if he were a hopeless chatterbox; there was no harm in being able to size him up at leisure.

"It should have been taken down as soon as the troops had finished marching past, but it would not come; see, there is a knot in the rope, and they pull and pull, but it will not come. So they say, 'Send for that worthless fellow Zimarra; he will be in the Café of the Guardian Angels just now; that is where you will find him.' So I came running from the café, Excellency, and it does not take me long to climb up a building like that. It was just as I was coming down that the clock of the Town Hall went Bim-boom, Bim-boom; you notice that, my faith, when you are within a few yards of it—it almost deafens you. It was half-past ten. That was when I was beginning to descend; and while I was descending, ah! This is where I ask for Your Excellency's attention."

"We are coming to the point? I hoped that we should, some time."

"I was looking across at the little balcony from which the Inspirer of the People had been taking the salute, such a short while ago. And I noticed this—that from the slope of the Town Hall roof you can do what you can do from no other quarter: you can look in through the windows of the chapel, that are set up so high in the wall."

Weinberg leaned forward: this was interesting. Yes; it was true that the chapel of the archbishops, a baroque affair, had panelling round it that went up to more than a man's height; only where the panelling stopped did the windows begin. From the street you would not be conscious of a fire in the chapel until it had already taken hold of the building; from the Town Hall roof, this preposterous little steeple-jack might have seen the first sparks flying much earlier. "And you saw?" he asked impatiently. He was growing tired of this mystery-making.

"I saw, Excellency, a sight altogether edifying. I saw the Inspirer of the people kneeling there and saying his prayers."

"His what? Come, Zimarra, you know as well as I do that the Inspirer was free-thinking."

"What do we know? Yes, to be sure I had heard that. It was only a few weeks ago that I said to the parish priest, 'Father, is the Inspirer of the people a good man?' And he said, 'But of course he is a good man.' So I said, 'How, then, is it we hear he does not go to Mass? Surely all good people go to Mass?' And the priest smiled, and said, 'You should pray for him, Pedro; then perhaps he will go to Mass more often.' That was good advice, Excellency, was it not? And now, as I sat astride the roof, I knew that the parish priest had been right. I think now that the Inspirer's angel guardian must have warned him he had a short time to live; so he went into the chapel to say his prayers. That is good; we should all be afraid of an unprovided death."

Weinberg stared at the preacher, and twirled his thumbs meditatively; not impressed, it is to be feared, by the sermon, but wondering how on earth this odd creature was deluded into such a mistake, or what object he could have in inventing such a story. Then he asked: "He was in the chapel; that is quite possible. But what makes you think he was saying his prayers?"

"Excellency, when I was a little boy I had a great privilege; I used to serve the Mass in the chapel of the Archbishop. And I know well that the altar is at the northern end; while the windows, of course, look out eastwards. I saw the Inspirer of the people a little from behind, but mostly, it will be understood, sideways, from his right. It will be seen, therefore, that the Inspirer had his face turned straight towards the altar. That is good. Moreover, his hands were lifted up as if he was in prayer; not clasped together, but held in front of him, just like the statue of San Taddeo where the tram-lines stop."

"Well, you saw what you saw. But how? It would have been dark by that time, too dark for you to see into the chapel. Do you tell me that the lights were lit?"

"The electric light, no; but there was light on the Inspirer's face, for all that. I will tell you what I think; I think the Inspirer of the people had lit a candle to San Taddeo, as we are taught to do when we want to pray for a good death.''

"And you are prepared to swear to all this? Mind you, I do not say that what you have told me is of any importance. But if it should be, you will have to take your oath upon it; and perjury, my friend, can be heavily punished.''

"Do I not know that? I will take all the saints to witness that that is what I saw. Then it occurred to me that I, a common fellow, had no right to sit there watching great people at their devotions. So I came down quickly, and they paid me a little for the trouble I had taken. I am a poor man, Excellency.''

"Go home; I will send for you again. Whether there will be a reward from the State, I do not know; for your trouble in coming here, I will compensate you out of my own purse. But, see here, there must be no gossiping among your friends about what you have just told me. Breathe a word, and there will be no reward, Zimarra.''

"Not a word, I swear it, though I should be as drunk as a pig when his Excellency sees fit to relieve my poverty a little.'' And with a languishing grimace the steeple-jack bowed himself out.

"It's possible, of course,'' said Weinberg to Almeda, an hour afterwards, "that the fellow may really have seen something. For instance, Don Gamba may have lit a candle or two to try the effect of such lighting on the new altar which, I understand, the talented señora carved for him. I am told it only arrived the day before; and it would be natural that he should wish to see how it looked by candlelight, so as to compliment the señora on its appearance. But that Don Gamba was at his devotions—no, you and I will not believe that, General.''

Almeda lifted his head slowly and cocked it sideways at the Colonel. "Do you know,'' he said, "I am not quite so positive about that. Mind you, Don Gamba had given up all that sort of thing since his student days, just as I did myself. We were of one mind in deploring the interference of the clergy in political matters. But he was—what shall I say? He was by temperament a little inclined to superstition. And, although I would not have mentioned it to anybody if this question had not come up, I may tell you this—he was very much unnerved by the Avenger's threat of burning down his house. *Don't make it a funeral oration,* he said, when I agreed to speak at the unveiling of the statue; he was joking, of course; but there was a real anxiety lurking in his eyes. Well, picture to yourself a man like that, who has just reached the summit of his ambition, been perpetuated in bronze for all time, and then finds himself shut in for the night alone, with a mysterious enemy threatening to burn his house down about his ears. Isn't it possible that the mind of a man in that position would hark back to the superstitious teaching of his childhood? I would not blame him, for one.''

Colonel Weinberg drew himself up a little in his chair. ''I think you know, General, that for myself I am of the old way of thinking. Nothing would please me better than to suppose what you suggest. But really, Don Gamba—it would be a miracle, that. However, you will tell me I am acting against my own principles, because I hold that you should never discredit good evidence when it conflicts with your preconceived ideas. Be it so; the fact that Don Gamba said his prayers, if he did say his prayers, has nothing to do with his murder. All the importance of the story lies, to my thinking, in the fact that a candle or candles were alight in the chapel, for whatever reason, at about half-past ten. That may, possibly, account for the fire breaking out—a candle has been badly set in its stick, falls sideways without being extinguished; a waxed altar-cloth catches from the flame. In that case, you see, the conflagration may have been an accident; and that means....''

''That means, you suggest, that there was no conspiracy beforehand; that one of the party who ran up when the door was broken in saw, quite on a sudden, the opportunity of gratifying some old animosity, fired on the spur of the moment, and tumbled the body out of the window in a panic-stricken desire to conceal his traces?''

''Yes, that is possible; all that is possible. But, General, it does not explain my anomalies. By the way, I have been conducting inquiries discreetly, and I have found a policeman who saw a man coming away from the direction of Don Gamba's house about nine; it might just be the visitor who left at that hour. But the man's face was hidden, in any case, because he wore the hood of his cloak up. I don't think we shall get any further along that line. Well, General, I will do myself the honour of reporting tomorrow.'' And he went off, to enrich the fortunes of Pedro Zimarra, steeple-jack, by a sum equivalent to fifty English pounds.

But the Chief of Police, in Magnolia, is seldom given a long respite from work. Weinberg was still at luncheon with Captain Varcos, at a restaurant in the Street of April the First, when he was summoned to a fresh interview, and found Almeda awaiting him in high discomposure. ''I must ask you, Colonel,'' he began, ''to prosecute your investigations with the utmost rapidity, unless indeed you are prepared to dismiss from confinement the young Englishman, James Marryatt. The Ambassador has been round again this morning; and he hints rather plainly that the incident is causing a hitch in the trade negotiations. The readers of this English rag, it appears, are signing a monster petition to the Government—Bah! What a Press!''

''To tell the truth, General, I shall be glad to see the last of him. Naturally he has to be treated differently from the other prisoners, because he will have a story to tell when he gets out. And that, the Prefect of Discipline assures me, always makes trouble. However, I have thought of a plan by which we might do a little elimination among the persons under suspicion, no later than this afternoon, if you prefer it. No, nothing new; the old psychometric test.''

''Ah, the machine, you mean, which registers reactions while the prisoner replies to a series of word-tests? I thought you did not place much reliance, Colonel, in those methods.''

''In the machine, no. But I have instituted a system by which the person under suspicion stands, while he answers the interrogation, holding hands with a representative of justice. He does not know why this is being done; and, if he is guilty, he is thinking only of the answers he makes, and the impression they will produce. Meanwhile, it is almost certain that he will wince slightly, that his hand will tremble just a fraction, when the words that provoke the guilt-association are pronounced. So we have the witness of the man, as well as the witness of the machine.''

''But a man, like a machine, can report inaccurately; in conveying his impressions, he may exaggerate or minimise them; he may be fanciful, or prejudiced. Surely we must recognise that?''

''It is the very point I was about to raise. In order to eliminate the human inconstant, I was wondering if you, General, could find time to come round to the Hall of Examination, and hold the hands of the suspects yourself? Then, you see, the tell-tale pulses of the malefactor will be reporting direct to the supreme authority.''

''Upon my word, Colonel, you bend all of us round your finger. Yes, I will come; about half-past three, will that suit? Let's see, it will mean interrogating the Englishman, the priest, Gomez, and the fireman—that is all, is it not?''

''General, I have been rather audacious. I was giving luncheon, just now, to Captain Varcos; and I represented to him that it would be a good thing, for the sake of completeness, if he also submitted to the test. Rather to my surprise, he agreed with alacrity. He knew, he said, that appearances were against him, because he was armed at the time of the fire, and there was no real check on his movements. He would welcome, therefore, any opportunity of establishing his innocence.''

''What! You tame even Varcos, then? Capital; be assured that I will be there punctually. And I have simply to hold the hand of the person who is being interrogated, and observe whether it shakes at all, or fidgets, or grows clammy, when this or that word is pronounced?"

"Exactly. Some of the words, of course, are just padding; it would not do to have them all incriminating. You will find it at least an interesting experience."

There is no need to describe the Hall of Examination. It is the only moderately humane part of the Magnolian police system, and is frequently shown to English and American visitors. Possibly the reader has even submitted, by way of pastime, to the ordeal of the psychometric machine. On this occasion, Captain Varcos (at his own wish) underwent the test first; then Marryatt, the priest Sanchez, Gomez the ex-anarchist, and Banos the fireman, in that order. The experiment was somewhat lengthy, for Weinberg believed in thoroughness; the following table, therefore, only gives a section of the actual proceedings. Each person under interrogation had to reply to the word given him by another word, which its associations called up; the word he used was noted down, with his reaction time. Meanwhile the machine buzzed, and his right hand was linked to that of General Almeda.

	VARCOS	MARRYATT	PRIEST	GOMEZ	FIREMAN
Staircase	Footstep	Carpet	Knees	Banisters	Ladder
Altar	Statue	Bride	Sacrifice	Superstition	Cross
Chapel	Balcony	Sermon	Relic	Stench	Roof
Water	Rum	Works	Baptism	Boat	Hose
Car	Body	Smash	Noise	Juggernaut	Wheels
Fire-engine	Brass	Alarm	Bucket	Barricade	Rails
Oil	Salad	Hair	Unction	Salad	Rust
Wax	Work	Candle	Candle	Honey	Candle
Lamp	Fuse	Shade	Switch	Post	Glass
Sentry	Revolver	Box	Prison	Blood	Salute
Good night	Absence	Dormitory	Repose	Dawn	Baby
Bedroom	Basin	Oilcloth	Window	Wall-paper	Window
Chalk	White	Cheese	White	Pavement	Cliff
Paint	Camouflage	Wet	Brush	Red	Red
Avenger	Bluff	Clubfoot	Angel	Justice	Danger

It was impossible, of course, to tell what the machine was making of it all; but certainly the five men answered without the appearance of confusion; stumbling over their words now and again, as we all do when we are in too much of a hurry to react, but not, so far as you could tell, picking one word in preference to another. The General was a little out of temper when it was all over; he was accustomed to long ceremonial performances, but this holding of hands had left him visibly impatient. "Well," he said, as the last of the prisoners had left, "it seems that the test has been a failure."

"That," objected Varcos, "depends on the point of view."

"It was very kind of you to help, General," said Weinberg. "And you too, Captain." He could afford to be polite; he had solved his problem.

investigates father ronald knox's crime

MURDER IN
UNIFORM

FATHER RONALD KNOX hasn't played fair. His perfect murder is so, not because the mystery can't be solved, but because, for political reasons, the crime must go unpunished—at any rate, for the time being. Very possibly retribution will come before very long, in the form of another murder.

That, at least, is how it seems to me. But perhaps I take a prejudiced view. My work as a detective has been done in a land where the law is no respecter of persons, and the course of justice cannot be deflected by political considerations. The writer of crime stories is, however, entitled to choose his own setting. Father Knox has chosen one which in certain circumstances might make the task of the police easier, because "third degree" methods, which would never be tolerated in Britain, would be accepted as a matter of course. On the other hand, the condition of affairs in Magnolia would enable certain persons to commit murder, even if the victim were the Inspirer, with impunity so long as there was no direct evidence against them.

In the present case there is no direct evidence against anyone. Gomez, because of his political opinions, inevita-

bly comes under suspicion. But he and the fireman corroborate each other's accounts of their movements. The
fireman's political views are unknown. I think it is safe to
say that in a country like Magnolia, had he been a member
of any of the Opposition parties, or had he even criticised
the regime at any time, that fact would be on record. Also,
it would be comparatively easy to check up whether he and
Gomez were known to each other. It is therefore safe to
assume that, as the Chief of Police accepted their story,
there was no reason to suppose that the two men were
accomplices.

The main difficulty in dismissing Gomez completely is a
psychological one. Would an anarchist take any action
because he thought it was "his duty as a citizen" to do so?
The central tenet of anarchism is the negation of government, and anarchists repudiate most, if not all, of what
ordinary people consider the duties of citizenship. It is not
stated whether Gomez was a "physical force" anarchist,
but, in a country like Magnolia, he probably was. I suspect, therefore, that Gomez' motive was murder, and the
psychometric test bears this out. "Lamp" to him suggests
"post," "fire-engine" suggests "barricade," "sentry"
suggests "blood," and "avenger" suggests "justice."
These reactions betray the violent nature of the man and
his dreams of "red revolution."

Nevertheless, I think that Colonel Weinberg is correct in
ruling him out. Had he shot the Inspirer, the weapon
would almost certainly have been found. It is possible also
that, regarding the deed as a laudable one, he would have
proclaimed and gloried in it. These facts, combined with
the fireman's evidence, suggest that Gomez arrived too
late. The murder had taken place before he came on the
scene.

Of the other outsiders who made their way into Gamba's
apartments, the priest may have had a motive in resentment at the disbandment of his Order or what would
appear to him the desecration of the chapel. But he and
Marryatt followed Varcos in his search for the Inspirer.

That means that none of these three could have committed the crime, supposing that it took place after the discovery of the fire.

This brings us back to the time factor. General Almeda left the Inspirer at about 10.20, and the body was found at about 11.15. The alarm of fire was given at 10.44. Gamba's wrist-watch stopped at precisely 10.54. According to the Chief of Police, "the shooting must have been done almost immediately after the door was broken in, or conceivably, of course, at some time earlier—though not earlier than 9.50."

Colonel Weinberg makes this statement to Almeda, who left Gamba about 10.20. Is he quoting the medical evidence or referring to the time when the Inspirer left the balcony? Or does he wish to indicate to Almeda that he also is under suspicion? When he arranges the psychometric test, is it really Almeda's reactions which he desires to observe?

Almeda was the last person, other than the murderer, to see Enrique Gamba alive. He had a powerful motive. An ambitious man, he was forced to play "second fiddle" to the Inspirer so long as the latter lived. But he had control of the army. He had been the dictator's right-hand man. If Gamba died, he was the natural, almost the inevitable successor. Possibly he had had that in mind when he joined forces with the dead man. Perhaps he had planned, all along, to use the Inspirer as an instrument, to be discarded as soon as opportunity offered.

Is there any way in which he could have committed the crime? He was at his house when the alarm of fire was given, and was summoned by telephone. On his return to Gamba's residence, he was met by Varcos, and then went upstairs, where he made a personal search of the Inspirer's apartments. He might have committed the crime then—had he found Gamba after the others had failed to do so. But the time at which the watch stopped suggests that the murder had already taken place, and Varcos, on his own account, discovered the body immediately after leaving Almeda.

Could Almeda have killed Gamba before, during his earlier visit? The Inspirer was heard saying: "Good night, my friends!" as Almeda appeared at the foot of the staircase which led to Gamba's private apartments.

That seems conclusive, unless Almeda had imitated the other man's voice so convincingly as to deceive Varcos and Lunaro, both of whom were in constant touch with the Inspirer. Also, to be convincing, the voice must have seemed to come from above. Therefore, either the voice was Gamba's, in which case he was still alive, or Almeda had arranged a gramophone record to produce the "Good night" at the exact moment he reached the lower floor.

In that case, the altar, which Almeda's wife had carved and which had been set up only the day before, might have contained some mechanism that was timed to start a fire after Almeda had left. We are told that the fire started in the chapel and that the altar was charred almost beyond recognition. And if Almeda used a silencer, no shot would be heard below.

This theory, however, would leave certain facts unexplained. Almeda could not possibly have thrown out the body. The steeplejack, Zimarra, saw the Inspirer kneeling at the altar at half-past ten. True, he might then have been dead, which would have explained an action which Colonel Weinberg found so much out of keeping with his character.

Could Gomez, on entering the chapel, have dragged the body from the altar, not realising Gamba was dead, but thinking him merely unconscious, and thrown it out of the window without being observed? The fireman may not have secured the extinguisher from the landing just at once; the place would be full of smoke, and his attention would be concentrated on dealing with the fire. He might not have seen Gomez till later, but still have thought, quite honestly, that the older man must have been beside him all the time. He would have accepted this idea all the more readily when he realised that Gomez' story gave him the alibi he required to clear himself.

If Almeda was the murderer, and Gomez acted in this way, the General had reason to congratulate himself.

In that case, was the Inspirer murdered before or after his broadcast? Perhaps before it. We are told that "the utterance, always a trifle raucous, was not much altered by traces of catarrh."

The difficulty of the "Good-bye" remains. I do not think that Almeda would have dared to speak the words himself, relying on his imitation of Gamba's tones, and on his hearers thinking that the voice came from above. But if a gramophone record had been used, the tell-tale evidence would have remained, unless the instrument had been in the chapel. The rest of the suite, we are told, had remained untouched by the fire. Had the gramophone been in the chapel, the people below might have been surprised that the Inspirer should speak from there—and, even if it were totally destroyed by the blaze, its absence from its accustomed place in the suite would be noticed. Obviously, Almeda would have to use a gramophone that was already in one of the rooms.

There is a further point. When Almeda is told of the chalked-up message, "Almeda next," he is silent for a moment, then squares his shoulders "as if to exorcise an imaginary terror." Is he acting, or is he really afraid? If he is the murderer, unless he or some friend of his is responsible for the Avenger's scribblings, he knows that the author of the threat had no part in making it come true.

That brings us to the Avenger. The prediction, "Gamba to be burnt out on Thursday evening," was fulfilled. Gomez might, on his past record, have been the author—but the fire had started before he appeared on the scene. Gamba's residence, too, was closely guarded—it was really a fortress rather than a house. It is inconceivable that, before the fire, any unauthorised person could have gained admission to it.

That seems to rule out the possibility of the Avenger

being the murderer unless, indeed, someone like Almeda had scrawled the warnings. But even suppose that Almeda were the murderer, why should he add to the risks he had to run others which were quite unnecessary?

On the whole, I incline to the opinion that the Avenger was simply an irresponsible person, trying to create a scare, but doing nothing to carry out his threats. His message, however, may have suggested the idea of the fire to the actual murderer.

Are there any other suspects? For the reasons Colonel Weinberg gives, we may dismiss the two mysterious visitors. There remains Varcos and his two henchmen. There is some uncertainty about the movements of these guards, and no doubt Colonel Weinberg investigated their stories very carefully. In his place, I should certainly have done so. I think, however, that they can hardly have been more than accomplices in the crime. It is doubtful if they were that.

Now, let us turn to Varcos. If Almeda had a motive, so had Varcos. We are told that it was the Free Youth Movement which had brought Gamba to power, and that, after his death, "Varcos must be presumed to be the head of it." True, while Almeda controlled the army, Varcos could not hope to seize the supreme power; but Almeda also might die. Was that why the latter was so thoughtful when he heard of the warning, "Almeda next"? Did he realise that if Varcos was the murderer of Gamba, his own life was in imminent danger?

We are told that the Inspirer's personal guard, of which Varcos was captain, consisted of gunmen. Presumably, therefore, Varcos was a gunman himself. His own station was just outside the door leading to the top floor and Gamba's apartments. During the period of Almeda's visit, he was waiting here with Dr. Lunaro. Presumably Dr. Lunaro left at about the same time as Almeda. If he had remained behind while Varcos made his tour of the sentries, the Chief of Police would undoubtedly have mentioned the fact and have taken his story.

About ten minutes elapsed between the time that Varcos returned to the upstairs landing and the alarm of fire. Was Varcos alone during that ten minutes? He seems to have been.

If this is so, it appears to me, on the evidence supplied by Father Ronald Knox, that the murder probably took place at some time in this short period.

It is possible, for instance, that the second of Gamba's mysterious visitors had brought him some information which showed that Varcos was unreliable, or even a conspirator. What we know of dictatorships abroad suggests that this is by no means unlikely. Suppose Gamba were unwilling to believe that his trusted lieutenant was playing him false. This was his first opportunity of placing these charges before him and asking for an explanation. Unknown to anyone else, he might have called Varcos upstairs.

His first words would reveal to Varcos that the truth was known. His expression may have convinced Gamba, at the same moment, that the charges were true. He would not want to continue the conversation.

"Very well, I shall see to it in the morning," he may have said and turned on his heel. Then Varcos, realising that if the Inspirer lived, he would be ruined, while if he died he might become leader of the movement and ultimately head of the State, shot him from behind.

It is just possible that he could have done this, dropped the body out of the window, and set fire to the place— either to burn some bloodstained article of his own or to cover up other traces, or because he remembered the Avenger's threat and wished to suggest its fulfilment—and got back to his post in the time at his disposal. Or the possibility already mentioned that Gomez threw out the body may still stand and give Varcos a little more time for his interview with the Inspirer and for starting the fire.

There is, of course, no direct evidence against Varcos. But the case against him seems stronger than that against Almeda, and he is the gunman type, while we are told that the other was a "genuine soldier." In my experience, it is rare for a "genuine soldier" to be a murderer. Also, Varcos' psychometric test does carry a suggestion of guilt. One of the things the man who threw the body out of the window must have been afraid of was being seen by someone in a passing car. Varcos fitted the word "body" to the word "car." He also replied "footstep" to "staircase"—would not his ears have been tensed, waiting for the possible sound of a footstep on the stairs, while he was busy at his grim work on the top floor? "Wax" suggested "work"—as he looked down on the body of his victim, may it not have suggested a waxwork figure to him?

None of these key words drew responses at all suspicious in the case of the others who were tested. And was not Varcos' "Bluff" to "Avenger" far more significant than the Anarchist's "Justice"? Others might think that the Avenger's threat had been fulfilled, but the real murderer knew that it had only been bluff, and the word rose automatically to his lips.

This, I know, is far from being conclusive. It would not satisfy a court of law. But I cannot help thinking that evidence which would have convinced judge and jury could have been found if the Chief of Police had looked for it. There is no record of any examination of the rooms for fingerprints. Yet there were probably fingerprints on the window from which the body was thrown, even if they occurred nowhere else.

Then, what happened to the bullet which killed the Inspirer? Was it extracted? Even if it had passed through the head completely it must have been somewhere. A search would have discovered it, perhaps, embedded in a wall. Then, supposing Varcos to have been the murderer, even if he had had time to remove all traces of recent use from his revolver before it was examined, a bullet fired from his gun would bear the same tell-tale markings as the bullet which killed Gamba.

He could not have objected to the test. Naturally, the Chief of Police would have had all the guards' revolvers dealt with in this way and would have taken all their fingerprints. General Almeda would also have been asked to produce his revolver.

I have no doubt that an investigation on these lines would have disclosed the culprit. Why wasn't it made? I can only assume that Colonel Weinberg suspected either Varcos or Almeda, or both, from the start, but knew that it was impossible to bring either of them to trial, and feared that too rigorous an inquiry might mean personal disaster. But, by a process of elimination and finally, by the psychometric test, he satisfied himself as to the guilty party.

"He could afford to be polite; he had solved his problem," is the concluding sentence of the story. And I have no doubt that, when he and Almeda were alone together, he told the General what his conclusions were, and they discussed together what steps it was necessary to take for Almeda's protection and Varcos' punishment.

Anthony Berkeley

THE POLICEMAN
ONLY TAPS ONCE
(with acknowledgments where due)

I

IT WAS A dull sort of day, cloudy and raw like they get it over here, so I thought I'd bump off Myrtle. She had it coming to her anyways.

Besides, the way I'd figured it, any dame with a dial like hers 'd be happier stiff. Myrtle certainly was a terrible looker. That was why I'd picked her. I'd had it all figured out.

There's no need to say how I'd got me into the position that a vacation from the States was going to be pretty good for my health; nor there's no need to say what my racket had been over there, except that it was a mighty good racket while it lasted. It was a private racket too. The bulls were never wise to me. They had no reason. It was a private racket, and it wasn't against any law, not even the Mann Act. I can tell you, it makes a guy feel good to know he doesn't figure on any police records; and I know that, because a pretty good friend of mine was a head-quarters' dick, and if there'd been any breeze stirring I'd have had the dope good and quick. I kept him sweet for the reason. But there was never a breath. I tell you, there was no need to be.

I was born in Connecticut when Connecticut was really tough. And was it tough! Believe you me, a guy that was born in Connecticut round about then wouldn't need any asbestos suit in the next world. Hell'd feel a sweet, cool breeze to him after Connecticut.

My old man was a cop, and I will say he did his darndest to keep me on the level. "Boy," he'd say, as he whacked me with his night-stick, "I'm telling you, it pays to be honest. There's more pickings to be got in one week by an honest cop who knows his racket than the tough guys can collect in a year. Think of it, boy. There's not a hold-up nor a bumping-off in this town but I get my rake-off, and I'm only a plain cop. When they make me a Lieutenant, I'll get double. That's pretty good, ain't it? You take my advice, boy, and stay honest. It pays like hell."

He never got to be a Lieutenant though. He slipped up on a big schemozzle there was one night between Joe Spinelli's boys and a bunch of wops that were trying to horn in on Joe's graft. The wops got cleaned up all right, but the old man let on that he'd seen one of Joe's gang somewhere around that evening and Joe rang up the Captain and had him broke. The old man was sore at that, but Joe wouldn't have him back in the force; he said he wouldn't have a man he couldn't trust taking his dough. So the old man slipped up on the honesty stuff himself after all.

Anyways, I'd gone my own road before the old man got in that jam. Before I could button my own pants I'd decided on my racket, and I was working it before I'd bought my first tuxedo. I worked it for pretty nearly fifteen years, too, up and down the country, before it went lousy on me. It was a swell racket while it lasted, and it never got me in bad with the bulls. There was no reason.

At that, I only quit just in time. If I'd left the quay five minutes later I'd have left it head-first into the water. As it was, I got up the gangway with just enough time to hide in the bilge, and the boys never thought of looking there. I stayed there two days, telling myself that if the rats could stick it I could, but the boys had gone ashore after all and I needn't have worried. I heard afterwards they'd made sure I wasn't on board, so I got to England with no one knowing.

There wasn't going to be any trouble about getting in, I knew that. There was no reason. My passport was all in order, and what it said was true. I was a private citizen of the United States, and nothing known against me. Independent means it said too, but maybe that wasn't so good. What with having to leave in a hurry, and the racket going stale during the last year or two, I was pretty short of dough. I reckoned I had enough to last me a few weeks, living not too high, but after that I'd have to get busy. The old racket wouldn't be any good either. You couldn't work a thing like that in England.

Well, the way I was fixed it meant I'd got to find a new one, and mighty quick at that. The scare I'd had, had kind of sobered me up. I'd got to get hold of enough dough to stay away for quite a while.

The rest of the trip I spent figuring how I could think up a new racket. It had to be a cast-iron one so far as the bulls went, though these English bulls aren't the tough babies like we've got at home; still, I didn't want to get in bad with them and maybe get shot out of the country before I'd had time to sweeten up. And it had to be a sure-fire starter, because I'd got no time to waste.

Before we docked I'd found what I was looking for. It was a pretty old racket, but when all's said and done the old rackets are still the best so long as you can pull them. I'd find some old dame who'd got dough of her own and a face like the back view of a cab-horse, and marry her. There's always some dames that look so terrible that no guy can put up with a dial like that over the coffee-pot of a morning even for the sake of the dough behind it, and I wasn't going to be particular. That was the plan I worked out, and the more I looked it over the better I liked it. I figured it oughtn't to be a difficult one to pull too, because as long as I can remember I'd always been the snake's step-ins with the dames: it seemed like they just couldn't say no to me.

Well, now, the way I thought it out was this. It wasn't going to be too good to make a set for anyone young. I didn't want any snoopy parents or guardians having their say-so; and however glad they may be to get a lousy looker off their hands, in-laws can be just hell once they've got the victim hooked, strapped, and delivered. No, not even if she'd got dough in her own rights I couldn't see myself putting up with the in-laws dropping in to breakfast just when they wanted, with me not daring to so much as sneeze at them in case I got cut off with a dime. I wasn't sure whether they'd let you sue your wife for alimony in these English courts, and I wasn't taking any risks.

That meant I'd got to look out for a dame old enough to have outgrown her family. That didn't worry me any. The older she was, the easier she ought to be. After a while a dame kind of gives up hope, and to offer her any then is just like feeding honey to a bear: she'll make just one jump and land at your side with all four feet. And if you begin pulling a line of sales-talk about gen-u-ine gold wedding rings on top of that, you'll wonder what that is frisking round your feet like a puppy chasing its tail. Leastways, that's how I saw it, and maybe I wasn't too wrong at that.

I figured it wasn't going to be difficult to meet up with the kind of dame I wanted. It was summer-time, and I worked it out that pretty well all I needed to do was to stay in some big dump by the sea and keep an eye on the swell hotels. So I asked a guy in the hotel in London what he reckoned was the real classy place to stay in by the sea in England, and he plumped for Folkestone. So I packed my grips and booked my ticket to Folkestone that same day. I knew I hadn't any time to waste.

Well, Folkestone sure is class all right. The Leas looked to me just lousy with millionaires, though maybe some of them weren't so sticky with dough as they looked. I registered in a real nice little hotel that the guy in London had told me about, and went out straight away to have a look around. I hadn't got any time to waste.

Well, there's no need to write about the next few days. What I like about Folkestone was that there was always plenty of wind. When I get a good line I stick to it, and I needn't say more than that my hat blew into about half a dozen laps a day, till I got real cute at making it land just where I wanted.

And was it easy? I'm telling you. I didn't get a single freeze when I sat down on the bench beside them and began spieling about the difference between Folkestone and Arizona. Not a one. That comes of picking them. I could always size up a dame with both eyes shut.

But when I began asking the questions, there was something wrong with all of them. Either they weren't staying at one of the really swell hotels, or it was out of their class, or there was something wrong with the way their dough was tied up. I wouldn't of believed there could be so many difficulties, when the dames themselves were so willing. I was beginning to wonder would I ever find the right one.

And then I found Myrtle. I could have nearly cried.

The way it happened was like this.

I'd been having tea in the swellest hotel of the lot just the day before, and keeping my eyes pretty wide open, too. Sitting over by one of the pillars was a big fat dame who looked just fierce. In fact, I don't mind saying that she looked so fierce I passed her over at first, though goodness knows I was getting kind of desperate. She had a sort of square face, with what looked like a couple of dozen chins under it, and it was the colour of the underside of a pumpkin pie that's been made by a cook who's just been stoking the furnace with her bare hands and forgotten to wash them. That's the colour it was; and she hadn't tried to cover it not even with a speck of powder. You'd almost have said she must be proud of it.

That was bad enough, but to add to it she was dressed kind of mannish. Leastways, she had on one of those flat black felt hats jammed down on her short, grey hair and a kind of square-cut coat of some darned dull grey stuff, and a short skirt to match, and a white silk waist, and a black knitted four-in-hand. She looked just fierce.

So when I found myself sitting on the next bench to hers the morning after, I don't mind admitting I kind of shuddered once or twice before I let fly with the derby. I had to keep telling myself that beggars can't be choosers, and if old man Henry VIII could stick it, I could: though I will say for that guy, when he didn't like it, he knew what to do with it. So I kind of breathed a prayer and braced myself up.

The shot was a beauty, and the derby landed slick as a coot. There was certainly plenty of lap for a landing-ground, but even so it was a nifty shot.

"Say, lady," I said, doing my stuff, "I certainly beg your pardon. That sure was dumb of me. I ought to of known by this time I should have been grabbing it with both hands, sitting here."

She handed it back, and it seemed to me there was a grim kind of look in her eye; but I couldn't be sure, and anyways, I hadn't finished my lines.

"But perhaps it warn't such an ill wind after all, mam," I says, pulling the Arizona line of talk. "Not if it allows me to make your honoured acquaintance. It sure is dull, setting here alone; and if you'll pardon the liberty, it looks like you're in the same boat. Perhaps we might spend half an hour in talking together? Ships that pass in the night, as the poet says: though it's certainly day with us." I stood looking kind of humble and questioning, like I did when all the other dames almost grabbed me and pulled me down on the seat beside them.

But Myrtle always was different. "My good man," she said, looking me up and down, "if you mean, may you sit on this bench, it belongs to the Corporation, not me. I have no say in the matter." And she kind of gives a cocky little snigger.

"That's certainly kind of you, mam," I said, sitting

down. "The seat may belong to the Corporation, but while you're on it you've got the right to say who may share it with you, and I take it kindly that you let me. Way back in Arizona, where I come from, we never force our company where it's not wanted."

"So you come from Arizona?" she said, in a sort of friendly way. She was real English, all right; she had the proper dude accent. I could tell she was a lady, whatever she looked like.

"I sure do, mam. Li'l old Arizona. Gee, it seems a long way away from here." And I heaved a pretty good sigh.

"My dear man," said the dame, "it *is* a long way from here."

Well, we didn't seem to be getting anywheres, so I thought I'd better liven things up with a compliment or two. I've found that's a thing a dame will always swallow. Even when a compliment on her dial would sound like a bad joke, she'll always be pleased to have one somewhere else. So I took a look at Myrtle's short fat legs in thick grey wool stockings, ending in outsize Oxfords, and said:

"If you'll pardon the liberty, mam, it certainly is a treat to see a neat pair of ankles. Way back in Arizona——"

"Hey!" she said. Just that. "Hey!"

"Mam?"

"If you're working up to the confidence trick, my good man, you can spare your breath. I'm wise."

"Mam!" I said. Well, it kind of took me aback.

"If you weren't—if you were just being infernally impertinent, I apologise," said Myrtle, and sniggered again.

I saw I'd made a mistake. I ought never to have made a pass at her at all. I might have known, from her hat. I thought I'd better beat it before she called a cop, so I jumped up and acted sore.

"Mam," I said, "it's for me to apologise. I see I should not have presoomed on the accident of the wind blowing my hat——"

"So it was the wind, was it?" she broke in like a flash.

"Certainly it was the wind," I said, all dignified.

"You lie," she said. "There isn't any wind this morning. Besides, I saw you flick it. Now sit down again and tell me why the heck you wanted to get off with an old frump like me, and why you're talking this stage American. Sit down, do you hear, my good man, or I'll call a policeman."

That was Myrtle all over. Bossy.

I sat down. There wasn't anything else to do.

II

Well, the funny thing is, after that, Myrtle and I got along fine. You see, I really had a ranch in Arizona, so I didn't come out of that so bad. I'd bought it when times were good, and it had surely looked like a little gold-mine then. I'd put in a guy to act as foreman and he had a bunch of boys to run it, and there was a tidy bunch of steers running there. But now times weren't so good it hadn't been doing much more than pay the boys' wages, so that was about as much use to me as horn-rims to a bustard; though I knew I'd be raking in the bucks from it again when times got better.

I explained all that to Myrtle, with pictures of me among the boys, wearing those woolly-mat pants to prove it. She saw then she'd got me wrong, though I allowed I'd overdone the Arizona line of talk. After that we were as sweet as two hicks in a flivver.

Well, I pretty soon saw I'd struck it swell. When I began edging my questions into the conversation, there wasn't a one that didn't get answered right. Myrtle never suspected a thing. Maybe that dame wasn't so smart as she'd figured, after all. She poured it all out to me; how she'd got almost more dough than she knew how to spend, and how she hadn't a living relative to give two hoots what she did with it or who she left it to, and how she wasn't such a tough girl as she looked and had a heart under that square-cut jacket just oozy with longing for a strong guy's love. Boy, was it easy! And in return I spilled the innocent beans about the swell ranch I had, and the dough I had stuffed away in the banks back at home, and the helluva big shot I was in the old home town. She lapped it up like a tough baby laps bourbon.

And could she take it!

That evening we met again, at her hotel, and when I saw the suite she had there I knew for certain I'd found what I was looking for. Anyways, Myrtle sent down for a pint, and we had it in her private parlour. They don't have bourbon in England, but the stuff was good, and after we'd had a few slugs each I felt good, too. Pretty soon Myrtle sent down for another pint, and I'm telling you she'd drunk level with me on the first. I didn't know they made 'em like that in England.

Well, to cut a good evening short, before I swayed out of that room Myrtle and I were engaged to be married. Yes, just like that. I always was a quick worker, and I will say for Myrtle she was pretty near as quick as me. I finished the second pint before I shut my eyes and kissed her, but it wasn't so bad, after all. And in any case, I was feeling pretty good just then, though I knew darned well I'd have to be sending out for bromo first thing the next morning.

So when a guy comes up to me as soon as I got outside Myrtle's parlour and looks like he wants to get fresh, I just slammed one into his stomach before I asked him what he wanted; but somehow he jerked his stomach to one side and my fist went past his hip, so he could grab my wrist.

"Now then, none o' that," he said, in his Limey accent. "I've been waiting for you, my lad."

"The hell you have," I said. "Come on outside, you son of a bitch."

"It's you that's coming with me," he said. "I know all about you. You're coming along with me to the clink." That's what they call the big house over here. "Confidence trick, eh? You can't get away with that kind of thing here."

"Well, what the hell are you?" I stalled. "A bull of some sort?"

"You bet I'm a bull," he said. "Now, then, are you coming quiet? Lucky Miss Frumm warned me. We know how to deal with your sort here."

Just then Myrtle herself appeared in the doorway. The guy still had me by the wrist.

"It's all right, Mr. Foster," she said. "I've decided not to charge him. I'm going to marry him instead. It'll be a worse punishment for him."

"Say, Myrtle," I said, "who is this guy, anyway?"

"Why, it's Mr. Foster, the hotel detective," Myrtle sniggered. "I told him all about meeting you this morning, and asked him to be on hand this evening, just in case. After all, a poor weak girl needs protection, doesn't she? And I haven't known you long. You might not have proposed marriage at all."

"Oh, that's his racket, is it?" said the bull, interested. "Well, miss, I'd better warn you that——"

"Say, Myrtle," I interrupted him, "this is just a private bull, you mean?" The guy had left hold of my wrist now.

"That's right," said Myrtle.

"Not a real cop at all?"

"Not an official one, no."

"Well, isn't that just too bad for him?" I said, and slammed him one again. This time it connected all right, because the guy wasn't expecting it. "How d'ya like that, punk?" I said. "Because there's another one coming to you from just where that one came from." And I slammed at him again, at his chin this time.

But he dodged it that time, and I took a belt on the chin instead myself that shook me up bad. The guy knew how to fight. I could see that.

"Come inside if you're going to fight," Myrtle said, holding the door open. "We can soon move the furniture." I had to hand it to her; she didn't look like she'd had a drop to drink all evening. Except that some of her chins were shaking a bit with excitement, you couldn't have told she'd been drinking slug for slug with me for nearly two hours.

Well, the guy and I went inside. We were pretty mad at each other, and before Myrtle had begun moving the furniture we took off our coats and started in. I felt like I must beat up this guy or get killed.

At first I thought he was going to have it all over me. I took another belt on the chin that knocked me over backwards. When I got up I was so crazy mad I began missing plenty. Then I slammed two into his face, right and left, and that didn't seem so bad. But I'd drunk so much I was off balance most of the time, and when I tried to close in with him he'd just stand back and let me have it. I began to think I was in for a swell lacing. The guy was beating hell out of me.

Once when he banged me on the side of the head and knocked the other side against the parlour wall, I heard Myrtle say:

"That's the stuff, Foster. Knock hell out of the matrimonial crook."

Well, I don't know why, but that made me madder than a trapped skunk. It sounded real raw. I just went in and I didn't care what he did to me; I couldn't pump 'em in fast enough. One of them landed on the point of his chin, and that was the finish.

While he was sleeping on the floor I turned to Myrtle.

"Did you tell that guy to lay for me?" I said.

You got to hand it to Myrtle. "I did," she said. "I saw through your little game when you were pumping me this morning. I knew you were going to have the darned impertinence to propose marriage, so I warned Mr. Foster about you."

"The hell you did," I said, and slugged her one for herself. She went down like a hippopotamus into a mudpool. I left them lying asleep across each other.

That was something Myrtle hadn't expected. Over here, I guess, they don't slug dames. Well, we're tougher where I come from, that's all.

I went back to my hotel and lay down across the bed. I was tired, and my jaw was sore where the bull had clipped me. I thought of Myrtle, and felt sorer than my jaw.

I figured I was about finished in Folkestone. Myrtle would see the story got spread around, and so would the bull; and after that the town would be too hot. It seemed like I'd better take the first train on somewheres else, if I was going to put my racket over before it got too late. But I felt sore. Myrtle had certainly seemed to fall for the dope that morning. Now I saw that when she was pretending to hand out all that information she was only razzing me along. I'd been the sucker right enough, and Myrtle had just played me for one. It makes a guy feel pretty sore when he's fancied he's tough and then finds he's fallen like a spent bullet for the first amachoor who tries to razz him.

When I woke up the next morning I didn't feel any better. I felt rotten. My mouth was as dry as the Arizona desert, and my lips were all swollen up, like I was trying to whistle and couldn't. One of my eyes was pretty near closed, too.

I had a pint in the cupboard, and after a couple of slugs I began to feel better. They didn't have running water in that hotel like they do in the civilised countries, but there was some water in the pitcher and I rinsed my face and doused my head in it. Then I sent down to the clerk for the bromo, and by the time I'd mixed that up and drank it I began to feel that I might be able to do some thinking again if I didn't do it too hard. So I sat down on the bed and tried to figure out what I was going to do next, and where I could go. I thought maybe they could tell me downstairs what was the next swell seaside town in England after Folkestone.

I was just going to try to make it, when the bell-hop came in to tell me there was a dame downstairs asking for me. Leastways, he said a "lady," but I guessed he meant a dame.

"Listen, sonny," I said, "I don't know any ladies here except one, and if it's her you can tell her to go fry herself. Is that the one?"

"That sounds like 'er, sir," said the bell-hop.

"Then tell her," I said.

The bell-hop reached for the door, but before he could get through it was slung open like a bison had charged it. The bell-hop got knocked into the wastepaper basket on the other side of the room. It was Myrtle, of course. She held the door open and gave one jerk with her thumb, and the bell-hop beat it quicker than I've ever seen a bell-hop move before.

Myrtle came and stood over me, and I covered up. I thought she'd come to slug me back for the belt I'd given her the night before, and I felt too sore to take another slam in the face.

But she didn't slug me. "Eddie," she said. "I got you into a hell of a jam last night." Leastways that isn't exactly what she said, I suppose, but it's what she meant.

I didn't say anything.

"I got you into a hell of a jam, and you slugged me for it, and I've come round to congratulate you."

"You've come round to do what?" I said.

"To congratulate you. You're the first man that's ever slugged me, and I never thought any man would ever have the guts. Congratulations, Eddie. And I apologise for doubting you."

"For doing what?" I said. I was feeling a bit nuts. I couldn't figure out what the hell Myrtle was doing.

"For doubting you, my good man," she shouted "Can't you understand English?"

"Not like the way you English talk it," I said.

"Well, tell me this. Did you mean what you said when you asked me to marry you last night, or were you too damned drunk to know what you were saying? That's a straight question, and I'd be obliged for a straight answer."

I stared at her. I'd thought at first I must be nuts; now I thought she must be.

She took off her hat and slung it on to a chair, and gave a sort of hitch with her elbows to her skirt. I made sure she was going to slug me.

"Well?" she said.

"Sure I meant it," I said hastily, before she could clip me.

"Do you love me?" she asked, and made a sort of movement with her feet. Her Oxfords looked bigger than ever.

"Of course I love you, Myrtle," I said quickly. I thought she meant to let out at my shins any minute.

"Then it's all on again," she said. "I'm sorry I doubted you, Eddie. I sent a cable yesterday to ask about your ranch, and I've just had the answer. I thought you were a crook, and I find you're only a mutt, or whatever you call a dumbbell in your language. I think I'd better marry you before you do something sillier still. You're quite sure you didn't want to marry me for my money, Eddie?"

"Aw, hell! Forget it," I told her.

"Very well, I will. And you'd better forget all I told you yesterday morning. I thought you were a crook pumping me, so I stuffed you up with a lot of nonsense. I haven't got any money."

"Sure you haven't," I said. I'd seen the wise look she shot at me and knew she was just trying me out. "What the hell? I've got plenty for two."

"Good!" said Myrtle, kind of briskly. "Then stop looking as if you were trying to whistle and get up and kiss me, even if it hurts."

Well, I didn't care which of us was nuts. I go up and clinched with her. I know a break when I see it.

III

So that's how Myrtle and I got fixed up.

You can bet I didn't waste any time. Myrtle didn't seem to want to waste any either. She was a quick worker, too. I will say that for Myrtle. The cable had put her properly to rights, and she was sure now I was a swell rancher and couldn't be after her dough. So she put me wise about the special licences and all those fool things you have to have over here when you want to get spliced in a hurry, and in three days Myrtle Frumm was Mrs. Eddie Tuffun.

And was she pleased? Well, it seemed like she was pretty near as pleased as me, and that's saying plenty. I lent her a couple of hundred bucks in advance of the contract to fix her trousseau and told her she needn't pay it back either, and that finished her. She knew I must be on the level to do that. I'd figured that was just how she would feel.

I didn't have to press her either. She was still pulling her stuff about being so darned poor you'd think she hardly knew where her next bucket of champagne was coming from.

"You shall never say I married you under false pretences, Eddie," she'd say. "I know they attach a lot of importance to money in your country."

"That's all right, Myrtle," I'd tell her. "I've got plenty for two."

"You'll need it," she'd answer. "I've got extravagant tastes, like staying in first-class hotels; and I warn you that I'm going to gratify them."

"You'll gratify 'em, all right, Baby," I'd say.

"I've told you before not to call me 'Baby,' " she'd snap out on me. "It sounds ridiculous." Then she'd go on to tell me about her house and gardens, and what alterations she was going to make with my dough.

I had a job not to smile. The way she talked you'd have thought it was a four-room bungalow, with a hired girl to do the work. Only she'd let out it was in London, and they don't have bungalows in London. I wasn't so green as all that.

Anyways, it made one thing easy. On the morning we were spliced we went to see an attorney and made new wills. Only a couple of dozen words, leaving everything to each other.

Myrtle never stalled at the idea. "My dear man, of course," she said, when I kind of delicately suggested it. "You needn't beat about the bush. I should expect it in any case. As for my few sticks, you're welcome to them; but I'm certainly not going to lose that ranch of yours the first time you get in the way of a motor-bus.'' That was Myrtle all over. She certainly had a raw way of putting things.

You'd think that after I'd got things all fixed like that the way I wanted them, I'd be feeling pretty good. But I don't know. Every time I had to kiss Myrtle, it seemed to get kind of harder. I tried good and plenty to give her the works as if I meant it, and it seemed like she couldn't tell the difference. I guess she couldn't too, at that. So I got away with it all right.

But I don't know. On the morning we were to get married, before we went to the attorney's, I began to wish I hadn't hit on the racket at all. I looked round my bedroom, with its narrow bed, and it didn't seem as if living with Myrtle was going to be worth all the dough in the world. I threw a couple of drinks into me and it wasn't so bad. I began feeling pretty high. I thought maybe I could get her dough into my own name, and then we could live apart. I'd give her a pretty good alimony too. It would be worth it.

Well, anyways, we got the wills signed and left them with the attorney for safe keeping. And then we got married. That was all there was about it. One minute we were married, the minute before we weren't. I felt like I was in a dream.

When we came out of the marriage office we looked at each other.

"What you say we have a drink, Myrtle?" I said.

"You look as if you needed one," said Myrtle.

We went back to her rooms and had a couple of slugs. That made me feel better, and I managed to kiss Myrtle kind of fierce, like they enjoy it.

I might have known Myrtle would be different. "Cut out the rough stuff, Eddie," she said. "You've socked me once, my lad, and that's going to last you for the rest of your life. If there's any more socking to be done, I'll do it."

Well, that made me feel a bit sore, so when Myrtle told me to get busy and help her pack her things I was all set for trouble.

"Pack your things hell," I said. "What do you want to pack your things for? We're staying right here."

"Nothing of the sort," she said. "What do you imagine? We're going on our honeymoon."

"Honeymoon hell," I said. "We're staying right here. I've brought my grips, haven't I?"

Well, would you believe it but Myrtle just took no notice at all. She just went on packing.

"Take it easy, baby," I said. "Take it easy, can't you? What's the big idea, anyways?"

She looked up for a minute. "I told you. We're going on our honeymoon. We're going to Slocum-on-the-Marsh. I've written for rooms there. We're catching the three-ten train. I've ordered the taxi.—Now, then, Eddie, put that bottle down. You've had quite enough to drink already, and you know you can't carry your liquor. I'm not going to arrive at Slocum with a drunk husband."

I threw the bottle at the fireplace, and it broke. It was a waste of good liquor, but I felt that way.

"And I'm not going to arrive at Slocum at all," I told her, and I didn't whisper it either.

From the way Myrtle acted, you'd have said she hadn't even heard.

Hell, what's the use? We went to Slocum.

There were twenty-seven people in Slocum while we were there, and twenty-six of them were dead. The twenty-seventh was Myrtle.

By the time our honeymoon was over there were twenty-eight dead, because I was dead three times over. Myrtle liked walking. There wasn't any need to walk, because there was nothing to see but more marsh after you'd walked there; but that didn't matter to Myrtle. And it wasn't any use to say I'd got a sore heel, because . . . oh, hell.

The only ten minutes I enjoyed out of our fortnight at

Slocum was when a guy beat me up for making a pass at him. He looked like he weighed about thirty pounds more than me and it was all muscle. He pretty near banged my head off. For the finish he knocked me ten feet into the marsh. Then he pulled me out, just to knock me in again. It was swell.

But Myrtle didn't like me fighting, and I'd figured out already that I'd got to do what she wanted for a while at any rate; and that stood for not doing what she didn't want.

The trouble was that doing what Myrtle wanted and not doing what she didn't want, seemed like there wasn't going to be room in my life for anything else. When I could give Myrtle the slip, I used to go and sit in the marsh and think about it. It looked like hell then, being ordered around by a fat dame for the rest of my life. I couldn't figure out where I'd slipped up, either. Maybe I hadn't had a break at all, or maybe the racket had been lousy from the start.

Then I'd go back to the bar and have three-four drinks, and it didn't look so bad after all. I'd gone out after the dough, and I'd got it. That was the big idea. I saw then that I'd had a lucky break. It was just I didn't know how to handle it. I'd be able to fix Myrtle to rights when I was ready. I just wasn't ready yet, that was all.

I didn't like to ask Myrtle much more about her mansion and grounds (they call a big house a mansion over here). She acted kind of queer sometimes when I did. I saw she'd got the economy-bug like lots of these rich guys. You have to be awful rich before you begin to worry over spending a couple of dimes. I've seen rich guys that way before. So I just pretended to agree with Myrtle when she kept saying we must economise, and thought what I'd do with her dough once I'd got my hooks on it.

I thought a good bit about Myrtle's mansion, too. I betted it was swell. I betted she had a butler too at that. I even worried whether I'd have to say "whisky and soda" to him instead of "highball" every time I wanted a drink.

By the day we were to leave Slocum and go to the
mansion I was like a jazz-drummer in a Harlem speakeasy
on Thanksgiving Night. Well, a guy doesn't step into
a mansion of his own and order his own butler to bring
him a couple of highballs (and make it snappy) for the
first time every day of his life, does he? I'll say he
doesn't.

Well we got away from Slocum, and was I glad to see
the end of that place? Myrtle told me to fix our bill, and I
still had a good few bucks left to buy the tickets to
London. I figured I'd better go on handing them out till we
were safe in the mansion. After that it wouldn't matter.

At London Myrtle gave the address to the taxi-driver,
and I followed her in so quick you might have thought I
was afraid of being left behind. Myrtle took up plenty of
room on the seat, but I crowded her a bit more still. I took
her hand too. I guess I came pretty near to being fond of
Myrtle just then.

"Ah," she said, leaning back, "this is nice, Eddie. It
isn't often I drive home in a taxi."

"Sure," I said. "Taxis run you to a lot of dough."

"A really good hotel once a year, that's my only weakness," said Myrtle, sounding sort of pleased with herself.
"You won't find me an extravagant wife, Eddie."

I gave her hand a squeeze. It was like squeezing a raw
chop. "That's all right," I said. "Just you wait till we
start hitting it up. Say, Myrtle, how far is it to this
mansion of yours?"

"Oh, a fair ride. I hope you're not going to be disappointed in my little house, Eddie. It's hardly the sort of
thing you've been used to."

I had to hide a smile. "Don't worry, Myrtle," I said. "I
guess I can make it do. Somewheres near Oxford Street,
did you say it was?" That was about the only swell street I
knew in London.

"Oh no. A long way," Myrtle said. "Now don't ask
any more questions. Wait and you'll see."

Well, I did wait, and it seemed like I was waiting a long

time. The taxi went on and on. Sometimes Myrtle told me the names of the districts we went through. "This is Fulham," she'd say. Or, "That's Putney Town Hall." I thought they must have their railway depots a long way from the swell parts in London, but it didn't look like the parts we kept driving through were getting any sweller.

At last we turned out of a long street into a little one where the houses were joined together in pairs instead of standing alone. The taxi stopped in front of one. It had about six feet of garden in front of it, and on the front gate was "Rapallo." When the taxi drew up, the hired help came bouncing out on the steps. She didn't wear a nice black dress and a white cap with streamers, like you see on the movies. She wore a sort of pink overall, and she looked like hell.

"Ah, there's Kate," said Myrtle.

I looked at her. "Say, Myrtle," I said, "what the hell are we stopping here for?"

"What do you think we're stopping here for, my dear man?" said Myrtle. "This is where I live."

Well, could you beat that?

IV

Now, I want you to get this plain. I never figured at the beginning to bump Myrtle off. I never have believed in bumping guys off unless you've got to, or dames either for that matter. It puts too much strain on a guy.

But I hadn't been Myrtle's husband for a month before I began to see it was more than flesh and blood could stand. At that I might have stood it if we'd been living in a mansion and Myrtle had as much dough as I'd figured. But all she had was about two-three thousand bucks a year, and this one-horse little shack "Rapallo." It certainly was a tough break.

As for Myrtle, you'd have thought she'd have been grateful to any guy that married her, with that dial of hers. But grateful hell! It seemed like she thought I ought to be down on my knees all the time being grateful to her for marrying me. It seemed like she thought she'd raised me up in the world, being associated with her. She was so pleased with herself she made me sorer than a split skull.

And bossy! Say, it was a wonder she let me breathe without her permission. It was "Eddie, do this," and "Eddie, I've told you you're not to do that," the whole time. And when I'd ask her who she thought she was ordering around, she'd say, "The meanest little skunk that ever came out of America, that's who."

The reason she called me mean was when she began to suspicion that maybe I hadn't got quite so much dough as I'd let on. I couldn't hide it up, either. By the time we got to London I hadn't much more than a dozen bucks left. Of course, I kept telling her I was expecting a draft any minute from home, but she was so darned mean she just didn't believe me.

After that she was always shooting off her mouth about her income only being enough for herself and not being able to keep an able-bodied husband in idleness, till I pretty near slugged her once or twice. But I don't know. I'd slugged her once, and I kind of had the feeling that I'd better not try it again. No dame fights fair, and Myrtle always seemed like she might grab up the poker and sock me with that. Hell, that dame had me pretty nearly scared.

So by the end of the month I'd figured out that I'd have to bump her off. There just wasn't anything else to do.

Of course I knew I could walk out on her, but where would I walk to? Besides, I didn't see why I should have had all that trouble for nothing. Myrtle certainly owed me something, and that was the only way she was likely to pay it.

Still, it wasn't going to be so easy, at that. They're liable to make quite a fuss here over the smallest case of assault if the guy craps out afterwards; and when a guy croaks, they don't give any bail either. It's not like it is back at home where you can put half a dozen guys on the spot in one evening, and only get a smile from the bulls; or if they do pull you in, just for the look of the thing, your attorney only has to lodge a writ of habeas corpus to have you out again in ten minutes. No, they don't give a guy much of a break over here.

So I knew I'd got to be plenty careful; and when Myrtle wasn't at me to chop up some wood or carry the coals to the kitchen or water the geraniums in the backyard or any other of the fool jobs she was always thinking up for me, I'd sit down and do some quiet figuring.

The way it seemed to me was this: it had got to look like an accident.

If it could be done that way, and the bulls didn't get suspicious, there was no one else to worry. I knew that was an important thing, because I read up the dope about some of the big cases they've had over here and it often looked like the guy was going to get away with it till some relative of the victim comes snooping around and asking awkward questions and then goes off and tells the bulls that things don't look too good. There was a guy called Seddon got his that way, and another guy called Crippen, and lots of other guys.

When things don't happen like that, it's some darned fool little mistake the guy makes that puts the dicks wise to him. Maybe he contradicts himself, or can't prove his alibi as well as he figured, or loses the check for the trunk he's left at the depot containing the body of the guy he's bumped off.

Well, except for Kate, who's too dumb to notice if anyone stole a pound of frankfurters out of her hand while she was putting them in her mouth, there's no one to come snooping around after Myrtle; and I wasn't going to do the job at all if it left any chance of making a mistake like the wise guys who get caught. I'd never bumped anyone off yet, and I certainly didn't intend to fry for the first.

That's why I figured it must look like an accident, so neither the bulls nor the reporters would ever suspicion a thing.

And another thing. It had to be an accident when I

wasn't anywhere around. These accidents don't look so good when a guy and his wife go walking along the cliffs and the guy comes back without the wife. Even a Broadway cop would scratch his block over that.

And another thing too. It had to be an accident over something Myrtle had the habit of doing, so there'd be no questions why she happened to be doing such a thing for the first time and croaked over it. That went for taking a moonlight row one night down the river and getting drowned; Myrtle doesn't take moonlight rows. And I was being so careful I meant it to go even for being run over by a car on a lonely road, just in case Myrtle hadn't the habit of being on lonely roads where there was no room for her and a car to pass abreast.

In fact, I thought up so many things it mustn't be, that it didn't seem like there was going to be much room left for anything it could be. But I was wrong at that. There was one thing.

The way I worked around to it was this. What was Myrtle in the habit of doing that might turn out dangerous?

For a time all I could think of was the Myrtle does the cooking herself, on the nights Kate's out, on a gas-stove; and from the number of guys who've bumped themselves off that way for the purpose you'd say that gas-stoves are more dangerous than a sawed-off shot-gun in the hands of Alvin Karpis. But I couldn't think up any plan of putting Myrtle on the spot that way without so much preparation and schemozzle that anyone would see there was something phoney.

It was queer the way I found the idea. Myrtle and I were talking over our lunch and all the time I was trying to think up a safe way of croaking her. When she began giving me my orders for the afternoon I loved her so much I could have strangled her.

"Oh, and you must find ten minutes to run down to the garage at the corner and get me a new tin of aviation petrol," she said. She meant gasoline, but she called it petrol; all these Limeys do. "And don't forget to take the empty tin with you.—Do you hear, Eddie?'' she snapped out.

I nodded. I guess I looked a bit glassy-eyed. Myrtle had just reminded me that every fortnight she washed her hair in petrol. I certainly felt grateful. That was going to mean curtains.

Well, after that it was just a choice of ways. At first I tried to work out how I could make a lighted match drop in the basin. It would have to be when Myrtle was about half-way through fixing her hair, so she'd have her eyes shut and her head over the basin. I didn't feel too good about burning Myrtle up, but it couldn't be helped. Then I thought that if I could get the match to light at the right time, and there was plenty of vapour in the room, she wouldn't burn up. She'd blow up. It would be a whole lot easier for her. That made me feel not so bad.

The time would be when she finished soaking her hair and was ready to dry it. I'd seen Myrtle on the job, and I knew she kept the towel on a glass shelf above the basin. When she was ready for it she just groped up with her hand; of course, she kept her eyes shut. That made me wonder whether I couldn't put something under the towel which would light up when Myrtle pulled the towel away, but I couldn't get it. I could fix the towel all right, and get out of the house and down the road a piece before she was ready to use it, but I couldn't figure out how to make something light up that way and be sure there'd be no trace left when the dicks examined the room.

Then I thought, if Myrtle was going to blow up anyways, why not blow her up with something else and everyone would naturally think it was the gasoline?

I knew I was getting pretty near it; and so I was. The next minute I saw the whole thing.

I'd help Myrtle get started and pour the gasoline over her head for her, like she'd made me do once before. Then, when she'd got her eyes shut and wouldn't be opening 'em again, I'd lay a bottle with some fulminate of mercury on top of the towel and beat it. When Myrtle

pulled the towel down, the bottle would drop on the floor.
The bathroom floor is tiled. Drop an ounce of fulminate of
mercury on it, and no one in that room is going to stand as
much chance as a drummer for electrically-heated pants in
hell. Everyone would naturally think it was the gasoline;
and if the plan went sour on me and Myrtle saw the bottle,
she'd have no more idea about the little crystals inside it
than a New York traffic cop has about the Einstein theory.

Well, I walked round that plan for days. I took it out for
walks with me, combed its hair and gave it all the beauty
treatment I could think up; and the more I looked at it, the
sweller it seemed.

The fulminate of mercury was easy. I'd made it a dozen
times over in the States. You can't be a tough guy and
work any kind of a racket without needing to know something about bombs and detonators and all that. All I needed
was some mercury, some nitric acid, and some spirits of
wine; and I guessed I could buy those pretty well anywhere, and no questions asked. All I had to say was I'm
an experimental chemist, or an experimenter in chemistry.

That's my plan, and I'm going out right now to buy
those chemicals. Myrtle's due to wash her hair again next
Wednesday, and I've got to be ready for it. I've been
taking a few dimes out of Myrtle's purse lately, and I've
still got a buck or two of my own left over. It looks like
I've got enough now for the mercury and fixings, so I'm
going out right this minute to get them.

And the reason I've written it all out this way is I find it
easier to see if I've overlooked anything. I don't aim to
make any mistake like the guys who got caught, and
setting it all out on paper makes it good and clear. I've
read through what I've written, and I can't see anything
wrong. The bottle with the fulminate in will be blown into
a million pieces. I'm not sure whether the detonation will
explode the petrol too, but I reckon there should be enough
flame to set off the vapour. Maybe I'll put some sulphide
of antimony and potassium chlorate in to make sure. Anyways, if that happens I guess the whole house may go up,

and I aim to be well down the road when it does. I'd pass the word to Kate if I could, but I can't. She'll have to take her chance.

Well, two thousand bucks a year is going to be plenty nice. Maybe if I sell out it will be nicer still. But nicest of all will be to get clear of Myrtle and be my own guy again. Plenty nice that will be. Plenty.

They say over here the bull only needs to tap you on the shoulder once. But over here they can't detain you as a material witness and then beat hell out of you till you come clean. Over here they've gotta prove it.

Yeah—I'll say they've gotta prove it!

[Eddie Tuffun's manuscript ends here.]

V

From *The Daily Tribune*, Wednesday, September 29th, 193—.

"A shocking explosion occurred yesterday at a house in Beverley Road, East Sheen, completely wrecking the bathroom and the walls of the adjoining rooms. The occupant of the bathroom at the time was literally blown to bits. It is reported that . . ."

POSTSCRIPTUM

I cannot refrain from adding a few words to the manuscript begun by my late husband, to satisfy my sense of artistic neatness, although I shall put the whole thing in the fire before the ink is dry.

My husband made a fatal mistake in not doing the same thing. It may have helped him to clarify his ideas by putting them down on paper, but he should have burned the results sooner. For naturally, when I noticed him engaged so prodigiously in an exercise so unusual to him as writing, my curiosity would not let me rest until I had found out what it was all about. I had already made the discovery that the key of a dispatch-case of my own fitted his bureau, so while he was out—actually buying his nitric acid and things—I took the opportunity of examining these papers.

To say that they interested me is to put it mildly. I had come to the conclusion already that I had made a fool of myself by marrying the little rat; but all women are prone to do that at my age. But I must confess that I had no idea what a real rat he was. For a few minutes it was quite a shock to me, although I am not easily shocked.

So when I had finished reading, I locked the manuscript away again and went up to my bedroom to think. I suppose that during the next hour I thought harder than I have ever done in my life before. After all, I had something to think about: what was I going to do?

I was not concerned for my life, of course. Now I knew, it was simple to escape the unpleasant end he had planned for me. I had only to take the manuscript to the police to ensure that, and at the same time bring on him the punishment he deserved.

But that did not satisfy me. I wanted to turn the tables on him more completely than that, and dole him out a more poetic justice than he was likely to receive from the law. Besides, there was that ranch of his. I have always wanted to live on a ranch, though I certainly saw no prospect of achieving it. If I merely handed the little skunk over to the police, I should never see that ranch. Whereas if it was Eddie who by a most unfortunate accident got blown up instead of me . . . well, his will was genuine enough. I may have made a fool of myself in one direction, but I am not a complete fool. I had taken steps to make sure about the will. He really had a ranch, and it really would come to me if he died.

Anyhow, to cut a long story short I devised a very simple plan.

My husband made another mistake. He assumed that I knew nothing about chemistry. In these days of higher education for women it is never safe to assume ignorance on the part of a woman in any branch of science. As it happens, I had done chemistry at school and found it extremely interesting; so interesting that I had progressed a good deal further than the school curriculum allowed, and used to help the chemistry mistress in her own private experiments. I still had my old text-books, in a trunk in the attic. I went up there and got them out.

The upshot was that when Eddie came back, very pleased with himself, I had my plan cut and dried. He went upstairs, and then came down to tea. Then I went upstairs—to get a handkerchief. Eddie, of course, did not offer to get it for me. Tough guys don't do things like that.

It didn't take me two minutes to find the bottles. He had hidden them behind some clutter on the top of the bathroom cupboard. I poured out a little of the nitric acid, and a little of the spirits of wine; I only wanted a very little.

The rest of tea we talked, funnily enough, about the ranch.

Afterwards Eddie went upstairs and locked himself in the bathroom. He didn't know that I went up and locked myself in the attic, any more than he knew that while he was busy making his fulminate of mercury I was just as busy dissolving a bit of a George IV silver teaspoon in nitric acid to make fulminate of silver. I was sorry about the teaspoon, which was one of a set, but it was all in a good cause. A sixpence of course has too much alloy.

Well, I suppose it was a curious situation that evening. Eddie was planning to murder me, and I was planning to get in first and murder Eddie; and we were as charming to each other as two snakes in love. In fact Eddie was so charming (Eddie could be charming when he wanted) that I nearly called the whole thing off, told him all about his little game, and suggested a fresh start with no murders on either side. But I knew it was only feminine weakness and fixed my thoughts on the ranch.

I didn't say anything the next day about washing my hair. My silver fulminate wasn't ready, and I wanted to give Eddie's mercury every chance. Eddie didn't say a word either. But the day after that I saw that the little two-ounce bottle hidden behind the clutter on the top of the bath-room cupboard was full of the grey crystals, and knew that Eddie's experiment had been successful and everything was in order. I couldn't help wishing, though, that he had managed to blow himself up during the process instead.

However, he hadn't; so at lunch I said, quite casually, that I was going to wash my hair that afternoon and would Eddie see that there was plenty of aviation petrol in the can. Eddie nodded, as cool as a cucumber, and said he would. I was annoyed, seeing Eddie's calmness, to notice how my own heart was thumping. I dislike weakness of any sort.

I knew Eddie would make for the bathroom directly after lunch. And he did. As soon as I saw him begin to go upstairs I hurried along to the kitchen. I wasn't sure how much damage would be done, and I wanted to get Kate out of the house. I was so intent on that, that I quite forgot to take a consciously last look at Eddie.

Now, what I had done was this. Fulminate of silver is a great deal more dangerous stuff than fulminate of mercury. It goes off almost if you look at it. I hadn't dared to make more than a pinch of it, but I could rely on that exploding at the slightest jar. So behind the clutter I had arranged a little see-saw. The bottle of fulminate of mercury weighed down one end of the little strip of wood that I had used as a cross-piece, and cocked up on the other end, but hidden behind a big jar of bath-salts, was the fulminate of silver, in a pill-box. As soon as Eddie took away the bottle, the pill-box, which was on its side with a match underneath to stop it rolling down the see-saw, would roll down the other way and drop on the tiled floor, where it would explode.

The explosion would make a sharp report, but of course so little of the stuff would do practically no damage. It was Eddie's own fulminate of mercury that was going to do the real job. And the way I had "figured it out," as Eddie would say, was this. Eddie would naturally be nervous. The loud pop by his feet while he was still taking down his own bottle, would make him jump violently. The jump would occur before he had got his bottle much below the level of the top of the cupboard, because he would be handling it slowly and with caution. So before putting his bottle on the see-saw, I greased it gently all over with butter and fixed a piece of thin white cotton under the cork, pushing the latter home not too tightly.

The theory was this. Eddie, starting violently when my fulminate of silver went off, would have one hand still above the level of his head. The inevitable reflex action would be to jerk that arm down. The jerk would encounter the resistance of the cotton under the cork—nothing very much, but enough to pull the slippery bottle out of his hand; and at the same time the jerk would have been enough to dislodge the not-very-securely-fastened cork from its place and so not leave the bottle dangling in the air. The bottle would therefore fall on to the tiled floor—and that would be the end of Eddie.

Naturally, I did not work entirely on theory. In the attic there was a shelf at just about the height of the top of the bathroom cupboard. I experimented there until I had found just how far to push the cork in over the cotton loop to make everything happen as it should.

And it did happen. Nothing much would have been lost if the trap had failed; I could have sprung it later another way. But it didn't fail. Even as I write I can feel the gratification of the theorist whose calculations work out exactly right. I suppose the designers of big guns feel much the same way, though their method of killing is more cumbersome than mine just as it is a great deal more expensive.

Kate apparently noticed nothing peculiar about my demeanour, for she has said nothing since and she would certainly have commented on the slightest deviation from the normal had she discerned it. Kate is very strong on premonitions and forebodings and all that kind of thing. In any case, when I told her to come out and let me show her the beans I wanted picked for dinner, as I should be busy and could not show her later, she came at once. We were actually among the beans when the explosion happened. Eddie could not have timed it for me better. What is more, I distinctly heard a little pop before the big explosion. The whole thing went precisely as I had planned.

Well, that is that, and they have been scraping Eddie off the shattered walls ever since. (Poor Eddie! He wasn't so tough after all. I might even be sorry for him if I didn't remember that ranch. And it was a perfect piece of poetic justice.)

And that, I submit, is the perfect murder. It is now past midnight; the police have gone; and not the slightest suspicion has been voiced that it might conceivably have been anything but an accident. The police have been remarkably active. They have traced Eddie's purchases of mercury, nitric acid, and the rest already. From that, and the nature of the explosion, they know that fulminate of mercury was the cause. They have my own information that he was amusing himself with some chemical experiments, though I do not know what. They have seen my horror at learning that he must have been making fulminate of mercury; and my suggestion that he did not tell me because he knew I should try to stop him owing to the danger, is a perfectly reasonable one. Nor have I attempted to hide the fact that I have some smattering of chemistry myself; I have even dug some dusty old text-books out of a trunk in the attic to prove it. But there is no trace in the attic of any experiment there: though even if there were, any such experiments would, of course, have been put down to Eddie.

They have no suspicion. I cannot understand how they ever could have any suspicion. And if they did, there is not the tiniest trace of proof. I repeat, it has been the perfect murder.

Now I am going along to the kitchen to burn this manuscript in the furnace, as I said, before the ink is dry. And in a month or two I shall be sailing for Arizona. As poor old Eddie would have put it: "Oh, boy!"

Ex-Supt. Cornish, C.I.D.

investigates anthony berkeley's crime

. . . AND THEN COME
THE HANDCUFFS!

MR. ANTHONY BERKELEY IS, I think, more successful in his clever and amusing parody of the new manner in American fiction than in his "perfect murder," ingeniously as he has worked it out.

True, on a first reading, many people will decide that Myrtle Tuffun is safe, and that no one will ever suspect that she is, in fact, the murderess of her husband. The American, at the time of his death, was himself preparing to commit murder. He was killed by the explosive with which he had planned to put an end to Myrtle. Police investigation will lay bare his antecedents and his true character. It will become obvious that he married Myrtle for the fortune which, in reality, she did not possess. Already his purchases of chemicals have been traced. The conclusion that he intended murder, and was killed by the premature explosion of the very dangerous substance he had manufactured, would appear to be natural. Why should the police bother to look further?

That, obviously, is Myrtle's own view. She has found the whole business easy. In my opinion, it was far too easy. And the sense of false security into which she has thus been lulled will make it more difficult for her to meet successfully any new and dangerous turn in the investigation, will increase the possibility of her giving herself away.

Already she has made certain mistakes which may have serious consequences. She has been too ready to assume, for instance, that Kate, the maid, has no suspicion of the true state of affairs. Like her husband, she apparently thinks that Kate is "dumb." A great many people do think that about their servants, but the average domestic is by no means as stupid as her employer imagines. She usually knows far more about the family in which she is working than its members would believe possible.

The police are aware of this, and the officer in charge of the case would give Kate every chance and every encouragement to talk. He would allow her to tell her story in her own way. A great deal of what she said would have no practical bearing on the case, but he would get a fairly accurate account of the relations between the strangely assorted husband and wife. And I should be considerably surprised if the following facts did not emerge:

(*a*) That two days before the death of Eddie Tuffun, while he had locked himself in the bathroom, Myrtle had locked herself in the attic.

(*b*) That one of Myrtle's George IV silver teaspoons had disappeared, and that Kate couldn't think where it had got to.

(*c*) That some days before the tragedy, Eddie had been very busy writing; something very unusual for him, and that he was at some pains to keep what he was writing secret.

(*d*) That Myrtle had been aware of, and interested in, this unaccustomed activity on the part of her husband.

(*e*) That immediately before the big explosion Kate had heard a "little pop." Myrtle records having heard it, and as Kate was with her at the time, she must have done so also.

These facts alone would provide food for thought, especially as the police would quickly discover about Eddie's will and the ranch, and Myrtle would no doubt announce her intention of going out to America. Then Kate and Myrtle would be interviewed separately, and it is quite certain that Myrtle would say nothing about the attic, the silver teaspoon, Eddie's manuscript, or the "little pop." Now, none of these things might be suspicious in itself, but taken together, they seem to call for some explanation, and Myrtle's silence about them underlines their significance.

But while Kate would almost certainly reveal those facts, which would in themselves be sufficient to give a new turn to the investigation, she might not stop there. She might also tell the police:

(*a*) That the key of Myrtle's dispatch-case fitted Eddie's bureau. (She might even have seen Myrtle open the bureau and read the manuscript.)

(*b*) That Myrtle had been in the bathroom shortly before the explosion.

(*c*) That Myrtle's manner had been strange when she hurried Kate out of the house just before Eddie met his death.

Myrtle, you remember, was sure that Kate had noticed nothing peculiar, because, if she had, being "very strong on premonitions and forebodings and all that kind of thing," she would certainly have remarked on it. That is true, if Myrtle's behaviour had suggested a premonition to Kate. If, however, the maid's suspicions had been aroused, she would say nothing to her mistress, but she would tell the police.

There is yet another possibility. Where, as in this case, husband and wife are at loggerheads, servants tend to take one side or the other. If Kate felt friendly towards Eddie—and the fact that he thought of trying to get her out of the way before the explosion which he planned occurred, suggests that there was at least no enmity between them—all that she said to the police would be coloured by that fact. She might even denounce Myrtle as a murderess.

Another point suggests itself. Would Myrtle be able to

burn the manuscript without Kate knowing about it? If Kate knew, she would certainly inform the police.

But here we may ask an interesting question. Kate, we have decided, would tell the police about Eddie's writing. After they had found that Myrtle was not going to volunteer any information about this, why did not the police question her regarding it? If the manuscript was still in existence, it might contain important evidence.

If no questions were asked on this point, it was because the police already suspected Myrtle, but did not wish to let her know that fact. In short, they were giving her the rope to hang herself.

In that case, it is probable that a man was left to watch the house. When Myrtle came downstairs to burn her manuscript, this officer would see her—or, at least, he would see lights going on. What would Myrtle's reaction be if he suddenly rang the bell or knocked at the door? He would have a story ready—something he had left behind, or an important question which had been overlooked. Perhaps a question about the manuscript, which Myrtle must have laid down somewhere before going to the door—and she could not ignore the summons without arousing suspicion. Nor could she put the manuscript in the furnace first without giving away the fact that she was burning a document.

What a dilemma for the woman who had just written: "And that, I submit, is the perfect murder!"

Suppose that the question is about the manuscript—and I think that, if I were the officer, that is the line I should choose. Myrtle might be clever and resourceful enough to produce it and tell the officer: "Yes, I found this after my husband's death, and I was trying to suppress it. If you read what he wrote, you will see why. I did not want to let the whole world know what a fool I had been, or what sort of man it was I had married."

That would have been highly irregular, but human and understandable. It might have gone far to explain Myrtle's previous equivocations, and helped to allay the suspicions against her. But—her own narrative was with Eddie's. Could she give the officer the one—and keep him from seeing the other?

Even if she managed to do this, if Kate knew that she had read it before the explosion, and had so informed police, Myrtle's quick thinking might not be of much service to her. Why had she not gone to the police? What answer could there be but that she had chosen to protect herself in another way—as a result of which her husband was dead?

But let us give Myrtle the benefit of the most favourable conditions possible. Let us suppose that she burns her own and Eddie's confession. The discrepancies between her statement and Kate's remain, and the police will not be satisfied until they have sifted the matter to the bottom.

Now we come to another of Myrtle's mistakes. "His will was genuine enough," she wrote. "I had taken steps to make sure about the will. He really had a ranch, and it really would come to me if he died."

These "steps" will certainly be traced. How are these inquiries going to look in the light of Eddie's subsequent death?

True, it was Eddie himself who bought the chemicals required to make the fulminate of mercury. But, with his manuscript destroyed, there is no evidence that he had been plotting murder, or that he knew anything about chemistry. On the other hand, Myrtle has admitted to a knowledge of that subject. It is known that she ordered Eddie about—sent him to make purchases for her. It might have appealed to the perverted mind of a murderess to make her prospective victim buy the materials by means of which she planned to launch him into eternity.

I can see a case against Myrtle taking shape on these lines—a case which, if proved to the satisfaction of a jury, would mean that there was no hope of her escaping the gallows. I think the very suggestion that the police were going to proceed on this theory would be sufficient to force Myrtle to confess—and to tell the true story.

It may be during further questioning by detectives that she will break down. It may be in the coroner's court, when she is giving evidence, and the coroner, apprised of the results of the police investigations, proceeds to interrogate her. But break down I think she will.

Very possibly this point will be reached, and she will make her confession, when she is confronted with a detailed reconstruction of the steps leading up to the murder. Personally, I am not an expert on explosives, but the police can command the services of men who are real authorities on this and on every other subject which may be useful in the investigation of a crime. These men would at once appreciate the significance of the missing silver teaspoon and the "little pop" that was followed by the big explosion.

Armed with the experts' report, backed, perhaps, by traces of Myrtle's experiments in the attic—I do not share her touching confidence that there was nothing there for the police to find—and, in any case, by the appropriate passages in her own text-books, detectives would tell her exactly how she had carried out her crime. I think that grim recital would be followed by a full confession.

Even if it were not, I believe that the police would have a strong enough case to secure a conviction. It would be based purely on circumstantial evidence—but if there is enough of it, circumstantial evidence is just as deadly as direct testimony.

No. The chances are heavily against Myrtle. Mr. Berkeley has told a very clever story, but he has not devised the perfect murder.

Russell Thorndike

STRANGE DEATH OF MAJOR SCALLION

I HAVE A CLEAR conscience, for if anyone deserved death it was Major Scallion. I cannot say exactly when first the idea of murdering him entered into my brain, but I remember the calm relief when the germ of that idea had grown into grim determination. This was during the first evening of his last visit to my home, and the first occasion on which he had met my wife. I remember how the heat of my wild resolution was cooled by my careful reasoning, and that very night I said to myself: "It is not clues only that I must beware of, but motive. I must conceal all motive. The first thing the police look for in a murder case is motive, for motive leads to the murderer. Therefore let me review the motive and then take steps to hide it."

The motive was disgust—a disgust that turned to hatred. A cold, terrible hatred. Add to this a jealousy and an irritation acute to the screaming point. I think that from the first I wished to kill him. I know that his mere existence, the sight of him, the thought of him, the knowledge of him and the growing irritation I suffered at either sight, thought or added knowledge, turned my wish to murder into a settled resolution, and so having reached this pass I made a close study of murder as an art. I carefully considered all the murders I could remember. I turned to the books of famous trails. I even delved back into the black print and crude woodcut records of the Newgate Calendar. I noted the silly blunders that had locked men and women in the condemned cell, and I asked myself the question: "Had that blunder not been committed, would this have been the perfect murder?" I explored the pages of fictional criminals, and from all these sources, I collected a number of murders that pleased me. Many of these I decided were not for me to attempt, because one should not play a part unsuited to one's temperament. So, one by one, I eliminated my list till it grew concise. I knocked this one off my list, then that. My list diminished till there were but ten left from which to choose. I took ten days with these, making a firm rule to knock off one a day till I achieved the favourite! I thought this out when I lay awake at night, chuckling to myself in the darkness. Upon the ninth night my decision was so difficult that I resolved to employ both methods in my perfect murder. One should support the other. Neither of these winning murders in my self-imposed competition had been discovered in their time, but I fully realised that since the day of their committal, the police had added science to their methods of sleuthing, and although I had been educated in chemistry I was well aware that the Home Office Experts had a greater knowledge. One of my chosen murders had been committed towards the end of the eighteenth century by that ingenious smuggler parson Doctor Syn, sometimes Vicar of Dymchurch-under-the-Wall in the county of Kent. It was a murder that appealed to me more than all the rest, and it appealed to my grim sense of the comical. But I cautiously recollected that Doctor Syn had only to deal with the authority of the local Beadle, a man of a no education. Also a friendly magistrate, a general practitioner, and his own cloak of parsonic sanctity. How would he have fared with such a man as Sir Bernard Spilsbury or that other enemy to murder, Mr. Cornish? No, I found that I must improve upon the methods of the eighteenth century or never get away with it, for I had to deal with far more dangerous antagonists. I therefore reviewed dispassionately my favourite murder and inspected the flaws. One joint in the armour of my defence would bring me to the scaffold, and so I set about the preparations which I shall hereafter describe.

But first let me give you a sketch of the man I had decided must die and by my hand.

Major Scallion was fat, full-blooded, loud-voiced, bearded and young. To be fat in youth is irritating to one who is lean and fit. But to be bearded and young, bloated and young, loud of voice and young, yes, surely that is terrible. There was also a strident heartiness about the Major, that as far as my nerves went sealed his death warrant. That and a conceit, a self-satisfaction that became unbearable. The man was not content with the title of Mister. He must be "Major" Scallion. What a name! What regiment he was major of I do not know. I never could bring myself to ask. I think there was no regiment in which he gained the title. Perhaps he was just christened Major, for though he was a distant cousin of mine, I never knew. I think he was everyone's cousin. He had a knack of digging out connections which would allow him a full familiarity. Save from his own lying lips I never discovered anyone who could tell me what he did in the War, though he would talk about it a great deal. But whenever you asked him any pertinent question, he would switch the conversation, and talk down any interruption. I'll give his invention the credit of being amusing and exciting. He compelled his listeners to be thrilled. As to his War yarns, he had a vast vocabulary of "Who's Who in the Divisions," but they were usually Divisions of which his hearers were ignorant. "You remind me of Colonel So-and-so," he would say. "We used to call him 'Old So-and-so.' Joined the So-and-so Division. Gunner on the Mespot Front." And if anyone of the company said: "I was there, and don't recollect," he would hedge glibly with: "Did I say Mespot? I'm scatty to-day. Too many chota pegs. I meant Salonika."

The mention of chota pegs reminds me of yet another nail in his coffin as far as I was concerned. He would use foreign idioms to convey that he was widely travelled, when I am pretty sure the extent of his voyaging did not exceed a cheap trip to Boulogne. He was too lazy to travel, even when in funds. Besides he had no need to attempt abroad when he knew there were mutts like myself at home that he could bleed for his own convenience. And what a hog he was over his food. No matter who was in the company, he treated every meal as though it had been prepared for his special benefit, his swinish self. A mouthful with him was a mouthful indeed, for he stoked in the food, and not wasting time to chew it, would swill it down with copious draughts of whatever alcohol there was to hand, and so long as it was strong enough, he could drink anything. Had he been dying of thirst, he would have preferred turpentine to water. "Anything with a kick in it," he would say, and this was fortunate for me and for the murder I had planned for him. He was no connoisseur, but he possessed a capacity. And then one other thing that was so helpful to me in what I had to do. Tobacco. He was a factory chimney. The greatest smoker I have ever met, inhaling the strongest shag, or the foulest cigars. There was no tobacco too rank for his lungs. His great strong teeth were discoloured with nicotine, so that when he smiled he put one in mind of an old hyena. When he failed to conjure money from other's pockets to supply him with cigars, he contented himself with Woodbines and talk about his old pal Woodbine Willie, when I am very sure that he had never met that saint. But that was the way of the Major. Anyone famous, he knew. Oh, yes, and very well too. He would refer to Lawrence of Arabia as 'Laurie,' and once had the effrontery to speak of Earl Haig as 'Doug.' I longed to shout out at his lying familiarity. I vowed that all his faults should be the means of his death, and it was his excessive misuse of tobacco that made me think of nicotine. I recalled the celebrated case of Count Bocarmé and how he killed his brother-in-law with nicotine in five minutes. I knew from reading that two or three drops of nicotine taken into the stomach would be fatal. There was also a case in the annals of medicine of a boy who died within three hours from smoking a pennyworth of twist. In the Major's case who could say that it was not his excess that killed him, when I knew that his whole system must be impregnated with smoke poison. But I was not going to depend on nicotine alone. It would have been too easy a death for my hog. I wanted him to die of a horror more acute. That horror I planned later.

Now the Major had no property, save the clothes he stood up in, and one black trunk. It was one of those black leather ones, shiny with a rounded top. The tray was filled with papers referring to many of his bogus businesses, signed photographs of women, who to their cost, he boasted, had had to do with him. There was also a vast collection of obscene postcards. Oh, yes, his faults were foul. They stank to Heaven, and I resolved to use every one of them to his undoing. Gluttony, drunkenness, excessive smoking, and God forgive me for trying the patience of the noblest woman that ever lived, my wife, but through her, I included his arrogant confidence where all women were concerned. Yes, under this last heading, I was to use my wife as a bait to his downfall. And oh, how easily he walked into the trap.

Now I have said that the Major claimed relationship with me. There was a very distant sort of connection I allow, but too remote to allow him any claim upon my purse and hospitality. He knew this well enough during the first years in which he crossed my path. But through my own stupidity, he was soon enabled to strengthen a claim upon my generosity. This claim was nothing more nor less than blackmail. The truth is that I had once got into a difficulty. There is no need for me to state the details, for it has no bearing on the murder. I confess, however, that a clever lawyer fighting against me might well have proved a criminal case which might have sent me to prison. In my adversity, fool that I was, I went to the Major for advice.

To give him his due, he extricated me from my dilemma
with great skill. But oh, how often I regretted this kind-
ness, for he forged it into a sword of Damocles, and I
knew that the blade would fall upon my defenceless head
the moment that I refused to fall in with his slightest wish.
He began to use my purse at his convenience. When things
were well with him, he left me severely alone, and my
estate was the more gracious. But no sooner did things go
awry with him than he descended upon me with his trunk.
I believe he regretted these necessities as much as I,
because I think no man's company bored him as mine did.
I did all I could to escape from him. During several of his
absences I would move my quarters, but he had an uncanny knack of nosing me out and subjecting me to some
new tyranny. And he would stay with me till I had seen to
it that his affairs looked up a bit. I suppose I should have
told him to do his damnedest, but I was cowardly enough
to value the world's opinion, and I knew that he would
expose me as a criminal and do it with revengeful relish,
because there was no sort of sneakery in which he would
not indulge. He knew well enough that I liked to be a good
citizen, that I paid my bills on the nail, and had a cowardly
dread of Income Tax Collectors and policemen.

It was this, my desire to be a good citizen, that made
my one lapse for which I was being blackmailed, so
cruelly bitter. So far I had paid up whatever he asked to
shut his swinish mouth. I think in those days of my
persecution there was heading a time when I would have
thrown all caution to the winds and told him that he would
not get another penny out of me; but a circumstance
arose, no doubt much to his delight, which as far as I was
concerned made exposure utterly impossible. I met my
dear wife. We fell in love instantaneously and deeply.
Except for the Major, of whom I told nothing, there was
no bar to our union. My patrimony, although somewhat
depleted by the blackmailer, was still a good deal more
than for my own immediate needs. My wife had an ample
income of her own. I own now to have been afraid of the

Major at that time. His continual cry of "Must let me have a pony, old son. No, make it a hundred," would embarrass my independence which I determined to keep against my wife's money. Nor did I want her to realise that from generosity or foolishness I was being sponged upon by a waster.

In addition to her private means my wife was the owner of a small farm upon the border of Dorset and Devon. Here we decided to live upon our joint income, which we planned to augment with the breeding of chickens and pigs. In addition to this I was a dabbler in literature, from which some day I hoped to derive benefit. In this farm cottage we therefore looked forward to an ideal existence. Indeed so keen were we to embark upon this new life that we resolved to curtail our honeymoon, and immediately to open house. I easily persuaded her not to acquaint her friends and relatives that we were setting up house so soon.

"Let us still be honeymooning, my dear," I said. "It is no lie, because what better honeymoon than that spent in getting ready our own home? We shall be gaining all the privacy that is denied to lovers in a hotel. Let our friends think that through our financial independence we are travelling abroad, and then we shall not be worried with visitors."

I did not tell her anything about the Major, who I confess was the real reason for my want of lying low. I had dreaded his appearance at the wedding, but he had not turned up. True he had not been sent an invitation, but what invitation was necessary to that gate-crasher. I never doubted but that he knew about the wedding in that uncanny way he had of nosing out other people's business, and it was a wonder to me that he kept away from the house where he would be sure of good hospitality and pretty girls with a chance to lord it as only the Major could. But he did not come. How was I to know that he happened to be embarrassed for the railroad fare.

Even when we had planned to bury ourselves in the

country, I don't think I ever flattered myself that we could escape from the Major: I did my best to cut all lines of communication by writing to mutual friends and telling them that my wife and I were planning to settle abroad and were embarked upon a world tour till we found somewhere in which to settle entirely after both our hearts.

My wife wrote in her innocence much after the same strain to her friends, and never suspected that it had been my guilt that had made the suggestion.

My wife's little farm-house was most remote. Standing half-way up a hill-side it commanded an uninterrupted view of the valley at the bottom of which ran a broad trout-stream. The hamlet, which consisted of a church and inn and one little general store, was upon the farther bank of the stream, crossed by a ford and stepping-stones. Car or cart had to ford the stream to reach our house. Working in our fields or garden it was possible to see anyone wishing to call upon us so long before they could reach us that if we wanted solitude we had only to slip behind the house and take cover in the spinneys that climbed to the summit of the hill. We did this many times successfully, returning to find a card in our letterbox with a "Sorry you were out" upon it. Incidentally we had to walk two and a half miles for the nearest telephone, which was installed in the official cottage of the local police constable.

Now there were two things that spoiled for me the serene happiness of those first weeks on our little farm. One was the certainty which I had in my mind that sooner or later the Major would appear and plant himself upon us, and the other was the knowledge, the guilty knowledge, that I had a secret from my wife of which the Major would one day take full advantage. Try as I would I could not bring myself to tell her of my one gap in an otherwise honest life. She was so honest herself, and took such a pride in what she called my goodness, that I feared to lose her respect and perhaps her love along with it. It was not long before she noticed that a melancholy often oppressed me, and put it down to the lack of company of my own sex. "I am selfish, my dear," she once said to me. "I have been so taken up with getting our home in order and doing the work myself so that we might not be interrupted with a servant, that I have quite forgotten how very dull it must be for you." I cried out against this, and vowed that I was never more happy in all my life, which was largely true, and yet that fault I had committed years before, and which had cost me so much money and patience to the blackmailing Major, ever seemed to rise like a cloud between me and my happiness. I remember one day resolving to tell her everything, and had I done so I think all would have been well. I should have blurted it out there and then, so that my awkward telling of it would have rung true, and convinced her of my sincerity. Instead, however, I thought to pick my words with care in the hope that my fault might appear to her as harmless as I could only wish it had been. To give myself the opportunity for thinking out this confession carefully, it was necessary to get alone for an hour or so, and so I told her that I was going into the market town to mix with the farmers and pick up useful information concerning the sale of our farm produce. My wife welcomed the suggestion, saying it would do me good and give her a chance of turning out the little den in which I kept my books. So I left the house, thinking of the speech I was to make on my return, and rallying my courage to make it.

I dropped down into the valley and made my way very cautiously across the somewhat shaky stepping-stones that spanned the ford. As I was occupied in the ticklish business the local carrier drove his cart into the river from the opposite direction. I gave him a "Good morning" as he passed, and he answered in a dialect so broad that I couldn't catch its purpose. I was negotiating some very slippery stones at that moment, but as soon as I reached a flat safe one I turned round and called to him, asking what he had said. He shouted something back to me which was also beyond my knowledge of translation, and patted a trunk in the open cart behind him. I saw it clearly. A shiny black leather trunk, with a rounded top. Just such a trunk as the Major used when on the move for money. "Confound the fellow," I thought. "There are thousands of such luggage about. Why should my heart hammer at the sight of it?"

It took me a good hour to walk to town, and I spent the rest of the morning in the market, and making the acquaintance of some of the local farmers, who, like myself, lunched at the Market Inn. It was mid-afternoon when I set off home, hoping to reach the cottage in time for tea.

Now whether it had been the sight of that trunk, or my plan to confess about the Major's hold on me to my wife, but I thought of that wretched man all day, and have never hated him so much. He seemed so vividly close to me that I felt no surprise, only a deadly sinking of spirit, when, on reaching home, I heard his loud and hearty laughter echoing through the open window of our parlour. Gripping my stout walking-stick the tighter, I went in quietly, with red murder in my heart.

He was lounging with his back towards me in the chimney corner, a comfortable seat which he ever afterwards annexed, and my wife was sitting on a stool on front of him. She was absorbed in what he was telling her and laughing at the lie he had been spinning for her amusement and his own conceit. I could see her face reflected by the sun, and I think I have never seen her look more beautiful. Her glorious auburn hair, her delicately-shaped face, smiling lips and large brown slanting eyes, that danced with pleasure in the belief of his lies.

"Oh, how funny," she was saying. "But oh, how brave of you. I am very proud of my new cousin. Really, I am. But I can't help laughing."

Then she saw me and sprang up delighted with: "Darling, look who's here. Why have you never told me about your soldier cousin?"

"Other things to do, and I don't blame him," laughed the Major, getting up and holding out his puffy hand. "How goes it, old man? Very well, I see. You've looked after Number One and no mistake. Your memsahib's been telling me that everything in the garden's a wow.''

Memsahib and *wow*. That such words should be used in our home.

''Then it was your trunk that I saw in the carrier's cart?'' I said.

''Yes, old son,'' he answered. ''And it's upstairs now in the nicest spare room I've seen for a long time. You see, I told the carrier to bring it here as I didn't know the name of your jolly old Local, and as there was no taxi, I walked. The last thing I thought of was parking myself on you, but my little cousin here insists that the local pub's not comfortable enough. But an old campaigner don't worry, and I honestly don't want to butt into the love-nest.''

''What nonsense,'' laughed my wife, blushing. ''Why, we're quite old married people now and very glad to welcome our first visitor.''

In her ignorance, my poor darling thought my so-called cousin would be company for me and cheer me up.

''And what brings you to these parts?'' I asked, knowing well enough.

''Rest from my labours, my boy,'' he replied. ''Been overdoing it in the work line lately. Heading for a jolly old break-down so the Doc says. Been forming a new company. I want to get you both in on the ground floor. Nice little nest-egg by the time the son and heir appears.''

He saw my scowl, no doubt, and noted that my wife was not amused at such a jest, so he added quickly: ''Don't mind me, little cousin. I'm a rough diamond. A man of the world. Knocking around in mining camps, cattle-ranches and other haunts of bad men is apt to scratch the polish off a chap. I say what I think and I certainly hope that my good cousins are going to have a great family. I want to see kids all over the place here. Can't have too much of a good thing, you know. That's always been my motto.''

It certainly was his motto and next instant he proved it by asking for a whisky and soda, and by the way he mixed it, whisky was obviously one of the things he classed as good.

He mixed another with a lady's portion of whisky and handed it to my wife, who said she never drank it, and he then had the impertinence to pass it on to me with a "Well, the boy will, anyway. And here's to my new-found cousin."

"I'll drink your health in tea," she said. "Would you rather have tea or whisky, dear?"

Because he was drinking whisky, I said "Tea," and set down the glass in a rage which I took pains to hide.

When she had gone to make the tea, the rascal winked at me and whispered: "You've not told her, of course."

"Not yet," I replied, "but I'm going to to-night."

"You'll do nothing of the sort," he went on, helping himself to another drink. "Man alive, you're not going to throw away the daintiest bit of love I've seen from here to 'Frisco? Don't fear me. I shan't split. We'll all get along together fine. But watch that girl of yours. I know the sex better than you, and she's not the sort to take a marriage made under false pretences lightly."

"What do you mean, you scoundrel?" I whispered.

"What I say, and it's the truth. Would she love you if she knew you'd been a criminal?"

"I'd trust her love for me through anything," I boasted.

"But you didn't and you haven't, and if you'll take my advice you won't. Keep mum, my boy, and see that I do too. I'll teach you how to keep my mouth shut, and not upset the love-nest."

And somehow I felt that he was right. As I watched him wolfing my wife's home-made cakes and swilling them down with whisky, I abandoned all idea of telling her about my past, and I vowed at the same time that I would take his advice and close his mouth against sneaking. But not in the way he would dictate.

He drank steadily while my wife went to prepare the hot dinner, watching me as I laid the table and I dare say congratulating himself that I was in his power. You may be sure that I was very careful not to let him suspect that the tables were reversed.

"Don't exactly relish laying a third place, do you?" he grinned. "Well, I guess you'll get used to it, for I'm staying here just until you make it worth my while to quit. You're both coming in on my new company see? Your wife's got a bit of dough, she tells me. So when you've bought your shares in cash, I'll trot up to London to watch your interests."

After dinner he drank more whisky and smoked a number of my cigars. He excused his drinking by telling my wife that he had a touch of his old complaint, malaria, and that whisky was the only way to drive it out. He winked at me as he said it, and then pretended to be affected by my wife's sympathy.

It was while he was smoking my cigars that I thought of death from nicotine. I recalled the cases I had read, and one especially gave me comfort, for the murderer was never discovered, but he left a confession which was read after his death. I remembered his statement. "So long as the victim can be proved to have been a great user of tobacco, there is very little chance of the crime being brought home to the murderer. But he must take pains in his preparation and use all caution in destroying evidence after the deed is done."

No pains would be too much trouble for me, and I promised myself to take all precautions afterwards. As I thought of these things, the Major kept us up late with his infernal stories, and my wife declared that she had never been so entertained in her life. As he chatted on—all lies I knew—I thought of other murders too. I had many books on criminology, and my wife was a great reader of detective fiction. Well, I would consider all the murder cases I could find and see which fitted to my need. That night I lay awake making plans. No need for hurry, I told myself, for the victim would be with us till he got his money for quitting. Well, I would temporise about that and endure his loathsome presence for the sake of keeping him safe inside the trap.

The next morning I got up earlier than usual and reviewed what was to be the scene of the crime. I had made up my mind that it would happen on the ground floor, and I walked from room to room wondering just where the corpse would lie.

The ground floor consisted of a cobble-floored linney used as a scullery, a good-sized kitchen and a large parlour. A small room leading out from the parlour I had for my own den, fitted throughout with bookshelves, and that in turn led into a spacious outhouse, which I used partly as a workshop and partly as a laboratory, for I was still keen on chemical experiments. The floors of all these rooms except the scullery and my workshop, which was bricked, were flagged with great slate slabs. My wife had complained of them, for they were uneven in many places, besides being cold and tiring for the feet. We had talked about flooring them with wood, and I had bought the planks, which I had stacked upon the open rafters of my workshop. As I was a good carpenter, I planned to do the job myself as soon as the weather broke, and it happened that this flooring was to play an important part in the murder.

Now, from the first night on which I had decided to kill the Major, I went out of my way to be charming to him in order to put him off his guard. My manner therefore had the like effect upon my wife. Though she must have resented his dictatorial manner, ordering this and that as though the house belonged to him, she went out of her way to be civil to him. She really thought that I was glad to have him with us, and for my sake played the gracious hostess. She excused his excesses in food, drink and smokes on account of his malaria. He called it Charleston fever, whatever that disease may be. At all events, I am quite sure he never suffered from it. But that again was the way of him. It was not enough to say he had malaria. No, he must give it a more high-sounding name.

Knowing him as well as I did, I was haunted by one dread which would have upset all my plans. I feared that he might become too familiar with my wife, so that I should be compelled to quarrel with him before the time was ripe. That would have ruined all. At first he contented himself with a cousinly attitude, going out of his way to please her with his manners. That he was impressed by her beauty I knew only too well, for once he urged me to hurry up and come down with the cash for our shares in his company. When I told him that married life had of necessity made me cautious over money, he said that it would be better for my happiness if I made it possible for him to depart, as he was in danger of falling very seriously in love with his pretty cousin. "And you know, old son, that I have a way with women, don't you?" I concealed my red rage under the cloak of not taking him seriously. I laughed and he laughed too, adding, "Well, don't say when it's too late that I didn't give you open warning."

For some weeks he did nothing but sit in the chimney corner, following my wife about with his protruding eyes. The whites of his eyes through drink had developed a bloodshot streak like those of a half-caste, and indeed when I looked at them and at his curly black hair and beard I began to suspect that he was not without a dash of the tar-brush.

During those weeks I never left the house unless my wife went with me, which she was always glad to do, for I would not trust the Major behind my back. He saw through this, and I think it amused him. But I had my grim amusements too. I remember how I chuckled to myself when I started to saw the floor-planks into their required lengths. He complained about the noise, and when I persisted he got annoyed.

"Yes," thought I, "and you'd be more than annoyed did you realise that I am preparing your scaffold." For by this time I had come to a definite decision of how his death should take place, and where.

Now my wife had one very natural objection to our

house, because it offended her cleanliness. Somewhere in the old wall between the fire-place in the parlour and my den there lurked a sinister family of house beetles, and despite traps and poison we had not been able to stamp them out. During the Major's stay with us she noticed that they seemed to be increasing. This was scarcely to be wondered at, since needing beetles for the greater torture of the Major's death, instead of warring against them, I encouraged their cultivation. I read up their habits, their likes and their dislikes, and instead of putting down the nightly poison I laid down food for their encouragement, and was delighted to see how rapidly the loathsome creatures bred. The Major noticed the increase of them too, and teased my wife about it, saying that beetles indicated a dirty house. She wanted me to pull out the hearth-bricks till I located them, but I said I was confident that traps and poison would do the trick. I showed her the well-filled traps, but did not tell her that I systematically emptied them and let the beetles live. The Major quite enjoyed them, and would finish up his nightly debauch by trying to harpoon them with the end of my walking-stick, but when he finally reeled off to bed I would lay down the food the beetles liked.

I will say that the Major took what pains he could to hide his drunkenness from my wife. He never replenished his glass if she were looking at him, but when she went to bed he would commandeer the bottle and tilt the raw spirit down his throat, for he never pretended to any virtue to me. In the mornings, when at last he condescended to put in an appearance, he would complain about his fever, to excuse the excesses written on his face.

In those nightmare days when the monster was our guest, I found that I gained considerable percentage in my wife's admiration. I knew that she was comparing me and all the work I did with my so-called relative, who did nothing whatever to make our daily life the easier. I remember her coming into the parlour when I had overturned her heavy elbow-chair in order to fix new webbing underneath the seat.

"An upholsterer now," she said. "Is there anything this clever husband of mine can't do?"

I saw the Major scowl at her praise of me, and I longed to say, "I'll tell you something I am going to do. Murder. That's why I am webbing. Webbing is one of the essentials. Strong webbing. And that is why I have laid this floor with wood. Slate slabs are no good for my murder. Must have wood, strong webbing and beetles, besides the deadly sins of my victim."

The Major meantime was loathsomely lazy. He was utterly unskilled except with his lying tongue, which wagged on with invented conceits. Could he have laid a wooden floor for his scaffold? No, for he had not the genius, the infinite capacity for taking pains, that I had. He despised my activities, and, I think, hated me at this time even more than I abominated him. He was bored with me too, and showed it plainly when my wife left us together. I could always escape from him by going into my study or workshop. The latter was too draughty for him, he said, and the study gave him no room in which to sprawl. Besides, he was no reader, and resented my well-filled shelves. He was not curious as to my books. I think he never read one title, and this was just as well, because my study of crime might have given him an inkling of what was in store for him.

Once, indeed, he intruded into my workshop and stood behind me as I worked upon the laboratory table. He wanted another bottle of whisky, and complained that I had locked the wine cupboard. I gave him the key and told him to help himself. I could afford to be generous at that moment by reason of the job I was employed on.

"And what do you think you're doing?" he asked, scornfully.

"Concocting some poison for the beetles," I lied.

He pointed to two stoppered glass vessels by my hand, and asked, "What's that stuff? Two sorts of gin?"

"They look like it, don't they?" I answered pleasantly. "This one Gordon's, that one Booth's, eh? But no, it is a harmless experiment I have been trying. Extracting the iron from water. You can see that this one has a slight resinous tinge, while this one is pure water."

"Pure water?" he repeated. "How damned dull."

"I give you my word that this liquid is absolutely pure," I added proudly. That at least was no lie, since the colourless liquid was absolutely pure nicotine unexposed to the air, while the other bottle I had exposed in order to see how quickly it discoloured.

That night I put a few drops into his whisky, and was overjoyed at the result. For he drank it down without criticism, but later, when I helped him to his room, he leaned more heavily than usual on my shoulder. "Been smoking a bit too much," he said. "Never affected me before. That doctor friend of yours read me a lecture on nicotine the other day. Damned cheek. I say, you don't think I'm in for nicotine poison, do you? Damned dangerous thing, you know."

I pretended ignorance on the subject, and asked him for information, professing to be vastly interested. This I did on purpose, for I knew that if he found he was making an effect talking about something which other people knew nothing about, he would not rest content with me for an audience. He would brag about his nicotine poisoning at the inn. In this I was right, for a few days later the innkeeper in passing asked after our guest. "Smokes too much," he said, shaking his head. "Told me he was suffering from nicotine poisoning. I could have told him that. When a man's teeth are so yellow with the juice you can reckon on nicotine trouble elsewhere. What's more, sir, though he carries his drink pretty well, he drinks a sight too much, and with all respect I should add alcoholic poisoning if I were the doctor diagnosing him. He's strong, but not strong enough for the way he goes. Killing himself by inches, to my mind."

The innkeeper was a Londoner of some education. An

old sergeant-major who had married a Dorset woman. His opinion on anything was taken for gospel in the neighbourhood. I knew to my joy that this news would spread about the Major killing himself.

A queer thing about the Major, which in my knowledge of men was unusual, was the fact that although such a drinker and smoker, he had yet preserved the sweet-tooth of his younger days. He would order suet puddings and heap the golden syrup on to his helpings. He once bought my wife a large box of chocolates on one of his rare visits to the market town, but he wolfed the lot of them on his way home and presented her with the empty box, laughing.

One day when he was returning from the inn he saw my wife and me in the shop. He lurched in after us and asked what was for dinner, saying that he was starving.

"Let's see what they've got in this antiquated hole, now. Show us your jams, Mrs. What's-your-name."

The dear old lady who kept the shop timidly pointed to the shelf where the preserves stood. I perceived a large pot of mincemeat.

"Can't think why we only eat mincemeat at Christmas," I said. "In America, I believe, they eat mince pies all the year, don't they, Major?"

How easily he swallowed the bait I had thrown out for him.

"They do," he replied, "and very good mincemeat it is too. Ate it every day of my life out there."

I knew very well that he never had been to America, but I let that pass. "I remember how you used to love it, Major," I went on, tempting him to knock just another nail into his coffin. "And believe me, Mrs. Partridge here can make it, and you should know the wife's pastry by now. This is your own make, isn't it, Mrs. Partridge?"

"All the preserves are my own make," answered the old lady. "Even to jutney. Of course, if you prefer the well-known manufactured brands, I can order them for you."

"Not as far as I'm concerned," I said.

"Nor I," added the Major. "Send us up some of this mincemeat, my good woman, and little cousin, you can get busy with the pastry again. It's pastry day to-morrow, isn't it?"

And on the morrow, to my extreme glee, I saw the Major putting one mince-pie after another into his mouth whole. If I could make him do that just when I wanted him to, I had improved upon the murder performed long ago by the Rev. Doctor Syn.

The use to which I was to put the mincemeat will appear in the proper sequence of the murder. When I had finished the flooring of the rooms I knew that now at any time the victim might precipitate the end. His excesses were by then the common talk of the neighbourhood, and opinion as regards myself was divided. Some, I discovered, praised me for my tolerance, and what they were pleased to call my Christian hospitality, while others thought me a crass fool to harbour such a monster in the same house as my young and beautiful wife.

Her attitude had been undergoing a gradual change. Her sympathy for the Major diminished, and her interest in his wild adventurous tales ceased. Before he died she had exposed him in her own mind as a liar, a cheat, and a gross liver, utterly worthless. I think then she hated him as much as I did. He was sensitive enough to feel the change in her, and his astonishment that she could prefer me to him galled him deeply. Wanting her money as well as mine, and still hopeful of getting it, he pursued the wrong policy towards that end. For resenting her changed attitude to him, he now openly solicited her favours. Of these insults my wife seemed to take no notice. She pretended not to understand them. But I now and then caught a look of pleading, a childlike appeal in her eyes directed towards me, which asked plainly but in dumb language, when was I going to rid the house of the monster.

On one of these occasions I whispered, "Not many days before the end now. Don't worry. He can't be with us long. He is killing himself. He will probably die of a

stroke. I have done all I can to help the poor fellow, while
you have been patience itself. We can hardly turn him out,
for where will he go? Of course, if he does have a stroke
we shall have to nurse him, but it's my impression that a
stroke will be fatal.''

''You think he will have a stroke?'' asked my wife.

''Everyone is of that opinion. But we must keep calm.
Yes, keep calm and do whatever we think is our duty.''

After dinner at night the atmosphere of the house became unbearable. I would bring in a book from the den
and pretend to read. My wife would take up her needle-
work or knitting, and he would sit staring at her, repeating
such insane invitations as ''Come and sit on your cousin's
knee, my dear.''

When she could not bear the strain any longer and went
to bed, he became ill-tempered, would grab the whisky,
drink deep and ask why the devil I didn't make my wife
kinder to him.

''I'll show her some of my naughty postcards tomorrow
night, to liven her up,'' he said. ''The ones you used to be
so shocked at. They'll teach her.''

''If you show her those,'' I said calmly, ''as sure as
there's a God above us, He'll strike you dead.''

''There isn't a God, you old-fashioned innocent,'' he
laughed. ''As to your wife, well, I tell you, I've got a
fancy for her, and why should you, a dirty criminal, keep
her from me? By God, I've always helped myself to what I
want, and I'll get her, see? And you shall help me.''

I brought him another bottle of whisky and told him to
help himself to that. It was laced with nicotine, and I
wondered how much I should have to increase the dose
before it took effect. Presently he complained that he had a
pain in his heart, and when he stood up he reeled with
giddiness. I told him it was through his drinking and
smoking, for which he went on cursing me as I led him up
to bed. ''It's not that at all, fool,'' he said. ''It's your
wife. Curse her, and you too. Why won't she love me? All

other women do. It's she that's upsetting me, to hell with her. But I'll show you yet.''

He was doomed to show us on the very next night, and I was destined to show him, too.

I somehow got him upstairs, and locked him in to snore himself out of his debauch as best he could. Then I went downstairs and performed my nightly ritual, which was to empty all the ash-trays of cigar stubs into a large box I kept for the purpose in the workshop. I then spread the usual food upon the floor and watched the first beetles dare to leave their hole to feast. I found that they were stupidly fond of golden syrup, getting their legs stuck in their greed. On this night I collected four of them, took them into the laboratory and poisoned them. My wife had been baking fresh mince-pies that day at the Major's orders. I took four of them from the larder, opened the pastry, and placed in each a dead beetle beneath the mince-meat. In case of a post-mortem, I was determined that the doctor should find at least one beetle in the monster's stomach. There was never any need to throw away the nicotined whisky, for he would always finish the bottle before going to bed.

I then saw that my hammer was in its usual place, and noted which drawer of my nail and screw cabin held the heavy-topped carpet-nails. Thus the stage was set for the murder, and the preparations and properties ready. The curtain went up on my drama the following night.

The next day the Major felt very ill, and his only cure for anything was more drink. I allowed him to help himself. He ate no breakfast, no lunch and no tea, but when six o'clock came he complained that he was starving. Now I had purposely asked my wife to delay dinner so that we should not have to endure that long torment of his company till he pleased to go to bed, so that when she announced that dinner could not possibly be served before eight, he flew into a rage and flung out of the house.

I knew well enough that he had gone down to the inn. So much the better, for I wished as many witnesses as possible to see his deplorable condition. At a quarter to eight the landlord and the local constable brought him back. They humoured him to his face, telling him that he was all right, and not to worry, but the constable whispered to my wife and me that he had been very offensive to the villagers, and that were he to visit the inn any more the landlord would be losing customers.

When they had gone the Major seemed to recover, began to laugh heartily, and said that country bumpkins couldn't understand a man of his calibre. Presently he flew into another rage because dinner was not ready. "You're not hungry," I laughed. "You've drunk too much. You couldn't eat a thing if you tried."

He swore that he had never been so ravenous, and at that I brought him in the mince-pies which I had so carefully prepared the night before. At the same time I set a fresh bottle of whisky in front of him. Then watching him covertly, I set about laying the dinner-table. To my huge delight, he ate two mince-pies as he always did, whole, at one chump and swallow of his capacious mouth. He washed them down with whisky: pastry, mincemeat, beetles, all together.

During dinner I marvelled at the man's appetite. What a constitution. I had asked my wife especially to make a treacle pudding that night, saying that I fancied it. The Major fancied it too, and helped himself to syrup bountifully. All the time he kept his eyes upon my wife. Suddenly he got to his feet, steadying himself by the table, and said huskily, "You've got to be nicer to me, by God. You look beautiful tonight. You've set me all on fire, you have. She's got to be nicer, hasn't she, you fool. Tell her so, or it'll be the worse for you."

I got to my feet and ordered him sharply to sit down. In his turn he ordered me to keep my mouth shut, and added, "Don't you know when you're not wanted. We want to be left alone, don't we, little cousin? Kissing and cuddling. And by God, we're going to do it now."

He drank off half a tumbler full of neat whisky. It was

laced. With a cry he sprang towards her. The time had come. I jammed the heavy table into him at his first movement. He overbalanced, clutched the armchair by the fire, and down he went, chair and all, upon the floor. He lay there gasping, and then the alcohol or nicotine got him. He twitched once convulsively, and lay still, his eyes rolling wide and then closing. As I moved forward to look to him, I contrived to knock over the tin of syrup. Yes, I thought of everything, and I knew that it was important that my wife should be a witness that the tin of syrup was thus spilled by accident.

"It's as I said," I whispered. "He's knocked out for the moment. It's the stroke that everyone said would happen. He may recover, and if he does he will be dangerous. I must see that he can do no further damage. Get me the third nail drawer from the cabinet and the heavy hammer."

Dazed with the horror of it, my wife obeyed. When she returned he had not moved, though his heavy breathing told us he was alive.

"What are you going to do?"

"Nail him to the floor till he's better," I replied. "Then we'll go for the policeman. We've had about enough of this scoundrel."

I tore off the webbing from underneath the overturned chair. Oh, yes, I had put it there in readiness. I had planned it all. I then rolled the unconscious brute over on his back and spread out his arms. "Pass me a thong," I said. "Now the hammer and nails."

I nailed the webbing securely to the wooden floor, stretching it tightly over his arms and legs. In like manner I secured his body and head. When I had finished it was obvious that he could not have moved had he been in full possession of his senses and strength.

"He'll do no more mischief now," I said.

When I had satisfied myself that each webbing was secure and every nail fast, I led my wife upstairs and persuaded her to lie down. "I'll go down and wait for the brute to come around, and then I'll give him a good talking to. It's no use losing one's temper with him, because he's mad. Mad and ill. I'm really sorry for him. But he shall not try any pranks like this again in our house. It may be a lesson to him.''

When I had calmed my wife, I told her that I would go and clear the dinner things, wash them up and at the same time keep an eye upon our guest. "I'll mop up that treacle mess too," I added. Once below, I acted quickly. I got a cloth and wiped up such syrup as had been spilled. Fortunately most of it remained in the tin. I took the precaution, though, to put on rubber gloves, so that I might not leave fingerprints on any tell-tale article. I then sprinkled a very thin line like the thread of a spider with the syrup. I trailed this from the bricks behind the hearth to the body, along one of his outpinned arms, and so to his black beard, which I spread thickly. It would be known that he had been wolfing treacle just before he fell. My wife had been witness to that. The rascal's mouth was hanging wide open, as it always did when he snored. With the help of a table-spoon, I wedged between his teeth a strong cork from a pickle-jar. I could feel his teeth pressing into it. Being assured that the cork could not be moved by the tongue, I poured a spoonful of whisky down his throat. I then saturated the cork with syrup, so that it trickled into his throat. It was then with a shudder and a gasp that he opened his eyes and stared at me bewildered.

At last my moment of triumph had come.

"Now listen to me, you lying, blackmailing hog," I whispered, "and listen well, for it's the last speech you'll hear this side of Hell's river. In a little while I am going for the police, but not yet. I shall go to them after you are dead. No, you cannot move. You are nailed tight to the floor. I built this floor for the purpose. You cannot knock nails into slate slabs. Yes, I have planned it all carefully, and no blame will fall on me. I shall not tell the police that you are dead. I shall let them find that out when I bring them back. My tale to them will be the truth. That you were violently dangerous and had a stroke. That I couldn't leave a madman loose to set the house on fire. By the time my wife and I bring the police your beard, mouth and throat will be alive with beetles. You've got two in your stomach now, you hog. They were in the mince-pies that you swallowed whole. I put them there. Look.''

Here I took the other two mince-pies and fished out before his eyes the dead bodies of the insects.

''The live beetles will soon be following the dead ones,'' I said as I dropped the nasty little bodies into his mouth. ''Another tot of whisky to wash them down? I think so. You've been drinking death all the time in that whisky. I've laced it with pure nicotine. The doctor will say one of two things. Either that you died of nicotine poisoning as he warned you was likely, or that when I left to get help, these poisonous beetles got into your throat, carrying their poison with them. Can't you imagine how shocked I shall appear? I who was doing everything to cure you of your excesses, to lose you like this. Too bad. I am now going to wash up the dinner things while the beetles get busy. Already I can see one or two bold ones creeping toward you on the syrup trail that I have laid. I don't think the coroner will find much good to say of you, and what a warning you will be to all excessive smokers. Good night. I wonder which will kill you. The nicotine or the beetles? It will be very interesting to hear the results of your post-mortem. They'll be sending bits of you up to London in jars. You'll be quite important for once, won't you?''

And with that I left him, for my rage had gone, and only cold disgust of him remained.

I took the dinner things with me to the kitchen, and the parlour lamp as well. I thought the beetles would be more at home in the dark. When I had shut and locked the door on him I called up to my wife that the Major was sleeping, and urged her to do the same. In between my washings up I would listen at the parlour door. Once I heard a throaty noise like a strangled gargle. Beyond that, nothing. I fancied, however, that I could hear the faint crackle of paper. I had pasted a piece of paper over the hole in the brickwork, out of which the beetles came. Needless to say that I had seen to it that they could still crawl out into the room, and it was the tiny scrambling of innumerable little legs that I could hear.

Presently I put out the kitchen light, and went into the parlour very cautiously, being careful to make no noise in the dark. I need not have taken such pains, because even when I turned on the electric torch I carried, the beetles were not scared. There they were as I had hoped to see them, swarming. With greedy, groping antennae, a host of them were working up the trail, while others were already fighting for the sweetness with which I had daubed the ugly beard. I could see the curly hairs of it stirring as the insects pushed here and there in search of the succulent syrup. Then I saw one of them venture along the hanging under-lip, crawl over the yellow teeth, and then down on the tongue to feast upon the cork. Others followed, and the gurgles that sounded from my victim's throat told me that the creatures were already at the uvula and tonsils. Could he contract his throat and keep them from a cavernous descent. I thought not, for I heard a gasp and a catch in his breath, and then a whimper of fearful horror. I kept the torch upon his face for a long time, horrified and yet triumphant until at last I saw the madness in his eyes. He had had enough to atone for all his horrid life. Loathsome as he still was to me, I was merciful enough to know that he could endure no more of the loathsomeness with which he crawled. Still wearing my rubber gloves, I took the nicotine bottle from its place, and emptied the contents down his open mouth. One dreadful swallow that swelled his throat, and he was gone. The horror of death glazed in his eyes, and I knew that he was dead. He could never publish his blackmailing secret now.

Immediately I went carefully along the depleted syrup trail and removed its sticky evidence. Then I wrenched out the cork gag, and put it in my pocket. His mouth was still wide open, and I lit up his teeth with my torch. I could see no fragments of bitten cork, but to be on the safe side I brushed his teeth with an old toothbrush I had ready. Having burnt the cork in the stove of my workshop, I put down some beetle poison on the parlour hearth. Everything was now ready for the Discovery.

After locking the parlour door from the outside, I went through the kitchen and up to my wife's room. She was lying down upon the bed, but still dressed and awake.

"I have been thinking over the situation downstairs," I said, "and the only thing to be done is to hand him over to the police. He's harmless enough at the moment, but we cannot endure another night like this. It's too frightening for you. Too insulting. Put on your things and come with me to the police. Do you mind the long walk?"

"I wouldn't stay here without you for anything," she answered. "But couldn't we go down to the inn and borrow their car?"

"I thought of that," I replied, "but they'll be in bed, and the less scandal we have the better. The police will take charge of him, and won't talk too much. He'll probably be put into a mental home, poor devil."

I think I shall never forget that walk through those high-hedged, winding lanes. My wife chatted all the way. She was relieved to know that the awful sojourn of our so-called cousin was to be over. She talked of the farming we were going to do, and made such plans that by the time we reached the constable's house she was in good spirits. The constable was a good fellow, and knew me well, so bore no resentment at being roused. He let us into his kitchen and made my wife a pot of tea, while we drank beer. I confess I should have preferred a strong brandy. He heard what we both had to say about our guest, and he commended me for my sudden brain-wave of pinning him to the floor. He was horrified at my wife's vivid description of the dinner. "He'll have to go into a strait-jacket if he plays those tricks with us," he said.

He phoned for the police van from the market town, which presently picked us up with a sergeant in charge, and drove us back to the farm.

"You can say in the village that he was took ill," advised the sergeant. "Took to hospital, see, sir? There's no need to set too many tongues wagging. A few months' detention will bring the Major to himself."

"With all respects, sir," said our constable, "but the Major goes it a good deal too far. I told him tonight he was heading for a fall, and he seems to have had it. You were too good, looking after such a rascal, sir."

I had certainly looked after him, and put a stop to his further sinning.

I was quite calm when I held the lighted lamp and turned the key in the parlour door. I went in first, bidding them follow me. My wife remained in the kitchen. As I put the lamp on to the table and stooped to adjust the wicks, I heard one of the policemen draw in his breath with a whistling sound. I longed to reply, "I know. The beetles have got him," but it was the sergeant who said, "He's been set on, done in, by these damned beetles. Look."

"It's the hand of God," muttered our constable.

Then the sergeant said, "He's dead right enough. We must get the doctor. Have you a phone, sir?"

I told him "No," so he sent the man who drove the van to fetch him. I went out into the kitchen to tell my wife that the Major was dead, and until the doctor arrived we had to listen to the two policemen discussing the cause of death.

The sergeant from the market town said there was no doubt in his mind it was the beetles, especially as I had pointed out some of them lying dead by the poison I had put down in the hearth.

The local constable, however, said he had watched the Major for some time, and had brought him home that evening, and death, to his mind, was due to a stroke brought on by alcoholic poisoning.

The doctor arrived, and after his examination held a different view. He also knew the dead man, and had strongly disapproved of his excessive smoking. To encourage this view, I showed them the box full of stubs. "Nicotine poisoning, without a doubt," he said. "He was a chain-smoker of cigars. Told me so himself, and I watched him inhaling. As to these horrible beetles, I must keep an open mind about them till I can examine the stomach. It's just possible that the brutes choked him and carried some of that beetle-poison on their legs into his system. On the other hand, he may have died from shock. I must reserve my opinion." He turned to me and added, "I'm afraid there will have to be an inquest, and the coroner will certainly order a post-mortem. I'm only sorry that such a thing should have happened in your house."

The doctor was right. The results of the inquest demanded a post-mortem. No thought of foul play seems to have entered the heads of any of the jury, and the coroner was sympathetic enough to regret such a tragedy should have occurred in the home of a newly-married couple. He even praised me for having done what I could for so disreputable a guest. As my wife and I are well liked in the neighbourhood, I believe that no thought of foul play will arise. We are now waiting to hear what the expert chemists will say. For my own part in the affair, I have no regret and very little fear. But I have got a burning curiosity to know whether my dead beetles will be found in the stomach, and whether any other of the brutes found their way into the body. In the meanwhile I have removed the bricks from behind the chimney and destroyed the pests in their lair. Needless to say, I have seen to it that no one shall find any proof of my having prepared those doses of nicotine. I feel quite happy that neither of my crimes will ever be known to the police or to my beloved wife. I await the immediate future with confidence.

DETECTIVES SOMETIMES READ

MR. RUSSELL THORNDIKE'S murderer is heavily handicapped by the fact that Mr. Russell Thorndike is a popular writer. Detectives sometimes read. They even read thrillers—though, quite often, they derive more amusement than thrills from them.

The Doctor Syn stories, however, are authentic thrillers, and the smuggling parson is one of the best-known characters in modern fiction. So Mr. Thorndike is much too modest—and his murderer much too optimistic—in assuming that neither the police engaged on the case nor the coroner who holds the inquest will have read of the sinister "sometime Vicar of Dymchurch-under-the-Wall."

I think, therefore, I can safely concluded that at least one of those who are investigating the strange death of Major Scallion will be struck by the resemblance between this event and the revenge taken by Dr. Syn on his enemy.

There might conceivably be the starting-point of the line of inquiry that would bring the murderer to the scaffold. He himself says of his victim: "He was not curious as to my books. I think he never read one title, and this was just as well, because my study of crime might have given him an inkling of what was in store for him."

Yet the Major was "no reader." To a detective who was "book conscious" the contents of the killer's bookshelves would mean much more.

I am not, of course, suggesting that any police officer would say: "Ha, this man has read a lot about crime, therefore he must be a criminal." That would be absurd.

But here is a man found dead in suspicious circumstances—and the explanation given of these circumstances does involve an admission that he had been pestering his hostess with unwelcome attentions. There is at least the suggestion of a possible motive for murder here.

Further, the stage-setting of the death recalls that of a murder in fiction, and the book describing this murder is one of those in the library of the man who, according to his own story, tied down the Major to the floor.

If I were in charge of the case this would interest me very much indeed. I should not allow my suspicions to appear on the surface, but I should certainly want to make a very full investigation. And even before the result of the post-mortem became known I might be in possession of some highly significant information.

I should certainly look through that shiny black leather trunk of the Major's. His murderer never seems to have considered the possibility of that containing something which would supply a clue to the real connection between himself and his victim.

True, we don't know the nature of the hold which Scallion had over the other man. But, for the threat of public exposure to be effective, there must be some proof of the "lapse" in existence. The Major's unsupported word, especially in view of his character, would have carried no weight whatever. Therefore, he must either have possessed some evidence himself, or he must have known where such evidence was to be found.

The latter is perhaps the more likely alternative. In that case, there might well have been some note on the subject among Scallion's effects. But even if there was nothing of this sort, my examination of the trunk would still tell me about the dead man's character and facilitate my inquiries into his past.

I would learn that Scallion was thoroughly disreputable and vicious—the last person whom a man who loved and respected his wife would introduce into his home. That alone would make me suspect that he must have had some sort of hold over his host.

This would be confirmed when I discovered the extent to which money had been extorted from the killer over a period of years. His patrimony, we are told, had been "somewhat depleted by the blackmail." Again, there is a reference to the Major's "continual cry of 'Must let me have a pony, old son. No, make it a hundred.'"

I should imagine that some of this money could be traced to Scallion. At least, there would be evidence of a severe and long-continued drain on the murderer's resources— and evidence also that the periods during which the dead man was in funds coincided with withdrawals from the bank by the other which could not be accounted for.

Then, Scallion was apparently a man much given to talking of himself. Among the lies which he told habitually, may there not also have been hints of the true state of affairs between himself and his host?

He might not, indeed, have said anything of this at the village inn, but inquiries would extend beyond the village, and some of his associates in town were probably aware that he had a hold over the killer.

It is also stated that the Major was fond of proclaiming his conquests among women. May he not have boasted that his hostess was one of these? The fact that there was no foundation for such a vaunt would not have stopped him. But the boast would be remembered—and might be believed—when he met his death.

You see how mistaken is the murderer's confidence that the police will be unable to find a motive for murder. It is, indeed, quite on the cards that the inquiries into his past, which will proceed simultaneously with those into his victim's, will reveal the incident which he has been so anxious to hide, and which gave Scallion his power over him. If Scallion's part in the business is also brought to light and some of the hush money traced to him, the case, so far as motive is concerned, will be complete.

Frankly, I should anticipate this to happen. It is sometimes said that there is at least one thing in everyone's life which he wants to hide. And most people with such secrets do manage to keep the skeleton safely in the cupboard.

That gives them an entirely wrong idea of the extent to which concealment may be practiced successfully. Their secrets remain their own because they have never attracted the attention of the police. But once the searchlight of detective investigation is turned upon any man—and it always is when there is suspicion of murder—there is very little of real importance about his private affairs that is not laid bare.

I think that the killer would discover this. Before the inquest was over—I assume that it is only the preliminary hearing of which the murderer writes, as there would be an adjournment until the result of the post-mortem was known— the police would be aware of his motive, and that part of the case against him would be strong enough to satisfy the most difficulty jury.

Nor is our criminal in any better plight as regards the manner of the murder. All his elaborate calculations and preparations break down on one simple fact—that a comparatively large dose of nicotine, a few drops of which are sufficient to kill a man, was administered while Scallion was lying, bound and helpless, on the floor.

"I took the nicotine bottle from its place, and emptied the contents down his open mouth," writes the killer. "One dreadful swallow that swelled his throat, and he was gone. The horror of death glazed in his eyes, and I knew that he was dead."

The post-mortem will reveal that, in addition to the slow nicotine poisoning, which extended over a long period, there was also this final fatal dose. The experts will have no difficulty in discovering this and in saying, quite definitely, that it could not have been caused by smoking, however excessive.

It will also be obvious that the dose was large enough to kill instantaneously. Now, according to the story told by the murderer and his wife, Major Scallion was alive when he was tied up on the floor. He was still secured when the body was discovered. So the poison could not have been self-administered.

The murderer took his wife upstairs while Scallion was still unconscious. "I'll go down and wait for the brute to come around and then I'll give him a good talking to," he said. And his story—not only as he relates it to us, but as he told it to the police—makes it quite clear that he was downstairs for some considerable time while his wife was in her room.

He thus had the opportunity to administer the poison. And the investigations into his past and Scallion's, to which I have already referred, have revealed the motive of the murder.

I can imagine his horror when, on the inquest being resumed, the coroner proceeds to put a series of questions which tells him that the truth is known. From statements made in the course of his narrative I should say that he is not a particularly convincing liar. Once he realises that the police have somehow uncovered his secret, he will either break down and tell the truth, or else he will stumble, contradict himself, be "caught out" in manifest perjury. Either way, his fate will be sealed. In a few weeks' time he will face judge and jury on the capital charge, and on the evidence only one verdict will be possible.

The only point which the prosecution may find difficulty in establishing is how the nicotine was obtained. According to the killer he prepared it himself, and saw to it that no traces were left of his having done so. But apparatus is required to extract nicotine from tobacco leaves, and if this were found in his workshop, that would suggest the manner in which the poison had been secured.

True, he might have disposed of the apparatus. But if it had been seen in his workshop, and had then disappeared, that very fact would tell against him.

No, very definitely this is not a perfect murder. And the man who committed it is congratulating himself too soon.

Dorothy L. Sayers

BLOOD
SACRIFICE

IF THINGS WENT on at this rate, John Scales would be a very rich man. Already he was a man to be envied, as any ignoramus might guess who passed the King's Theatre after eight o'clock. Old Florrie, who had sat for so many years on the corner with her little tray of matches, could have given more than a guess, for what she didn't know about the King's was hardly worth knowing. When she had ceased to adorn its boards (thanks to a dreadful accident with a careless match and some gauze draperies, that had left her with a scarred face and a withered arm) she had taken her stand near the theatre for old times' sake, and she watched over its fortunes, still, like a mother. She knew, none better, how much money it held when it was playing to capacity, what its salary list was like, how much of its earnings went in permanent charges, and what the author's share of the box-office receipts was likely to amount to. Besides, everybody who went in or out by the stage door came and had a word with Florrie. She shared good times and bad at the King's. She had lamented over lean days caused by slumps and talkie competition, shaken her head over perilous excursions into highbrow tragedy, waxed tearful and indignant over the disastrous period (now happily past) of the Scorer-Bitterby management, which had ended in a scandal, rejoiced when the energetic Mr. Garrick Drury, launching out into management after his tremendous triumph in the name-part of *The Wistful Harlequin,* had taken the old house over, reconditioned it inside and out (incidentally squeezing two more rows into the reconstructed pit), and voiced his optimistic determination to break the run of ill-luck; and since then she had watched its steady soaring into prosperity on the well-tried wings of old-fashioned adventure and romance.

Mr. Garrick Drury (Somerset House knew him as Obadiah Potts, but he was none the less good-looking for that) was an actor-manager of the sort Florrie understood; he followed his calling in the good old way, building his successes about his own glamorous personality, talking no nonsense about new schools of dramatic thought, and paying only lip-service to "team-work." He had had the luck to embark on this managerial career at a moment when the public had grown tired of gloomy Slav tragedies of repressed husbands, and human documents about drink and diseases, and was (in its own incoherent way) clamouring for a good romantic story to cry about, with a romantic hero suffering torments of self-sacrifice through two and three-quarter acts and getting the girl in the last ten minutes. Mr. Drury (forty-two in the daylight, thirty-five in the lamplight and twenty-five or what you will in a blond wig and the spotlight) was well fitted by nature to acquire girls in this sacrificial manner, and had learnt the trick of so lacing nineteenth-century sentiment with twentieth-century nonchalance that the mixture went to the heads equally of Joan who worked in the office and Aunt Mabel up from the country.

And since Mr. Drury, leaping nightly from his Rolls saloon with that nervous and youthful alacrity that had been his most engaging asset for the past twenty years, always had time to bestow at least a smile and a friendly word on old Florrie, he affected her head and heart as much as anybody else's. Nobody was more delighted than Florrie to know that he had again found a winner in *Bitter*

Laurel, now sweeping on to its hundredth performance. Night by night she saluted with a satisfied chuckle each board as it appeared: "Pit Full," "Gallery Full," "Dress Circle Full," "Upper Circle Full," "Stalls Full," "Standing Room Only," "House Full." Set to run for ever it was, and the faces that went by the stage door looked merry and prosperous, as Florrie liked to see them.

As for the young man who had provided the raw material out of which Mr. Drury had built up this glittering monument of success, if he wasn't pleased, thought Florrie, he ought to be. Not that, in the ordinary way, one thought much about the author of a play—unless, of course, it was Shakespeare, who was different; compared with the cast, he was of small importance, and rarely seen. But Mr. Drury had one day arrived arm-in-arm with a sulky-looking and ill-dressed youth, whom he had introduced to Florrie, saying in his fine, generous way: "Here, John, you must know Florrie. She's our mascot—we couldn't get on without her. Florrie, this is Mr. Scales, whose new play's going to make all our fortunes." Mr. Drury was never mistaken about plays; he had the golden touch. Certainly, in the last three months, Mr. Scales, though still sulky-looking, had become much better dressed.

On this particular night—Saturday, April 15th, when *Bitter Laurel* was giving its ninety-sixth performance to a full house after a packed matinée—Mr. Scales and Mr. Drury arrived together, in evening dress and, Florrie noted with concern, rather late. Mr. Drury would have to hurry, and it was tiresome of Mr. Scales to detain him, as he did, by arguing and expostulating upon the threshold. Not that Mr. Drury seemed put out. He was smiling (his smile, one-sided and slightly elfin in quality, was famous), and at last he said, with his hand (Mr. Drury's expressive hands were renowned) affectionately upon Mr. Scales's shoulder, "Sorry, old boy, can't stop now. Curtain must go up, you know. Come round and see me after the show—I'll have those fellows there." Then he vanished, still smiling the elfin smile and waving the expressive hand; and Mr. Scales, after hesitating a moment, had turned away and came down past Florrie's corner. He seemed to be still sulky and rather preoccupied, but, looking up, caught sight of Florrie and grinned at her. There was nothing elfin about Mr. Scales' smile, but it improved his face very much.

"Well, Florrie," said Mr. Scales, "we seem to be doing pretty well, financially speaking, don't we?"

Florrie eagerly agreed. "But there," she observed, "we're getting used to that. Mr. Drury's a wonderful man. It doesn't matter what he's in, they all come to see him. Of course," she added, remembering that this might not sound very kind, "he's very clever at picking the right play."

"Oh, yes," said Mr. Scales. "The play. I suppose the play has something to do with it. Not much, but something. Have you seen the play, Florrie?"

Yes, indeed, Florrie had. Mr. Drury was so kind, he always remembered to give Florrie a pass early on in the run, even if the house was ever so full.

"What did you think of it?" inquired Mr. Scales.

"I thought it was lovely," said Florrie. "I cried ever so. When he came back with only one arm and found his fiancée gone to the bad at a cocktail party——"

"Just so," said Mr. Scales.

"And the scene on the Embankment—lovely, I thought that was, when he rolls up his old army coat and says to the bobby: 'I will rest on my laurels'—that was a beautiful curtain line you gave him there, Mr. Scales. And the way he put it over——"

"Yes, rather," said Mr. Scales. "There's nobody like Drury for putting over that kind of line."

"And when she came back to him and he wouldn't have her any more and then Lady Sylvia took him up and fell in love with him——"

"Yes, yes," said Mr. Scales. "You found that part moving?"

"Romantic," said Florrie. "And the scene between the two girls—that was splendid. All worked-up, it made you feel. And then in the end, when he took the one he really loved after all——''

"Sure-fire, isn't it?" said Mr. Scales. "Goes straight to the heart. I'm glad you think so, Florrie. Because, of course, quite apart from anything else, it's very good box-office.''

"I believe you," said Florrie. "Your first play, isn't it? You're lucky to have it taken by Mr. Drury.''

"Yes," said Mr. Scales, "I owe him a lot. Everybody says so, so it must be true. There are two fat gentlemen in astrachan coats coming along to-night to settle about the film rights. I'm a made man, Florrie, and that's always pleasant, particularly after five or six years of living hand-to-mouth. No fun in not having enough to eat, is there?''

"That there isn't," said Florrie, who knew all about it. "I'm ever so glad your luck's turned at last, dearie.''

"Thank you," said Mr. Scales. "Have something to drink the health of the play." He fumbled in his breast-pocket. "Here you are. A green one and a brown one. Thirty bob. Thirty pieces of silver. Spend it on something you fancy, Florrie. It's the price of blood.''

"What a thing to say!" exclaimed Florrie. "But you writing gentlemen will have a bit of a joke. And I know poor Mr. Milling, who wrote the book for *Pussycat, Pussycat* and *The Lipstick Girl* always used to say he sweated blood over every one of 'em.''

A nice young gentleman, thought Florrie, as Mr. Scales passed on, but queer and, perhaps, a little bit difficult in his temper, for them that had to live with him. He had spoken very nicely about Mr. Drury, but there had been a moment when she had fancied that he was (as they said) registering sarcasm. And she didn't quite like that joke about the thirty pieces of silver—that was New Testament, and New Testament (unlike Old) was blasphemous. It was like the difference between saying: "Oh, God!" (which nobody minded) and "Oh, Christ!" (which Florrie had never held with). Still, people said all kinds of things nowadays, and thirty bob was thirty bob; it was very kind of Mr. Scales.

* * *

Mr. John Scales, slouching along Shaftesbury Avenue and wondering how he was going to put in the next three hours or so, encountered a friend just turning out of Wardour Street. The friend was a tall, thin young man, with a shabby overcoat and a face, under a dilapidated soft hat, like a hungry hawk's. There was a girl with him.

"Hullo, Molly!" said Scales. "Hullo, Sheridan!"

"Hullo!" said Sheridan. "Look who's here! The great man himself. London's rising dramatist. Sweet Scales of Old Drury."

"Cut it out," said Scales.

"Your show seems to be booming," went on Sheridan. "Congratulations. On the boom, I mean."

"God!" said Scales, "have you seen it? I did send you tickets."

"You did—it was kind of you to think of us amid your busy life. We saw the show. In these bargain-basement days, you've managed to sell your soul in a pretty good market."

"See here, Sheridan—it wasn't my fault. I'm just as sick as you are. Sicker. But like a fool I signed the contract without a controlling clause, and by the time Drury and his producer had finished mucking the script about——"

"He didn't sell himself," said the girl, "he was took advantage of, your worship."

'Pity," said Sheridan. "It was a good play—but he done her wrong. But," he added, glancing at Scales, "I take it you drink the champagne that she sends you. You're looking prosperous."

"Well," said Scales, "what do you expect me to do? Return the cheque with thanks?"

"Good Lord, no," said Sheridan. "It's all right. Nobody's grudging you your luck."

"It's something, after all," said Scales defensively, "to get one's foot in at all. One can't always look a gift horse in the mouth."

"No," said Sheridan. "Good Lord, I know that. Only I'm afraid that you'll find this thing hang round your neck a bit if you want to go back to your own line. You know what the public is—it likes to get what it expects. Once you've made a name for sob-stuff, you're labelled for good or bad."

"I know. Hell. Can't do anything about it, though. Come and have a drink."

But the others had an appointment to keep, and passed on their way. The encounter was typical. Damnation, thought Scales, savagely, turning in to the Criterion bar, wasn't it enough to have had your decent play cut about and turned into the sort of thing that made you retch to listen to it, without your friends supposing you had acquiesced in the mutilation for the sake of making money?

He had been a little worried when he knew that George Philpotts (kindly, officious George, who always knew everybody) had sent *Bitter Laurel* to Drury. The very last management he himself would have selected; but also the very last management that would be likely to take so cynical and disillusioned a play. Miraculously, however, Drury had expressed himself as "dead keen" about it. There had been an interview with Drury, and Drury, damn his expressive eyes, had—yes, one had to admit it—Drury had "put himself across" with great success. He had been flattering, he had been charming. Scales had succumbed, as night by night pit and stalls and dress circle succumbed, to the gracious manner and the elfin smile. "A grand piece—grand situations," Garrick Drury had said. "Of course, here and there it will need a little tidying up in production." Scales said modestly that he expected that—he knew very little about writing for the stage—he was a novelist—he was quite ready to agree to alterations, provided, naturally, nothing was done to upset the artistic unity of the thing. Mr. Garrick Drury was pained by the suggestion. As an artist himself, he should, of course, allow nothing inartistic to be done. Scales, overcome by Drury's manner, and by a flood of technicalities about sets

and lighting and costing and casting poured out upon him
by the producer, who was present at the interview, signed
a contract giving the author a very handsome share of the
royalties, and hardly noticed that he had left the management with full power to make any "reasonable" alterations to fit the play for production.

It was only gradually, in the course of rehearsal, that he
discovered what was being done to his play. It was not
merely that Mr. Drury had succeeded in importing into the
lines given to him as the war-shattered hero, a succulent
emotionalism which was very far from the dramatist's idea
of that embittered and damaged character. So much, one
had expected. But the plot had slowly disintegrated and
reshaped itself into something revoltingly different. Originally, for example, the girl Judith (the one who had "gone
to the bad at a cocktail party") had not spurned the
one-armed soldier (Mr. Drury). Far from it. She had welcomed him and several other heroes home with indiscrimi-
nate, not to say promiscuous, enthusiasm. And the hero,
instead of behaving (as Mr. Drury saw to it that he did in
the acted version) in a highly sacrificial manner, had gone
deliberately and cynically to the bad in his turn. Nor had
"Lady Sylvia," who rescued him from the Embankment,
been (as Mr. Drury's second leading lady now represented
her to be) a handsome and passionate girl deeply in love
with the hero, but a nauseous rich elderly woman with a
fancy for a gigolo, whose attentions the hero (now thoroughly deteriorated as a result of war and post-war experience) accepted without shame or remorse in exchange for
the luxuries of life. And finally, when Judith, thoroughly
shocked and brought to her senses by these developments,
had tried to recapture him, the hero (as originally depicted)
had so far lost all sense of decency as to prefer—though
with a bitter sense of failure and frustration—to stick to
Lady Sylvia, as the line of least resistance, and had ended,
on Armistice Day, by tearing away the public trophies of
laurel and poppy from the Cenotaph and being ignomini-
ously removed by the police after a drunken and furious

harangue in denunciation of war. Not a pleasant play, as originally written, and certainly in shocking taste; but an honest piece of work so far as it went. But Mr. Drury had pointed out that "his" public would never stand the original Lady Sylvia or the final degradation of the hero. There must be slight alterations—nothing inartistic, of course, but alterations, to make the thing more moving, more uplifting, more, in fact, true to human nature.

Because, Mr. Drury pointed out, if there was one thing you could rely on, it was the essential decency of human nature, and its immediate response to generous sentiments. His experience, he said, had proved it to him.

Scales had not given way without a struggle. He had fought hard over every line. But there was the contract. And in the end, he had actually written the new scenes and lines himself, not because he wanted to, but because at any rate his own lines would be less intolerable than the united efforts of cast and producer to write them for themselves. So that he could not even say that he had washed his hands of the whole beastly thing. Like his own (original) hero, he had taken the line of least resistance. Mr. Drury had been exceedingly grateful to him and delighted to feel that author and management were working so well together in their common interest.

"I know how you feel," he would say, "about altering your artistic work. Any artist feels the same. But I've had twenty years' experience of the stage, and it counts, you know, it counts. You don't think I'm right—my dear boy, I should feel just the same in your place. I'm terribly grateful for all this splendid work you're putting in, and I know you won't regret it. Don't worry. All young authors come up against the same difficulty. It's just a question of experience."

Hopeless. Scales, in desperation, had enlisted the services of an agent, who pointed out that it was now too late to get the contract altered. "But," said the agent, "it's quite an honest contract, as these things go. Drury's management has always had a very good name. We shall keep an eye on these subsidiary rights for you—you can leave that to us. I know it's a nuisance having to alter things here and there, but it *is* your first play, and you're lucky to have got it with Drury. He's very shrewd about what will appeal to a West End audience. When once he's established you, you'll be in a much better position to dictate terms."

Yes, of course, thought Scales—to dictate to Drury, or to anybody else who might want that type of play. But in a worse position than ever to get anybody to look at his serious work. And the worst of it was that the agent, as well as the actor-manager, seemed to think that his concern for his own spiritual integrity didn't count, didn't matter—that he would be quite genuinely consoled by his royalties.

At the end of the first week, Garrick Drury practically said as much. His own experience had been justified by the receipts. "When all's said and done," he remarked, "the box-office is the real test. I don't say that in a commercial spirit. I'd always be ready to put on a play I believed in—as an artist—even if I lost money by it. But when the box-office is happy, it means the public is happy. The box-office is the pulse of the public. Get that and you know you've got the heart of the audience."

He couldn't see. Nobody could see. John Scales's own friends couldn't see; they merely thought he had sold himself. And as the play settled down to run remorselessly on, like a stream of treacle, John Scales realised that there would be no end to it. It was useless to hope that the public would revolt at the insincerity of the play. They probably saw through it all right, just as the critics had done. What stood in the way of the play's deserved collapse was the glamorous figure of Garrick Drury. "This broken-backed play," said the *Sunday Echo,* "is only held together by the magnificent acting of Mr. Garrick Drury." "Saccharine as it is," said the *Looker-On, "Bitter Laurel* provides a personal triumph for Mr. Garrick Drury." "Nothing in the play is consistent," said the *Dial,* "except the assured skill of Mr. Garrick Drury, who——''. ''Mr. John Scales,'' said the *Daily Messenger,* ''has constructed his situations with great skill to display Mr. Garrick Drury in all his attitudes, and that is a sure recipe for success. We prophesy a long run for *Bitter Laurel.*'' A true prophecy, or so it seemed.

And there was no stopping it. If only Mr. Drury would fall ill or die or lose his looks or his voice or his popularity, the beastly play might be buried and forgotten. There were circumstances under which the rights would revert to the author. But Mr. Drury lived and flourished and charmed the public, and the run went on, and after that there were the touring rights (controlled by Mr. Drury) and film rights (largely controlled by Mr. Drury) and probably radio rights, and God only knew what else. And all Mr. Scales could do was to pocket the wages of sin and curse Mr. Drury, who had (so pleasantly) ruined his work, destroyed his reputation, alienated his friends, exposed him to the contempt of the critics and forced him to betray his own soul.

If there was one living man in London whom John Scales would have liked to see removed from the face of the earth, it was Garrick Drury, to whom (as he was daily obliged to admit to all and sundry) he owed so much. Yet Drury was a really charming fellow. There were times when that inexhaustible charm got so much on the author's nerves that he could readily have slain Mr. Drury for his charm alone.

Yet, when the moment came, on that night of the 15th–16th April, the thing was not premeditated. Not in any real sense. It just happened. Or did it? That was the thing that even John Scales could not have said for certain. He may have felt a moral conviction, but that is not the same thing as a legal conviction. The doctor may have had his suspicions, but if so, they were not directed against John Scales. And whether they were right or wrong, nobody could say that it had made any difference; the real slayer may have been the driver of the car, or the intervening hand of Providence, sprinkling the tarmac with April showers. Or it may have been Garrick Drury, so courteously and charmingly accompanying John Scales in quest of a taxi, instead of getting straight into his own car and being whirled away in the opposite direction.

In any case, it was nearly one in the morning of Sunday when they got the film people off the premises, after a long and much-interrupted argument, during which Scales found himself, as usual, agreeing to a number of things he did not approve, but could see no way to prevent.

"My dear John," said Mr. Garrick Drury, pulling off his dressing-gown (he always conducted business interviews in a dressing-gown, if possible, feeling, with some truth, that its flowing outline suited him), "my dear John, I know exactly how you feel—Walter!—but it needs experience to deal with these people, and you can trust me not to allow anything inartistic—oh, thank you, Walter. I'm extremely sorry to have kept you so late."

Walter Hopkins was Mr. Drury's personal dresser and faithful adherent. He had not the smallest objection to being kept up all night, or all the next morning for that matter. He was passionately devoted to Mr. Drury, who always rewarded his services with a kind word and the smile. He now helped Mr. Drury into his coat and overcoat and handed him his hat with a gratified murmur. The dressing-room was still exceedingly untidy, but he could not help that; towards the end of the conversation the negotiations had become so very delicate that even the devoted Walter had had to be dismissed to lurk in an adjacent room.

"Never mind about all this," went on Mr. Drury, indicating a litter of grease-paint, towels, glasses, siphons, ash-trays, tea-cups (Mr. Drury's aunts had looked in), manuscripts (two optimistic authors had been given audience), mascots (five female admirers had brought Mickey Mice), flowers (handed in at the stage-door) and assorted fan-mail, strewn over the furniture. "Just stick my things together and lock up the whisky. I'll see Mr. Scales to his taxi—you're sure I can't drop you anywhere, John?—Oh! and bring the flowers to the car—and I'd better look through that play of young what's his name's—Ruggles, Buggles, you know who I mean—perfectly useless, of course, but I promised dear old Fanny—chuck the rest into the cupboard—and I'll pick you up in five minutes.''

The night-watchman let them out; he was an infirm and aged man with a face like a rabbit, and Scales wondered what he would do if he met with a burglar or an outbreak of fire in the course of his rounds.

''Hullo!'' said Garrick Drury, ''it's started to rain. But there's a rank just down the Avenue. Now look here, John, old man, don't you worry about this, because—Look out!''

It all happened in a flash. A small car, coming just a trifle too fast up the greasy street, braked to avoid a prowling cat, skidded, swung round at right angles and mounted the pavement. The two men leapt for safety— Scales rather clumsily, tripping and sprawling in the gutter. Drury, who was on the inside, made a quick backward spring, neat as an acrobat's, just not far enough. The bumper caught him behind the knee and flung him shoulder-first through the plate-glass window of a milliner's shop.

When Scales had scrambled to his feet, the car was half-way through the window, with its driver, a girl, knocked senseless over the wheel; a policeman and two taxi-drivers were running towards them from the middle of the street; and Drury, very white and his face bleeding, was extricating himself from the splintered glass, with his left arm clutched in his right hand.

''Oh, my God!'' said Drury. He staggered up against the car, and between his fingers the bright blood spurted like a fountain.

Scales, shaken and bewildered by his fall, was for the moment unable to grasp what had happened; but the policeman had his wits about him.

''Never mind the lady,'' he said, urgently, to the taxi-men. ''This gent's cut an artery. Bleed to death if we ain't quick.'' His large, competent fingers grasped the actor's arm, found the right spot and put firm pressure on the severed blood-vessel. The dreadful spurting ceased. ''All right, sir? Lucky you 'ad the presence of mind to ketch 'old of yourself.'' He eased the actor down on to the running-board, without relaxing his grip.

''I got a 'andkercher,'' suggested one of the taxi-men.

''That's right,'' said the policeman. '' 'Itch it round 'is arm above the place and pull it as tight as you can. That'll 'elp. Nasty cut it is, right to the bone, by the looks of it.''

Scales looked at the shop-window and the pavement, and shuddered. It might have been a slaughter-house.

''Thanks very much,'' said Drury to the policeman and the taxi-man. He summoned up the ghost of the smile and fainted.

''Better take him into the theatre,'' said Scales. ''The stage-door's open. Only a step or two up the passage. It's Mr. Drury, the actor,'' he added, to explain this suggestion. ''I'll run along and tell them.''

The policeman nodded. Scales hurried up the passage and met Walter just emerging from the stage-door.

''Accident!'' said Scales, breathless. ''Mr. Drury—cut an artery—they're bringing him here.''

Walter, with a cry, flung down the flowers he was carrying and darted out. Drury was being supported up the passage by the two drivers. The policeman walked beside him, still keeping a strong thumb on his arm. They brought him in, stumbling over the heaps of narcissus and daffodil; the crushed blossoms smelt like funeral flowers.

''There's a couch in his dressing-room,'' said Scales. His mind had suddenly become abnormally clear. ''It's on the ground floor. Round here to the right and across the stage.''

''Oh, dear, oh, dear!'' said Walter. ''Oh, Mr. Drury! He won't die—he can't die! All that dreadful blood!''

''Now, keep your 'ead,'' admonished the policeman. ''Can't you ring up a doctor and make yourself useful?''

Walter and the night-watchman made a concerted rush

for the telephone, leaving Scales to guide the party across the deserted stage, black and ghostly in the light of one dim bulb high over the proscenium arch. Their way was marked by heavy red splashes on the dusty boards. As though the very sound of those boards beneath their tread had wakened the actor's instinct, Drury opened one eye.

"What's happened to those lights?" . . . Then, with returning consciousness, "Oh, it's the curtain line. . . . Dying, Egypt, dying . . . final appearance, eh?"

"Rot, old man," said Scales hastily. "You're not dying yet by a long chalk."

One of the taxi-drivers—an elderly man—stumbled and panted. "Sorry," said Drury, "to be such a weight . . . can't help you much . . . find it easier . . . take your grip further down. . . ." The smile was twisted, but his wits and experience were back on the job. This was not the first or the hundredth time he had been "carried out" from the stage of the King's. His bearers took his gasping instructions and successfully negotiated the corner of the set. Scales, hovering in attendance, was unreasonably irritated. Of course, Drury was behaving beautifully. Courage, presence of mind, consideration for others—all the right theatrical gestures. Couldn't the fellow be natural, even at death's door?

Here, Scales was unjust. It was natural to Drury to be theatrical in a crisis, as it is to nine people out of ten. He was, as a matter of fact, providing the best possible justification for his own theories about human nature. They got him to the dressing-room, laid him on the couch, and were thanked.

"My wife," said Drury, ". . . in Sussex. Don't startle her . . . she's had 'flu . . . heart not strong."

"All right, all right," said Scales. He found a towel and drew some water into a bowl. Walter came running in.

"Dr. Debenham's out . . . away for the week-end. . . . Blake's telephoning another one . . . suppose they're all away . . . whatever shall we do? . . . they oughtn't to *let* doctors go away like this."

"We'll try the police-surgeon," said the constable. "Here, you, come and 'old your thumb where I've got mine. Can't trust that there bandage. Squeeze 'ard, mind, and don't let go. And don't faint," he added sharply. He turned to the taxi-men. "You better go and see what's 'appened to the young lady. I blew me whistle, so you did oughter find the other constable there. You (to Scales) will 'ave to stay here—I'll be wanting your evidence about the accident."

"Yes, yes," said Scales, busy with the towel.

"My face," said Drury, putting up a restless hand. "Has it got the eye?"

"No, it's only a scalp-wound. Don't get excited."

"Sure? Better dead than disfigured. Don't want to end like Florrie. Poor old Florrie. Give her my love. . . . Cheer up, Walter. . . . Rotten curtain, isn't it? . . . Get yourself a drink. . . . You're certain the eye's all right? . . . You weren't hurt, were you, old man? . . . Hell of a nuisance for you, too . . . stop the run. . . ."

Scales, in the act of pouring out whisky for himself and Walter (who looked nearly as ready to collapse as his employer), started and nearly dropped the bottle. Stop the run—yes, it would stop the run. An hour ago he had been praying for a miracle to stop the run. And the miracle had happened. And if Drury hadn't had the wits to stop the bleeding—if he had waited only one minute more—the run would have stopped and the film would have stopped, and the whole cursed play would have stopped dead for good and all. He swallowed down the neat spirit with a jerk, and handed the second glass to Walter. It was as though he had made the thing happen by wishing for it. By wishing a little harder—Nonsense! . . . but the doctor didn't come and, though Walter was holding on like grim death (*grim death!*) to the cut artery, the blood from the smaller vessels was soaking and seeping through the cloth and the bandages . . . there was still the chance, still the likelihood, still the *hope*——

This would never do. Scales dashed out into the passage

and across the stage to the night-watchman's box. The policeman was still telephoning. Drury's chauffeur, haggard and alarmed, stood, cap in hand, talking to the taximen. The girl, it appeared, had been taken to hospital with concussion. The divisional police-surgeon had gone to an urgent case. The nearest hospital had no surgeon free at the moment. The policeman was trying the police-surgeon belonging to the next division. Scales went back.

The next half-hour was a nightmare. The patient, hovering between consciousness and unconsciousness, was still worrying about his face, about his arm, about the play. And the red stain on the couch spread and spread. . . .

Then, with a bustle, a short, stout man came in, carrying a bag. He took a look at the patient, tested his pulse, asked a few questions, shook his head, muttering something about loss of blood and loss of time and weakness. The policeman, somewhere in the background, mentioned that the ambulance had arrived.

"Nonsense," said the doctor. "Can't possibly move him. Got to deal with it here and now." With a few brisk words of commendation, he dislodged Walter from his post. He worked quickly, cutting away the sodden sleeve, applying a proper tourniquet, administering some kind of stimulant, again assuring the patient that his eye was not damaged and that he was suffering from nothing but shock and loss of blood.

"You won't take my arm off?" said Drury, suddenly visited with a new alarm. "I'm an actor—I can't—I won't—you can't do it without telling me—you——"

"No, no, no," said the doctor. "Now we've stopped the bleeding. But you must lie still or you might start it again."

"Shall I have the use of it?" The expressive eyes searched the doctor's face. "Sorry. But a stiff arm's as bad as no arm to me. Do your best . . . or I shall never play again. . . . Except in *Bitter Laurel*. . . . John, old man . . . funny, isn't it? Funny it's this arm. . . . Have to live on your play for the rest of my days . . . the only, only play. . . ."

"Good God!" cried Scales, involuntarily.

"Now, I must have this room clear," said the doctor, with authority. "Officer, get these people out and send me in those ambulance men."

"Come along," said the policeman. "And I'll take your statement now, sir——"

"Not me!" protested Walter Hopkins, "I can't leave Mr. Drury. I can't. Let me stay. I'll help. I'll do anything——"

"The best way you can help," said the doctor, not unkindly, but with determination, "is by giving me room to work. Now, please——"

Somehow they got Walter, struggling and hysterical, into the dressing-room across the passage. Here he sat, gathered together on the edge of a chair, starting at every sound from outside, while the constable interrogated and dismissed the two taxi-men. Then Scales found himself giving a statement, in the midst of which the doctor put his head in to say:

"I want some of you to stand by. It may be necessary to make a blood transfusion. We must get that arm stitched, but his pulse is very weak and I don't know how he'll stand it. I don't suppose any of you know which blood-group you belong to?"

"I'll do it!" cried Walter, eagerly. "Please, sir, let it be me! I'd give all the blood in my body for Mr. Drury. I've been with him fifteen years, Doctor——"

"Now, now," said the doctor.

"I'd sacrifice my life for Mr. Drury——"

"Yes, I daresay," said the doctor with a resigned look at the constable, "but there's no question of that. Where do people get these ideas? Out of the papers, I suppose. Nobody's being asked to sacrifice any lives. We only want a pint or so of blood—trifling affair for a healthy man. It won't make the slightest difference to you—do you good, I shouldn't wonder. My dear sir, don't excite yourself so much. I know you're willing—very naturally—but if you haven't the right kind of blood, you're no good to me."

"I'm very strong," said Walter, palpitating. "Never had a day's illness."

"It's nothing to do with your general health," said the doctor, a little impatiently. "It's a thing you're born with. I gather there is no relation of the patient's handy? . . . What? Wife, sister and son in Sussex—well, that's rather a long way off. I'll test the two ambulance men first, but unfortunately the patient isn't a universal recipient, so we may not get the right grouping first go-off. I'd like one or two others handy in case. Good thing I brought everything with me. Always do in an accident case. Never know what you may need, and time's everything."

He darted out, leaving behind him an atmosphere of mystery and haste. The policeman shook his head and pocketed his note-book.

"Dunno as blood-offerings is part of my dooty," he observed. "I did oughter get back to me beat. But I'll 'ave to give that there car the once-over and see what my chum 'as to say about it. I'll look in again when I done that, and if they wants me they'll know where to find me. Now, then, what do *you* want?"

"Press," said a man at the door, succinctly. "Somebody phoned to say Mr. Drury was badly hurt. That true? Very sorry to hear it. Ah! Good evening, Mr. Scales. This is all very distressing. I wonder, can you tell me . . . ?"

Scales found himself helplessly caught up in the wheels of the Press—giving an account of the accident—saying all the right things about Drury—what Drury had done for him—what Drury had done for the play—quoting Drury's words—expatiating on Drury's courage, presence of mind and thought for others—manufacturing a halo round Drury—mentioning the strange (and to the newspaper man, gratifying) coincidence that the arm actually wounded was the arm wounded in the play—hoping that Roger Brand, the understudy, would be able to carry on till Mr. Drury was sufficiently recovered to play again—feeling his hatred for Drury rise up in him like a flood with every word he uttered—and finally insisting, with a passion and emphasis that he could not explain to himself, on his own immense personal gratitude and friendship towards Drury and his desperate anxiety to see him restored to health. He felt as though, by saying this over and over again he might stifle something—something—some frightful thing within him that was asserting itself against his will. The reporter said that Mr. Scales had his deepest sympathy. . . .

''Mr.—ha, hum——'' said the doctor, popping his head in again.

''Excuse me,'' said Scales, quickly. He made for the door; but Walter was there before him, agitatedly offering his life-blood by the gallon. Scales thought he could see the pressman's ears prick up like a dog's. A blood-transfusion, of course, was always jam for a headline. But the doctor made short work of the reporter.

''No time for *you*,'' he said, brusquely, pulling Scales and Walter out and slamming the door. ''Yes—I want another test. Hope one of you's the right sort. If not,'' he added, with a sort of grim satisfaction, ''we'll try bleeding the tripe-hound. Learn him not to make a fuss.'' He led the way back into Drury's dressing-room where the big screen which usually shrouded the washstand had been pulled round to conceal the couch. A space had been cleared on the table, and a number of articles laid out upon it; bottles, pipettes, needles, a porcelain slab oddly marked and stained, and a small drum of the sort used for protecting sterilised instruments. Standing near the wash-basin, one of the ambulance men was boiling a saucepan on a gas-ring.

''Now then,'' said the doctor. He spoke in a low tone, perfectly clear, but calculated not to carry beyond the screen. ''Don't make more noise than you can help. I'll have to do it here—no gas-ring in the other room, and I don't want to leave the patient. Never mind—it won't take a minute to make the tests. I can do you both together. Here, you—I want this slab cleaned—no, never mind, here's a clean plate; that'll do—it needn't be surgically sterile.'' He wiped the plate carefully with a towel and set it on the table between the two men. Scales recognised the pattern of pink roses; it had often held sandwiches while he and Drury, endlessly talking, had hammered out new dialogue for *Bitter Laurel* over a quick lunch. "You understand"—the doctor looked from one to the other and addressed himself to Walter, as though feeling that the unfortunate man might burst unless some notice was taken of him soon—"that your blood—everybody's blood—belongs to one or other of four different groups." He opened the drum and picked out a needle. "There's no necessity to go into details; the point is that, for a transfusion to be successful, the donor's blood must combine in a particular way with the patient's. Now, this will only be a prick—you'll scarcely feel it." He took Walter by the ear and jabbed the needle into the lobe. "If the donor's blood belongs to an unsuitable group, it causes agglutination of the red cells, and the operation is worse than useless." He drew off a few drops of blood into a pipette. Walter watched and listened, seeming to understand very little, but soothed by the calm, professional voice. The doctor transferred two separate droplets of diluted blood to the plate, making a little ring about each with a grease pencil. "There is one type of person"—here he captured Scales and repeated the operation upon his ear with a fresh needle and pipette—"Group 4, we call them, who are universal donors; their blood suits anybody. Or, of course, if one of you belongs to the patient's own blood-group, that would do nicely. Unfortunately, he's a Group 3, and that's rather rare. So far, we've been unlucky." He placed two drops of Scales's blood on the other side of the plate, drawing a pencil-mark from edge to edge to separate the two pairs of specimens, set the plate neatly between the two donors, so that each stood guard over his own property, and turned again to Walter:

"Let's see, what's your name?"

As though in answer, there was a movement behind the screen. Something fell with a crash, and the ambulance man put out a scared face saying urgently: "Doctor!" At the same moment came Drury's voice: "Walter—tell Walter——!" trailing into silence. Walter and the doctor dived for the screen together, Scales catching Walter as he pushed past him. The second ambulance man put down what he was doing and ran to assist. There was a moment of bustle and expostulation, and the doctor said: "Come, now, give him a chance." Walter came back to his place at the table. His mouth looked as though he were going to cry.

"They won't let me see him. He asked for me."

"He mustn't exert himself, you know," said Scales, mechanically.

The patient was muttering to himself and the doctor seemed to be trying to quiet him. Scales and Walter Hopkins stood waiting helplessly, with the plate between them. Four little drops of blood—absurd, thought Scales, that they should be of so much importance, when you remembered that horrible welter in the street, on the couch. On the table stood a small wooden rack, containing ampoules. He read the labels: "Stock Serum No. II." "Stock Serum No. III"; the words conveyed nothing to him; he noticed, stupidly, that one of the little pink roses on the border of the plate had been smudged in the firing—that Walter's hands were trembling as he supported himself upon the table.

Then the doctor reappeared, whispering to the ambulance men: "Do try to keep him quiet." Walter looked anxiously at him. "All right, so far," said the doctor. "Now then, where were we? What did you say your name was?" He labelled the specimens on Walter's side of the plate with the initials "W.H."

"Mine's John Scales," said Scales. The doctor wrote down the initials of London's popular playwright as indifferently as though they had been those of a rate-collector and took from the rack the ampoule of Serum II. Breaking it, he added a little of the contents, first to a drop of the "J.S." blood and, next, to a drop of "W.H." blood, scribbling the figure II. beside each specimen. To each of the remaining drops he added, in the same way, a little of Serum III. Blood and serum met and mingled; to Scales, all four of the little red blotches looked exactly alike. He was disappointed; he had vaguely expected something more dramatic.

"It'll take a minute or two," said the doctor, gently

rocking the plate. "If the blood of either of you mixes with both sera without clumping the red corpuscles, then that donor is a universal donor, and will do. Or, if it clumps with Serum II and remains clear with Serum III, then the donor belongs to the patient's own blood group and will do excellently for him. But if it clumps with both sera or with Serum III only, then it will do for the patient in quite another sense." He set the plate down and began to fish in his pocket.

One of the ambulance men looked round the screen again. "I can't find his pulse," he announced helplessly, "and he's looking very queer." The doctor clicked his tongue in a worried way against his teeth and vanished. There were movements, and a clinking of glass.

Scales gazed down at the plate. Was there any difference to be seen? Was one of the little blotches on Walter's side beginning to curdle and separate into grains as though some one had sprinkled it with cayenne pepper? He was not sure. On his own side of the plate, the drops looked exactly alike. Again he read the labels; again he noted the pink rose that had been smudged in the firing—the pink rose—funny about the pink rose—but what was funny about it? Certainly, one of Walter's drops was beginning to look different. A hard ring was forming about its edge, and the tiny, peppery grains were growing darker and more distinct.

"He'll do now," said the doctor, returning, "but we don't want to lose any time. Let's hope——"

He bent over the plate again. It was the drop labelled III that had the queer, grainy look—was that the right way or the wrong way round? Scales could not remember. The doctor was examining the specimens closely, with the help of a pencil microscope. . . . Then he straightened his back with a small sigh of relief.

"Group 4," he announced; "we're all right now."

"Which of us?" thought Scales (though he was pretty sure of the answer). He was still obscurely puzzled by the pink rose.

"Yes," went on the doctor, "no sign of agglutination. I think we can risk that without a direct match-up against the patient's blood. It would take twenty minutes and we can't spare the time." He turned to Scales. "You're the man we want."

Walter gave an anguished cry.

"Not me?"

"Hush!" said the doctor authoritatively. "No, I'm afraid we can't let it be you. Now, you"—he turned to Scales again—"are a universal donor; very useful person to have about. Heart quite healthy, I suppose? Feels all right. You look fit enough, and thank goodness, you're not fat. Get your coat off, will you, and turn up your sleeve. Ah, yes. Nice stout-looking vein. Splendid. Now, you won't take any harm—you may feel a little faint perhaps, but you'll be right as rain in an hour or so."

"Yes," agreed Scales. He was still looking at the plate. The smudged rose was on his right. Surely it had always been on his right. Or had it started on his left? When? Before the blood-drops had been put on? Or after? How could it have altered its position? When the doctor was handling the plate? Or could Walter have caught the plate with his sleeve and swivelled it round when he made his mad rush for the screen? If so, was that before the specimens had been labelled? After, surely. No, before—*after* they were taken and *before* they were labelled. And that would mean . . .

The doctor was opening the drum again; taking out bandages, forceps, a glass flask. . . .

That would mean that his own blood and Walter's had changed places before the serum was added, and if so . . .

. . . scissors, towels, a kind of syringe. . . .

If there was the smallest doubt, one ought to draw attention to it and have the specimens tested again. But perhaps either of their bloods would have done equally well; in that case, the doctor would naturally give the preference to John Scales, rather than to poor Walter, shivering there like a leaf. Clump with II, clear with III;

clump with III, clear with II—he couldn't remember which way it went. . . .

"No, I'm sorry," repeated the doctor. He escorted Walter firmly to the door and came back. "Poor chap—he can't make out why his blood won't do. Hopeless, of course. Just as well give the man prussic acid at once."

. . . The pink rose. . . .

"Doctor——" began Scales.

And then, suddenly, Drury's voice came from behind the screen, speaking the line that had been written to be spoken with a harsh and ugly cynicism, but giving it as he had given it now on the stage for nearly a hundred performances:

"All right, all right, don't worry—I'll rest on my laurels."

The hated, heart-breaking voice—the professional actor's voice—sweet as sugar plums—liquid and mellow like an intoxicated flute.

Damn him! thought Scales, feeling the rubber band tighten above his elbow, I hope he dies. Never to hear that damned awful voice again. I'd give anything. I'd give . . .

He watched his arm swell and mottle red and blue under the pressure of the band. The doctor gave him an injection of something. Scales said nothing. He was thinking:

Give anything. I would give my life. I would give my blood. I have *only* to give my blood—and say nothing. The plate *was* turned round. . . . No, I don't know that. It's the doctor's business to make sure. . . . I can't speak now. . . . He'll wonder why I didn't speak before. . . . Author sacrifices blood to save benefactor. . . . Roses to right of him, roses to left of him . . . roses, roses all the way. . . . I will rest on my laurels.

The needle now—plump into the vein. His own blood flowing, rising in the glass flask . . . somebody bringing a bowl of warm water with a faint steam rising off it. . . .

. . . His life for his friend . . . right as rain in an hour or two . . . blood-brothers . . . the blood is the life . . . as well give him prussic acid at once . . . to poison a man with one's own blood . . . new idea for a murder . . .
MURDER. . . .

"Don't jerk about," said the doctor.

. . . and what a motive! . . . Murder to save one's artistic soul . . . who'd believe that? . . . and losing money by it . . . your money or your life . . . his life for his friend . . . his friend for his life . . . life or death, and not to know which one was giving . . . not *really* know . . . not know at all, *really* . . . too late now . . . absurd to say anything now . . . nobody *saw* the plate turned round . . . and who would ever imagine . . . ?

"That'll do," said the doctor. He loosened the rubber band, dabbed a pad of wool over the puncture and pulled out the needle, all, it seemed to Scales, in one movement. He plopped the flask into a little stand over the bowl of water and dressed the arm with iodine. "How do you feel? A trifle faint? Go and lie down in the other room for a minute or two."

Scales opened his mouth to speak, and was suddenly assailed by a queer, sick qualm. He plunged for the door. As he went, he saw the doctor carry the flask behind the screen.

Damn that reporter! He was still hanging round. Meat and drink to the papers, this kind of thing. Heroic sacrifice by grateful author. Good story. Better story still if the heroic author were to catch him by the arm, pour into his ear the unbelievable truth—were to say: "I hated him, I hated him, I tell you—I've poisoned him—my blood's poison—serpent's blood, dragon's blood——"

And what would the doctor say? If this really had gone wrong, would he suspect? What *could* he suspect? He hadn't seen the plate move. Nobody had. He might suspect himself of negligence, but he wouldn't be likely to shout *that* from the housetops. And he *had* been negligent— pompous, fat, chattering fool. Why didn't he mark the specimens earlier? Why didn't he match-up the blood with Drury's? Why did he need to chatter so much and explain things? Tell people how easy it was to murder a benefactor?

Scales wished he knew what was happening. Walter was hovering outside in the passage. Walter was jealous—he had looked on enviously, grudgingly, as Scales came stumbling in from the operation. If only Walter knew what Scales had been doing, he might well look. . . . It occurred to Scales that he had played a shabby trick on Walter—cheated him—Walter, who had wanted so much to sacrifice his right, his true, his life-giving blood. . . .

Twenty minutes . . . nearly half an hour. . . . How soon would they know whether it was all right or all wrong? "As well give him prussic acid," the doctor had said. That suggested something pretty drastic. Prussic acid was quick—you died as if struck.

Scales got up, pushed Walter and the pressman aside and crossed the passage. In Drury's room the screen had been pushed back. Scales, peeping through the door, could see Drury's face, white and glistening with sweat. The doctor bent over the patient, holding his wrist. He looked distressed—almost alarmed. Suddenly he turned, caught sight of Scales and came over to him. He seemed to take minutes to cross the room.

"I'm sorry," said the doctor. "I'm very much afraid— you did your best—we all did our best."

"No good?" Scales whispered back. His tongue and palate were like sawdust.

"One never can be certain with these things," said the doctor. "I'm very much afraid he's going." he paused and his eyes were faintly puzzled. "So much hœmorrhage," he muttered as though explaining the trouble to himself. "Shock—cardiac strain—excitable"—and, in a worried voice—"he complained almost at once of pain in the back." He added, with more assurance: "It's always a bit of a gamble, you see, when the operation is left so late— and sometimes there is a particular idiosyncrasy. I should have preferred a direct test; but it's not satisfactory if the patient dies while you wait to make sure."

With a wry smile he turned back to the couch, and Scales followed him. If Drury could have acted death as he was acting it now! . . . Scales could not rid himself of the notion that he *was* acting—that the shine upon the skin was grease-paint, and the rough, painful breathing, the

stereotyped stage gasp. If truth could be so stagey, then
the stage must be disconcertingly like truth.

Something sobbed at his elbow. Walter had crept into
the room, and this time the doctor made way for him.

"Oh, Mr. Drury!" said Walter.

Drury's blue lips moved. He opened his eyes: the di-
lated pupils made them look black and enormous.

"Where's Brand?"

The doctor turned interrogatively to the other two men.
"His son?"

"His understudy," whispered Scales. Walter said: "He'll
be here in a minute, Mr. Drury."

"They're waiting," said Drury. He drew a difficult
breath and spoke in his old voice:

"Brand! Fetch Brand! The curtain must go up!"

Garrick Drury's death was very "good theatre."

Nobody, thought Scales, could ever know. He could
never really know himself. Drury might have died, anyhow, of shock. Even if the blood had been right he might
have died. One couldn't be certain, now, that the blood
hadn't been right; it might have been all imagination about
the smudged pink rose. Or—one might be sure, deep in
one's own mind. But nobody could prove it. Or—could
the doctor? There would have to be an inquest, of course.
Would they make a post-mortem? Could they prove that
the blood was wrong? If so, the doctor had his ready
explanation—"particular idiosyncrasy" and lack of time
to make further tests. He *must* give that explanation, or
accuse himself of negligence.

Because nobody could prove that the plate had been
moved. Walter and the doctor had not seen it—if they had,
they would have spoken. Nor could it be proved that he,
Scales, had seen it—he was not even certain himself,
except in the hidden chambers of the heart. And he, who
lost so much by Drury's death—to suppose that *he* could
have seen and not spoken was fantastic. There are things
beyond the power even of a coroner to imagine or of a
coroner's jury to believe.

Ex-Supt. Cornish, C.I.D.

investigates dorothy l. sayers' crime

THEY WOULDN'T BELIEVE HIM!

I CAN IMAGINE many readers laying down *Blood Sacrifice* with the exclamation: "At last the perfect murder!"

It is certainly true that, on the facts as Miss Dorothy L. Sayers has given them, I could not hope to prove, either to a jury's satisfaction or to my own, that John Scales was guilty of the crime of murder. Neither could any other detective—not even, I think, that distinguished amateur, Lord Peter Wimsey. None of us could prove, indeed, that murder had been committed.

On the face of it, this does suggest that the conditions necessary to the perfect murder have been fulfilled. But I respectfully submit, addressing myself to that large and highly intelligent jury, the readers of Miss Sayers' detective stories, that a crime which Lord Peter cannot distinguish as such can be no crime.

The truth is, I am afraid, that for once Miss Sayers has been too clever. She has been so concerned to make the "crime" of John Scales detection-proof that she has failed to establish the fact of murder. That does not, of course, detract in any way from the interest of her story as a story or as a psychological study. But my criticism is not concerned with these things. Neither am I concerned with the verdict of the reader, sitting at home in his arm-chair. He may very well decide to take this narrative at its face value and to say that John Scales has committed the perfect murder.

But . . . transport the same reader from his arm-chair to the jury-box of a criminal court and place before him all the facts which are given by Miss Sayers in her story. Would he bring in a verdict of "Guilty" against John Scales, the prisoner in the dock?

Frankly, I don't think that he would. And that is why, examining this story purely from the angle of the detective, I say that this "perfect murder" is not murder at all.

I don't base this upon the fact that there is no evidence that Garrick Drury has been murdered. There are circumstances in which Drury might have died, after the blood transfusion, when there would be no more suggestion of foul play than in the present instance, but when murder would have been done. For instance, had Scales deliberately turned round the plate before the specimens were labelled, he would have been guilty of the crime of murder. Yet, at least at first, no suspicion would have been aroused.

That is not to say that Scales would then have committed the perfect murder. Unknown to him, the action might have been seen by someone who, unaware of its significance at the time, would yet realise it later on. Or, because Scales is not, as Miss Sayers has depicted him, a criminal type, he might be driven by remorse to confess his guilt. If he made such a confession, he would certainly be arrested.

But Scales did not touch the plate—unless he did so accidentally and unconsciously.

Let us examine what he did do. Let us think in terms, not of who is going to suspect him of murder and why, but of what would occur if he went to Scotland Yard and told the story of Garrick Drury's death as Miss Sayers has told it in *Blood Sacrifice*.

When a murder is committed, it may happen that a number of persons go to the police and accuse themselves

of the crime. Sometimes they tell highly circumstantial
stories. All such "confessions" are checked and again and
again it is found that the people making them have had
nothing—and could have had nothing—to do with the
killing. Their reasons for making these false statements are
of different kinds. Sometimes they suffer from delusions.
Sometimes they are actuated by a craving for notoriety—
they want to see their name in the newspapers; they want
to become a centre of public interest.

But what is behind these confessions matters less to us
at the moment than the way in which they are received.
They are not treated as in themselves a proof of guilt.
They are carefully investigated. They are carefully weighed
and analysed. They are checked against the known facts.

This would certainly be done in the case of any confession made by John Scales.

The first question that would suggest itself to me if I
were interviewing him is: Was the plate actually turned?
Apparently neither the doctor nor Walter saw anything
amiss and the doctor at least was a trained observer. If the
plate had been turned, of those three men the doctor is the
one most likely to have noticed it.

But the doctor didn't notice it—and John Scales did?
Here the important point to my mind is that Scales was not
sure. When he first wondered about the pink rose, there
was no more than a formless doubt, a suspicion that
something was not exactly as it should be, in his mind.
This doubt had hardly taken shape before the blood transfusion began. He was hardly sure even after Drury's death.
Not intellectually sure, only emotionally sure, "in the
hidden chambers of his heart."

Now, of the three men, if the doctor was the trained
observer, Scales was, I think, indubitably the most imagi-
native. If the transposition had actually taken place, I
should have expected the doctor to notice it. But I should
not be at all surprised by Scales imagining it.

This possibility becomes a probability when we consider
the emotional state in which Scales found himself at the

time, the conflict which had been going on in his mind throughout the run of his play and the shock of the accident.

I expect that Miss Sayers knows more about psychology than I do, but I am told by doctors who have studied the subject that most neuroses have their origin in mental conflict and emotional repressions. Scales had been repressing his instincts as a creative artist, trying to fight down his artistic conscience. He had been at war with himself. It is obvious from Miss Sayers' narrative that he was in a very "nervy" state. It would not be surprising, therefore, if he showed certain neurotic symptoms other than those which appear on the surface.

Now, I gather that one of the most common of neurotic symptoms is an over-anxiety, an uncertainty about things concerning which healthy people have no doubts. A neurotic will lock up automatically on retiring, then rise in the middle of the night because he is quite sure that he has left doors or windows open. He will put two letters into envelopes correctly—and then worry himself sick in case he has sent the wrong letter to the wrong person. And the more he thinks about it, the more he wonders what has happened, the more certain will he be that he has, in fact, made this mistake.

It seems to me that the doubts and suspicions concerning the plate which Miss Sayers describes as passing through Scales' mind follow this neurotic pattern.

But the fact remains that Drury did die—and die in a way which was quite consistent with the plate having been turned. His death, however, was consistent with other things as well. The doctor enumerates some of them. And I would draw particular attention to his words: "It's always a bit of a gamble, you see, when the operation is left so late. And sometimes there is a particular idiosyncrasy. I should have preferred a direct test; but it's not satisfactory if the patient dies while you wait to make sure."

The transfusion had already been delayed. Suppose that Scales had voiced his doubts—as he ought to have done—that involved new tests . . . a very real risk of the patient dying while the doctor was "making sure." That might have been just as effective a way of killing him as giving him the wrong blood. Had Scales suggested new tests—and Drury died while they were being made—would he not have accused himself in his own mind of murder in just the same way?

These considerations would, I think, make it impossible, even if Scales made a confession on the lines of Miss Sayers' story, to take any action against him. No detective would arrest him. If he were arrested and brought to trial, no jury would convict him.

Some detectives might even wonder whether he were not telling the story simply as a "stunt"—in order to interest the public in his play as originally written—and so pave the way for its production in place of the Garrick Drury version.

The case would be different had Scales actually *known* that the plate had been turned and the specimens of blood wrongly labelled. Then, just as surely as if he had turned the plate himself, he would have been guilty of murder. But he did not know and therefore, though we may consider that a degree of moral guilt attaches to him, I do not think that it would be possible to sustain a charge of murder, even if it were proven that Drury's death was due to the blood transfusion. So far we have only the suggestion that this was the case—no actual proof.

In the circumstances, I am afraid that I cannot admit this to be the perfect murder. True, I have not been able to discuss it with Lord Peter Wimsey. But if he could convince me that murder had, in fact, been committed, I feel that in doing so he would also show me how to lay the criminal by the heels. And then, again, it couldn't be the perfect murder.

But I enjoyed reading *Blood Sacrifice*.

Freeman Wills Crofts

THE PARCEL

I

STEWART HASLAR'S FACE was grim and his brow dark as he sat at the desk in his study gazing out of the window with unseeing eyes. For he had just taken a dreadful decision. He was going to murder his enemy, Henry Blunt.

For three years he had suffered a crescendo of torment because of Blunt. Now he could stand it no longer. He had reached the end of his tether. Everything that he held dear, everything that made life endurable, was threatened. While Blunt lived he would know neither peace nor safety. Blunt must die.

It was when he was turning into the road from the drive of his house one afternoon just three years ago that the blow had fallen. He had got out of his car to close the gate behind him and had met the old man. Something familiar about the long face and the close set eyes had stirred a chord of memory. In spite of himself he had stared. Blunt had stared too: an insolent leer which changed slowly to a look of amazed recognition. That had been the end of Haslar's peace of mind. But now he was going to get it back. Blunt would trouble him no longer.

It was an old story, that which had given Blunt his power, the story of a happening which Haslar had believed

was dead and buried in the past. It went back five and
thirty years, back to when he, Haslar, was a youth of
twenty and Blunt had just passed his thirty-first birthday.

Five and thirty years ago Haslar's name was John Matthews and he was a junior clerk in the head office of the
Scottish Counties Bank in Edinburgh. Henry Blunt was in
the same department, but in a more responsible job. Matthews was a good lad, well thought of by his superiors.
But Blunt was of a very different type. With charming
manners, he was wholly selfish and corrupt.

Owing to a run of bad luck at cards, Blunt's finances
were then at a very low ebb. Ruin indeed was staring him
in the face. He decided on a desperate remedy. In the bank
he was handling money all day. If only he had the help of
a junior clerk he believed he saw a way in which he could
transfer a large sum to his own pocket. He decided to use
Matthews and made overtures of friendship. Matthews was
flattered at the notice taken of him by the older man and
responded warmly. He did not know that Blunt merely
wanted a dupe.

Blunt had weighed up the young fellow's character ac-
curately. He didn't think he would be troubled by moral
scruples, but he feared he might refuse his help through
fear of consequences. Blunt was taking no risks. He decided to prepare the ground before sowing his seed. With
skill he introduced Matthews to his gambling friends and
with fair words got him to play. After that matters were
simple. In a few weeks Matthews' position was as desperate as his own.

The psychological moment had come. Blunt put up his
scheme. There was a chance of being caught, yes, but it
was so slight as to be negligible. But without the scheme
there would be certain ruin. Which would Matthews choose?

The result was a foregone conclusion. Matthews joined
in. The attempt was made. It failed. Matthews was taken
red-handed.

At the inquiry Matthews told the truth. But he had not
reckoned on the diabolical cunning of Blunt. Blunt had

prepared evidence to prove that Matthews and Matthews alone was guilty. He had intended to collar and hide his share of the money before producing the evidence. But events forced his hand. To save himself he had to forgo the profits and make his statement at once.

In the face of the evidence Matthews was found guilty and sentenced to eighteen months imprisonment. No official suspicion fell on Blunt, but it was privately believed he had been mixed up in the affair. Between the cold shouldering he received in consequence and his debts, Edinburgh grew too hot to hold him. He resigned his position and disappeared.

When Matthews was released he took the name of Haslar and at once shipped before the mast for Australia. It was a hard passage, but it was the making of him. When he reached Sydney he was a man.

For a few years he lived an adventurous life, meeting the ups and downs of fortune with a brave front. Then with borrowed capital he started a small fruit shop. From the first it was a success. He soon paid back what he owed and then put all his profits into the concern. One shop after another was opened, till at last he found himself the owner of a chain of stores, all doing well. For the first time he relaxed and went, so far as he could get the entry, into Melbourne society. There it was that he met his wife Gina, out on a holiday from England. They were married two months later. Gina did not, however, like Australia, and presently at her request he sold his business and returned with her to England, a comparatively wealthy man. She wanted to be near London, and he bought a house in a delightfully secluded position near Oxshott.

Here both of them enjoyed life as they had never done before. Haslar was pleasant and unassuming and soon grew popular with the neighbours. Gina had many friends in Town and rejoined the circles which she had left on her trip to Australia. The couple got on well together and had pleasant little week-end parties at their home. Everything was friendly and pleasant and secure. Haslar had never imagined anything so delightful.

Until Blunt came.

The meeting with Blunt gave Haslar a terrible shock. Instantly he saw that his security, his happiness, the security and happiness of his wife, everything in fact that was precious to him, was at the mercy of this evil-looking old man. Once a whisper of his history became known, his life in this charming English country was done. That he had fully paid for his crime would count not one iota. The righteous people among whom he lived would be defiled if they met a person who had been in prison. Both he and Gina would be cut to their faces. Life would be impossible.

And it would not meet the case to leave Oxshott for some other district, for some other country even. In these days of universal travel their identity could not long remain hidden. No, Blunt had both of them in his hands. If he chose, he could ruin them.

And Blunt was equally well aware of the fact. At that disastrous meeting, as soon as the man realised that the fine little estate from which Haslar had emerged was the latter's own property, Haslar had seen the realisation grow in his face; wonder, incredulity, assurance, exultation: it had been easy to follow the thoughts which passed through his mind. And they had soon been put into words. "Like coming home in my old age, this is," Blunt had said, adding with an evil leer that he would now have no further troubles, as he knew his old pal would see him comfortable for the rest of his time.

Haslar had acted promptly. "Get in," he had said, pointing to the car. "We can't stand indefinitely on the road. I'll run you wherever you want to go and we'll have a good chat on the way." Blunt had hesitated as if he would prefer to be taken to the house, but Haslar's determined manner had its effect and he climbed in. By a stroke of extraordinary luck no one had seen the meeting.

What might have been expected then took place. During the drive Blunt made his demand. They were old pals.

Haslar had gone up in the world while Blunt had gone down. For the sake of old times Haslar couldn't see his old pal go where he was now heading—to the Embankment seats or the fourpenny doss. Blunt didn't want much. He had no intention of sponging on his friend. A tiny cottage and a few shillings a week for food were all he asked.

Though Blunt had all gone to pieces and seemed suffering from senile decay, he was discreet enough in his conversation. He made no mention of the force which gave his somewhat maundering requests their compulsion. His only reference to it was veiled. "I hate talking of unpleasant things," he declared with his evil leer. "We're good pals, you and I. Let's not mention anything that's disagreeable."

Haslar indeed was surprised at the man's moderation, though as they talked he realised that the tiny cottage and few shillings a week were rather a figure of speech than an exact description of Blunt's demand. However, what the man asked for could be given him with a negligible outlay. Haslar promised he would see to it.

"But look here, Blunt," he went on, "this is an agreement for our mutual benefit. I'll do my part if and as long as you do yours, and no longer. I admit that the information you have is worth something to me and I'm willing to pay for it. I'll get you a small cottage and I'll make you an allowance so that you'll be comfortable on one condition— that you keep my secret. That means more than not telling it. It means that you must do nothing by which people might find it out. You mustn't ever come near Oxshott. If you want to see me, telephone, giving some other name. What name are you going under now?"

"Jamison. I reckon Blunt died in Edinburgh."

Haslar nodded. "So did Matthews. I'm now Haslar. Matthews is never to be mentioned. See?"

Blunt, who appeared overwhelmed by his good luck, swore by all his gods that he would keep his bargain. Haslar thought he meant it. All the same he rubbed in his point of view.

"I admit, Blunt, that you can injure me if you want to. You spill your story and this place gets too hot for me. I have to go. I don't want to, so I'll pay you as long as you hold your tongue. But talk: and see what else happens. I leave here and go abroad and settle down where I'm not known. My money goes with me and I remain comfortable. But your money stops. You hurt me slightly, but you destroy yourself."

In the end Haslar gave the man money to take a tiny cottage in a country backwater near Rickmansworth. He made an estimate of what it should cost him to live in reasonable comfort, including the daily visit of a woman to "do" for him. To this sum Haslar added ten per cent. Handing over the first instalment, he undertook to pay a similar amount on the first Monday of every month. On his part Blunt expressed himself as well satisfied and pledged himself as long as the payment continued never to approach or annoy Haslar.

It was bad, Haslar thought grimly when all this had been arranged, but it was not so bad as it might have been.

II

The arrangement between Haslar and Blunt worked well— for nearly a year. Every first Monday of the month Haslar folded ten £1 notes into a cheap envelope, bought each time specially for the purpose, and at precisely half-past one o'clock left a certain prearranged telephone booth in an unobtrusive position in Victoria Station. Blunt on these occasions was always waiting to telephone, and the envelope hidden in the red directory by the one was duly found by the other.

But before the year was up Haslar's fears were realised. Blunt made a fresh demand. One evening he rang up and asked in a surprisingly cultivated voice where they could meet. Haslar fixed a point on the Great North Road and picked the other up in his car.

Blunt was cynically complaisant as he explained his

desires. His manner suggested his certainty that he could have what he chose to ask. He was now so comfortable that he had grown bored. No longer faced with the need for work, time hung heavily on his hands. He wanted money to amuse himself. Not much—Haslar need not be alarmed. A very little would satisfy him. All he wished was to be able to go two or three times a week to the pictures, to take an occasional excursion on a bus, and to pay for his glass and stand his treat at the "Green Goat."

To Haslar the additional amount was negligible, but he was disturbed by the principle of the thing. He had never before been blackmailed, but all the tales he had read about it stressed the inevitable growth of the demands. What might be insignificant at first swelled eventually to an intolerable burden.

During ten miles of slow driving Haslar considered whether he should not now, at once, make his stand. Then very clearly he saw three things. The first was that he couldn't really make a stand. He could only bluff. If Blunt called his bluff, as he certainly would, he, Haslar, would be done for. He would have to give way. He would be worse off than he was now, for his weakness would have actually been demonstrated.

The second point was that Blunt's demands still remained moderate. In this Haslar could not but consider himself lucky.

The third was that the proposal was really to his, Haslar's advantage. The more fully occupied was Blunt's time, the less dangerous he would be. Contented, he would think of fewer grievances than if he were bored.

Haslar decided that when he had already gone so far, he would be a fool to fight on so small an issue. But if he were going to give way, he must do it with a good grace. Blunt must not be allowed to suppose there had been any trial of strength. He still further slackened speed and turned to the old man.

"I wasn't hesitating about the money," he said pleasantly. "I don't think what you want is unreasonable and I don't mind the small extra. But I was trying to put myself in your place. With all that time on my hands I should fish. What do you think of that? If you'd like it, I'll put up the outfit.''

Blunt was obliged, though always there was that ugly sardonic leer in his eye. He considered himself lucky that his relations with his old pal were so satisfactory. But he was not and never would be a fisherman. If he had the other two or three little things he had asked for, he would be content.

From this time the ten pounds a month became fourteen. The arrangement again worked well, this time for six months. Then Blunt telephoned for another interview. That telephone message was the beginning of Haslar's real trouble. The amount asked for again was small: an extra lump sum of £20 to go a motor trip to Cornwall. Haslar gave it, but said in half joke, whole earnest, that he was not made of money and that Blunt must not forget it would only pay him to help his friend up to a certain amount. Blunt had replied by asking what was £20 to a man of Haslar's wealth? and had stated in so many words that he was reckoning that to keep his present position would be worth many hundreds a year to his old pal.

Four months later came a further demand: that the £14 a month should be increased to £20. This time the request took more the form of an ultimatum than a prayer. Moreover Blunt was at less pains to justify it. He simply remarked carelessly that he found he couldn't do on the smaller sum.

At last, Haslar felt, it was time to make a stand. He made it—with the result he might have foreseen, with the result that in his secret mind he had foreseen. Blunt for the first time showed his hand. He swept the other's protestations aside. His demands, he declared, were over-moderate. The secret was worth vastly more than he was getting for it. He was surprised at Haslar being so unreasonable. Instead of asking a beggarly £250 a year he might have had a couple of thousand. And he would have a couple of thousand if there was any more trouble about it. He would have his £20 a month, or would Haslar rather make it £25?

Increasingly Haslar felt his bondage. Not that the payments incommoded him. They had still to mount a long way before he would really feel them. But now fear for the future was growing. Blunt was not exactly an old man. He might live for another twenty years. And if his demands went on increasing—as Haslar believed they were pretty certain to do—how would things end?

The realisation of his power now seemed to intoxicate Blunt. His demands grew more frequent and they were made with less regard for Haslar's feelings. Still worse, the old man ceased to show the scrupulous care to keep their meetings secret which he had done at first and which Haslar demanded. No harm had come through this, but it was disconcerting.

Blunt's first large request, not very politely worded, was for a fifty-guinea radio gramophone and a mass of records. The money again didn't much trouble Haslar, though he could no longer say he was not feeling the drain. But he was beginning to see that this state of things could not go on indefinitely. Sooner or later the man would demand something which he could not give, and then what would happen?

After an ineffectual demur, for which he despised himself, Haslar handed over the price of the gramophone. From that moment Blunt's demands increased in geometrical progression. The more he was given, the more he asked. Haslar was now parting with quite a considerable proportion of his income, and he began to envisage either cutting down his own expenses or drawing on his capital. The former he wished to avoid at all costs, as at once his wife would have begun to suspect something amiss. The latter he could do for a while without feeling it, but not for very long.

However, though Haslar was a good deal worried, he did not as yet consider his case really serious. So long as

Blunt's demands remained anywhere about their present scale, he could meet them and carry on. Any small retrenchment that might be necessary he could account for by saying that his shares had fallen.

But now at last, within this very week, a fresh blow had fallen, by far the heaviest of all. It left Haslar stunned and desperate.

Blunt had once again rung up and asked to see him. Haslar supposed it meant some fresh extortion, but always afraid that the old man might turn up at Oxshott, he had agreed to meet him at the rendezvous on the Great North Road. He had kept the appointment and had picked up Blunt in his car.

At once to his horror he saw that the man was drunk. He was not hopelessly incapacitated, but he was stupid and maudlin and spoke in a thick voice.

Here was a new and dreadful complication! To have his security at the mercy of an evil and selfish old man was bad enough: to have it in the keeping of a drunkard was a thousand times worse. In a certain stage of intoxication men of Blunt's type grew garrulous. Even if Blunt's intentions remained good, his actions were no longer dependable.

Haslar for the first time felt really up against it. His home, his wife, his friends, his pleasant circumstances, all were in danger. Never had his mode of life seemed so sweet as now that it was threatened. Security! That was what mattered. His security was gone. What would he not give to get it back!

And all this menacing misery and wretchedness would be the fate not only of himself but of his wife. Gina thought more of social prestige than he did. She would feel their disgrace the more. He had never told her he had been in jail. She would feel cheated. Not only would they be driven from their happy surroundings, but their own good comradeship would be gone. The more Haslar considered it, the more complete appeared the threatening ruin.

And all of it depended on the existence of one evil old man: a man guilty of the loathsome crime of blackmail: a man whose life was of no use or pleasure to himself or to anyone else: a man who was an encumbrance and a nuisance to all who knew him. It was not fair, Haslar thought bitterly. The happiness of two healthy and comparatively young people should not be in the power of this old sot.

And then the thought which for a long time had lurked in the recesses of Haslar's mind, forced itself to the front. It was not right that he and Gina should suffer. It was his job to see that Gina didn't suffer. Well, she needn't. She wouldn't—if Blunt were to die.

When first the dreadful idea leaped into his mind Haslar had crushed it out in horror. A murderer! No, not that! Anything rather than that! But the thought had returned. As often as he repulsed it, it came back. If Blunt were to die. . . .

It would be a hideous, a ghastly affair, Blunt's dying. But if it were over? Haslar could scarcely conceive what the relief would be like. Security once again! An escape from his troubles!

But could he pay the price?

Haslar played with the horrible thought. But all the time, though he didn't realise it, his mind was made up. Blunt was old, he must die soon in any case. He was infirm, his life was no pleasure to him. A painless end. And for Haslar, security!

Then Haslar told himself that his solution mightn't mean security at all. There was another side to the picture. He broke into a cold sweat as he thought of the end of so many who had tried to attain security in this way. The sudden appearance of large men with official manners; the request to accompany them; the magistrates; the weeks of waiting; the trial. And then—Haslar shuddered as he pictured what might follow. *That* was what had happened to so very many. Why should he escape?

Escape depended on the method employed. From that moment his thoughts became filled with the one idea—to find a plan. Was there any way in which he could bring about his release without fear of that awful result? Could murder be committed without paying the price?

He was convinced that it could—if only he could find the way.

III

Whatever Stewart Haslar undertook, he performed with system and efficiency. In considering any new enterprise, he began by defining in his mind the precise object he wished to obtain, so as not to dissipate his energies on side issues. Then he made sure that he had an accurate knowledge of all the circumstances of the case and the factors which might affect his results. Only when he was thus prepared did he begin to consider plans of action. But when at last he reached this stage he gave every detail the closest attention, and he never passed from a scheme until he was satisfied it was as flawless as it was possible to make it. Finally, like a general planning a campaign, he considered in turn all the things which might go wrong, thinking out the correct action to be taken in each such emergency.

In this latest and most dreadful effort of his life, the murder of Henry Blunt, he pursued the same method. Here also he began by asking himself what did he want to attain?

This at least was an easy question. He wanted two things. First, he wanted Blunt to be dead. He wanted his tongue to be silenced in the only way that was entirely and absolutely effective. Secondly, he wanted this so to happen that no connection between himself and the murder would ever be suspected.

The next point was not so simple. What were the precise circumstances of the case and the factors which might affect his results?

First, as to his past dealings with Blunt. As things were, how far, if at all, could skilled detectives connect him with his victim?

He considered the point with care, and the more he did so the better pleased he became. He had been more discreet even than he had supposed. There was nothing that anyone could get hold of. He had always insisted on his communications with the old man being carried out secretly. When telephoning, Blunt never gave his name, ringing off after making his call unless he recognised Haslar's voice. Moreover, he always spoke from a street booth, so that his identity should remain untraceable. Haslar then had never allowed himself to be seen talking to the old man. Provided no one else was close by, he had stopped his car momentarily on an open stretch of the Great North Road, to pick Blunt up and set him down again. Sitting back in the closed car, he, Haslar, could not have been recognized even if there had been anyone to recognise him. During the drive it was unlikely that either of them would be recognised, but even supposing someone had seen them from a passing car, it was impossible that *both* should have been recognised, for the simple reason that no one knew both of them.

Haslar had been insistent that neither party should write to the other, and the only further way in which they came in contact was during the monthly payments. But these meetings Haslar was satisfied could not under any circumstances become known. In the first place, nothing could be learnt from the banknotes. They were all of the denomination of one pound and could not be traced. Moreover, Haslar never drew the whole £10 or £14 or £20 from his bank at one time, but collected the notes gradually. It was clearly understood that Blunt should not pay them into a bank, but should keep them at his cottage and use them for his current expenses. Finally, the method of utilising the directory in the telephone booth at Victoria was secrecy itself. Not only was the booth in an inconspicuous place and neither man went to it if another user were present, but also they never spoke or communicated with one another in any visible way.

It seemed then to Haslar that so far as his dealings with

Blunt in the past were concerned he was absolutely safe. But could Blunt have done anything which might call attention to him, Haslar?

Haslar didn't see how he could. Even if in a moment of carelessness Blunt had spoken of his rich friend, he would never have been so mad as to mention Haslar's name. Blunt knew perfectly well that the revelation of the secret would end its cash value to himself, that to give it away would be to kill the goose that was laying the golden eggs. Nor had Blunt a photograph or any paper which might lead to an identification.

Haslar again had been very careful not to appear in any of the negotiations the other had carried on. Blunt had bought the house and engaged the daily help. Except in an advisatory capacity and in the secret passing of one pound banknotes via the Victoria telephone booth, Haslar had had no connection with any of Blunt's affairs.

So far everything seemed propitious, but there was one point which gave Haslar very furiously to think. Had Blunt written anywhere a statement of the truth, perhaps as a sort of guard against foul play?

This was a serious consideration. If such a document were in existence, to carry out his plan might be simply signing his own death warrant.

Haslar gave the point earnest thought and at last came to the conclusion that he need have no fears of such a contingency. Blunt would not be disposed to put his ugly secret in writing, lest the document should accidentally be found. For the truth would injure him in precisely the same way as it would Haslar. Besides losing Haslar's payments he also would personally suffer. If the circumstances under which he left Edinburgh became known, he also would be cold shouldered out of his little circle of acquaintances. He wouldn't get a daily help or a welcome to the bar of the "Green Goat." Revelation would not be so disastrous as in Haslar's case, but still it would be pretty unpleasant.

Further and more convincingly, the only motive Blunt could have had for making a written statement would be that Haslar had already considered—as a safeguard against foul play. But this safeguard would be inoperative unless Haslar knew of its existence. Now Blunt had never mentioned such a document. This silence seemed to Haslar conclusive proof that nothing of the kind existed.

Reviewing the whole circumstances Haslar felt convinced that nothing had taken place in the past which could possibly connect him with Blunt. So far, so good. But what of the future? Could a method of murder be devised which would leave him equally dissociated?

This wasn't an easy problem. The more Haslar thought over it, the more impossible it seemed. To murder Blunt involved becoming associated with him. The man would have to be met, personally. Haslar began to visualise picking him up on the Great North Road on the occasion of his next demand, and driving him to some lonely spot where the dreadful deed could be carried out and the body hidden. But this would be horribly dangerous. He, Haslar, might be seen; he might drop something traceable; the car might be observed; the wheel marks might be found. The whole thing indeed was bristling with risks. And if he, Haslar, were asked where he was at the time, what should he say? He could put up no alibi and the absence of one would be fatal.

But was he not going too fast? Had he considered all the circumstances of Blunt's life? To do so might give him the hint he required.

He had never seen the cottage bought with his money, but Blunt had shown him a photograph and described it. It was a small bungalow with three rooms, which Blunt used as kitchen, sitting-room and bedroom. It had electric light and water, but not gas. It stood in a field alongside a lane, surrounded by trees and with a tiny garden. It was very secluded and yet was within a hundred yards of a main road. Anything might happen there unknown to neighbours or passers by. A shot could even be fired with a fair chance of its being unheard.

Haslar considered paying the place a nocturnal visit. He

could park up the lane, knock at the door, hit Blunt over the head when he opened it, and drive back to Oxshott. He might manage that part of it all right. But he could never get secretly away from home. Gina would wake and miss him. The taking out of the car might be heard. . . . . No, that didn't seem a possibility.

His thoughts returned to Blunt. How did the old man spend his day? Here again his information was scanty. The picture he was able to build up from the few remarks Blunt had dropped was incomplete. And yet he knew so much that he thought he could fill in the blanks.

The first thing which took place in the morning was the arrival of Mrs. Parrott, the daily help. She prepared breakfast and when Blunt came down it was waiting for him. During the morning she cleaned the house, prepared Blunt's midday and evening meals and left them ready for him to heat, and washed up the previous day's dishes. She left about noon. Blunt smoked, read the paper, listened to his wireless, went down to the "Green Goat," pottered in the garden, or went for a bus ride as the humour took him. He warmed up his evening meal and retired to bed, where he read himself to sleep.

He was not, so Blunt had himself said, socially inclined. The "Green Goat" gave him all the companionship he wanted. Seldom or never did he offer hospitality to his neighbours.

It was beginning to look to Haslar as if the only way he could carry out his dreadful purpose was by an evening or night visit. By parking some distance away and walking to the cottage he might manage the actual murder safely enough. But he couldn't see how to overcome the difficulty of getting away from Oxshott. The more he thought of this, the more insuperable it seemed.

For days Haslar pondered his problem. Under all the special circumstances of Blunt's life, was there no way in which the man could be removed with secrecy? He could think of none.

And then one morning an idea suddenly flashed into his

mind. Was there not, after all, a very obvious way in which a man could be done to death with complete and absolute safety to the murderer?

Haslar's heart began to beat more rapidly. He sat stiffly forward, thinking intently. Yes, he believed there was such a way. Admittedly it would only work under certain circumstances, but in this case these circumstances obtained.

He went to his table and picked up a book a friend had lent him. It was a popular account of the application of science to detection and told of the use that is being made of such things as fingerprints, the microscopic examination of dust, ultra-violet photography, chemical analysis and criminal psychology. Eagerly he turned the pages. He thought he remembered the details of what he had read, but he must check himself. He found the paragraph.

Yes, he was right. The method he had in mind was very commonly used by criminals. It had been tested a good many times and was fool-proof. Of course he would not use it exactly as it had been used before. He would add his own modification, and it was this modification which would make the affair so absolutely safe.

Safe! By this plan he would be as secure as if he took no action at all. He could never be suspected. But even if he were suspected, even if Blunt left a statement of the secret, he was safe. If the police were convinced of his guilt he was safe. Never, under any circumstances, could they prove what he had done.

If Blunt's fate had been in doubt before, it was now sealed beyond yea or nay.

IV

To Stewart Haslar his idea as to how Henry Blunt might be safely murdered soon became an impersonal problem like those he had dealt with when managing his chain stores in Australia. Once its thrill and horror had worn off he set to work on it with his customary systematic thoroughness. He began by a general consideration of the details of the plan and then made out a list of the various things he had to do. In the main these consisted of three items: he had to buy or otherwise obtain certain materials; he had to make a certain piece of apparatus; and he had to ensure that Blunt would do nothing to upset the scheme.

The most risky part of the plan was the purchase of two chemicals. One was easy to obtain, the other might be more difficult. He decided to begin by buying these, as if he failed on this point he need proceed no further.

Carefully he worked out two disguises. He invariably appeared in tweed suits and Homburg hats. In a large establishment in the City he bought a ready-made suit of black and a cheap bowler, and in a second-hand clothes shop an old fawn waterproof and a cap. He did not wear glasses: therefore in a theatrical supplies shop he secured a couple of pairs of spectacles, both with plain glass, but one with dark rims and the other with light. From a piece of soft rubber insertion he cut two tiny pairs of differently shaped pads for his cheeks. All these, together with a brush and comb, he packed in a suitcase, which he placed in his car.

On the next convenient day he drove to Town, saying he would lunch at his club and do some shopping. He did both of these: lunched with acquaintances, who in case of need could certify that he was there, and bought a number of articles which he could, and afterwards did, show to his wife. But he did more.

In the car he put on the old waterproof, which he buttoned up round his neck. He took off his hat, brushed his hair back from front to rear in a way in which he never wore it, put on the cap and light spectacles, and slipped one pair of the rubber pads into his cheeks. Thus prepared, he set out.

On a previous occasion he had noted two or three large chemists' shops near Paddington and Liverpool Street respectively. Selecting one near Paddington, he parked in an adjoining street and walked round. As he had hoped, it was well filled with customers.

"I want a little potassium chlorate, please," he said, "to mix my own gargle."

"Potassium chlorate, yes," the assistant returned. "About what quantity?"

Haslar made a gesture indicating a package about 3 ins. X 2 ins. X 2 ins. "I don't know," he admitted. "I suppose about that size."

The assistant nodded and weighed out the white powder, handed over the little package, gave the change, said "Good afternoon" in the usually politely perfunctory manner, and turned to serve the next customer. Haslar walked quietly out. The first of his two principal fences was taken!

But this first was easy. The second, which he was now going to attempt, was the most difficult and dangerous item in his whole programme.

Parking outside Paddington, he went with his suitcase into the station lavatory and there changed to his black suit and bowler hat. He rebrushed his hair, put on the dark-rimmed spectacles and exchanged the pads in his cheeks. Then, slipping out while the attendant's back was turned, he regained the car and drove to Liverpool Street. Again he parked at a convenient distance and walked to another of the chemists.

"I want some picric acid for burns, please. The powder, if you have it. I like to make up my own ointment."

The assistant looked along his shelves. "We have it, in solution," he said, "and on gauze. I'm afraid we're out of the powder."

This was what Haslar had feared. "Then give me the gauze," he answered. "It'll do well enough."

He bought a roll of gauze which he didn't want, stored it in the car, parked in a new place and tried a second shop. He was prepared to go on visiting shop after shop for the entire afternoon, but to his delight, at this second establishment he got what he wanted. Without any formality or suggestion that his request was unusual, he obtained a small bottle of the brilliant yellow powder. As this seemed scarcely enough, he got a second bottle in another shop.

Six more purchases Haslar made before changing back to his normal garb. One was at still another chemist's. There he bought a dozen small test tubes, about 3 ins. long by ¼ in. diameter, and a dozen rubber "corks" to fit. The second was at a garage, where he got a small bottle of sulphuric acid, "to top up my batteries." The third purchase was a couple of sheets of brown paper and the fourth a ball of twine, both at small stationer's. The fifth and sixth were a steel pen and a cheap bottle of ink, each obtained at a different establishment.

Haslar breathed more freely as he reached home and locked his purchases in his safe. His great difficulty had been overcome. He had obtained everything that he required to complete his apparatus. A mixture of potassium chlorate and picric acid was inert and harmless, but this mixture in contact with sulphuric acid became a powerful explosive. He believed he had enough chemicals to blow half his house to pieces. And he had obtained them *secretly*. He was satisfied that his purchases had attracted no special attention and that under no circumstances could they be traced to him.

The next step was to make his apparatus. He was something of a carpenter and metal worker and he had a fair outfit of tools in his workshop. Wearing his rubber gloves, he took some ⅜ in. plywood and made himself a small flat box with outside dimensions of about the size of an ordinary novel. One of the long edges he made to open on a hinge and to fasten with a small hook and eye. He was careful not to use a plane or chisel, as he was aware that cuts made by these tools could be identified.

Before fastening on the sides he made and fixed the operating machinery. This consisted of a steel lever some 3 inches long, with one end bent round and chisel-pointed and mounted on a pivot at the opposite end so that the pointed end could swing from close to the lid to near the base. A strong spring coiled round the pivot kept the lever down in the latter position. Fastened to the base beneath the unpivoted end of the lever was a little block of oak to act as an anvil. The arrangement was that if the lever were lifted towards the lid and let go, it would immediately snap its chisel-point down on the anvil.

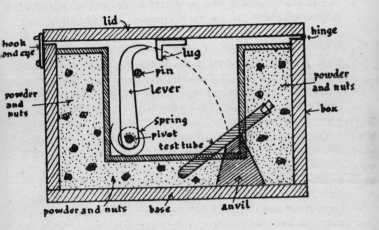

Through the sides Haslar bored a hole so that if the lever were raised towards the lid, a pin pushed through these holes would keep it in that position. To the lid he fixed a small projecting lug of steel, so that when the lid was closed it would come down in front of the raised lever and prevent it dropping. Above is reproduced Haslar's original diagrammatic sketch of the apparatus.

Haslar now conducted some tests. First he raised the lever, slipping in the pin to hold it in place. Filling a test tube with water, he corked it and fastened it in the box across the anvil. Then he closed the lid and withdrew the pin. Driven by the spring, the lever slipped forward till it was held by the lug projecting from the lid.

Then Haslar raised the lid. This freed the lever from the lug, it snapped down on the anvil, smashed the test tube into fragments, and spilled the water.

Haslar was delighted. He repeated the experiment several times. Not once did the raising of the lid fail to break the test tube.

Then he put in his chemicals. Having pinned up the lever, he put some sulphuric acid into a test tube and secured it firmly on the anvil. Next he mixed the white potassium chlorate with the yellow picric acid and filled it in, inserting also a number of old bolt nuts to act as projectiles. Thin wooden divisions kept the powder from getting out of place and preventing the lever from falling.

With the utmost care Haslar now closed the lid, hooked it fast and withdrew the pin. Then, taking a sheet of his brown paper, he parcelled up the box, finally tying it with a length of his twine.

One further operation remained, one to which he had given a lot of thought. He must address his parcel. But if it should happen that the parcel fell into the hands of the police, the writing must not be traceable to himself.

A box of sporting cartridges had reached him a few days earlier, of which the label had been addressed in block capitals. He had kept this label, and now, using his steel pen and the cheap ink, he set himself to copy the letters. Slowly he printed:

MR. SAMUEL JAMISON,
"GORSEFIELD,"
HENNIKER ROAD,
RICKMANSWORTH,
NR. LONDON.

Then he weighed the parcel and put on the required stamps.

Locking away the box in his safe, he proceeded to destroy all traces of what he had done. The remainder of the plywood, the sporting cartridge label, the brown paper, the ball of string and his rubber gloves he burnt, scattering the ashes. The test tubes, the bottles which had held the chemicals, the pen and ink and all the remaining nuts he threw into the nearest river. He was careful to see that nothing he had used in connection with the affair remained.

Nothing left to connect him with the affair! And if the bomb failed to go off, nothing about it traceable and no fingerprints anywhere upon it! So far he was absolutely safe!

The third part of his scheme only remained: to make sure that Blunt would open the box. This he had already arranged. At their last interview he had brought the conversation round to the question of the furnishing of Blunt's cottage and had learnt that the man was badly off for a clock. Any other small object would have done equally well, and Haslar would have gone on talking till one was mentioned. But a clock was entirely suitable.

"Oh," he said, "I have a clock that I don't want. It's a small thin one, little bigger than a watch in a stand, but beautifully made. I'll bring it along next time I see you. Or rather I'll send it, for I'm going to be away from home for a few weeks."

As he had anticipated, Blunt's greed blinded him to Haslar's departure from his usual refusal to use the post. Haslar described the sort of parcel he would send and he had no doubt Blunt would immediately open it.

And when he opened it! An explosion! Swift and painless death! Complete destruction of the parcel: perhaps complete destruction of the cottage—a fire might easily be started. And under no circumstances could anything be connected with him, Haslar!

Going again to lunch in Town, Haslar slipped the parcel into the large letter-box of a post office on his way to the club. It would be delivered that evening—when Blunt would be alone in the house.

That evening Haslar would be free.

V

Stewart Haslar had supposed that once he had posted his bomb, his personal interest in the death of Henry Blunt would be over. He soon found he had been mistaken. It was from that moment, when action was over, that his real anxiety began.

While he was lunching at his club things were not so bad. Several hours must elapse before anything could happen, and the conversation of his friends helped him to put the affair to some extent out of his mind. But as the afternoon dragged on and the time for the evening delivery at Rickmansworth drew near, he found he could no longer control his agitation.

On the way home he realised that his excited state of mind could not fail to attract his wife's attention. This, he saw even more clearly still, would be a disaster. Under no circumstances must she be allowed to suspect that he had anything special on his mind.

For a time he simply tried to force himself to forget what he had done. To some extent he succeeded, but in spite of all his efforts, he found he could not make his manner normal.

His longing to know what had happened grew till it became positive pain. Over and over again he pictured the probable scene. The postman's knock, Blunt opening the door, a word or two about the weather, Blunt returning to his sitting-room, unwrapping the paper, opening the lid. . . . And then, what? Was Blunt dead? Was the box and paper burnt? Was the cottage burnt? Had anyone yet discovered the affair? Haslar, his hands shaking, grew more and more upset. For the first time in his life he understood the urge which tends to drive a murderer back to the scene of his crime.

He wondered how he could find out what really was taking place, then sweated in horror that such a thought should have come to him. He couldn't find out. Above all things, he mustn't try. He could read the papers he was accustomed to read, and those only. If there was nothing about the affair in them he would have to remain in ignorance.

But curse it all, he told himself, he *must* know. He must know if he was safe. Up till now he had never for a moment doubted that the explosion would kill Blunt instantaneously. But now fears assailed him. He began to picture the man in a hospital—recovering. *And knowing who sent the parcel.*

Haslar stopped the car. He was sweating and trembling. This would never do. He had carried out a perfect plan and he must not wreck it now by lack of self-control. Then he saw that it was all very well to think such thoughts. The thing was stronger than he was. His anxiety was insupportable and he could not hide it.

As he sat, thinking, he suddenly saw his way. He was still within the limits of Town and he stopped at the first grocer's he came to and bought a package of common salt. With this he thought he could prevent any suspicion arising.

Arrived at his home, he garaged the car and went to his room. There with the salt he prepared himself an emetic. Putting it beside him, he lay down on his bed.

Gina, he knew, had been going out in the afternoon and the absence of her car told him that she had not yet returned. He lay waiting. Then at last he heard the car. At once he drank the salt and water, washed the glass and left it in its place, and lay down again. When shortly afterwards Gina came upstairs, he was just being violently sick.

She was upset about it, for such an attack was unusual.

"It's all right," he assured her. "Must have had something that disagreed with me for lunch. Been feeling seedy all afternoon. I'll be better now."

She wanted to send for the doctor, but this he scouted. Then she insisted on his lying on his bed and not going down for dinner. He protested, but with secret satisfaction gave way. The lowering effect of the sickness had reduced his nervousness so that he really felt practically normal. He was sure his manner was unsuspicious.

Next morning he found it a matter of extreme difficulty to avoid rushing down the drive and snatching the paper from the newsboy. But he managed to restrain himself. He did not open it till his normal time, and then he forced himself to make his usual comments on the outstanding news before slowly turning away from the centre pages.

He was on tenterhooks as he searched the sheets. If anything had gone wrong with his scheme and Blunt had escaped, there would be no paragraph. If the plan had succeeded perfectly so that only accident was suspected, there might be no paragraph. Only would a notice be certain if a partial success had taken place: if Blunt had died, but under suspicion of foul play.

Then on an early page Haslar saw a short paragraph. It was headed "FATAL EXPLOSION," and read: "Through an explosion in his cottage last evening, Mr. Samuel Jamison, Henniker Road, Rickmansworth, lost his life. The report was heard by a passer-by who entered and found Jamison lying in his wrecked sitting-room. The cause of the explosion is unknown."

Haslar had now almost as much trouble in hiding his relief as before he had had in covering his anxiety. Cause unknown! This was better than anything he could have hoped for. He had a convenient fit of coughing and by the time it was over he felt himself once again under control.

All that day he oscillated between exultation and fear. To steady his nerves he went for a long tramp. But he was careful to be back when the evening paper arrived. The only fresh news was that the inquest was to be held that afternoon.

Another night of suspense and another period of stress in the morning and Haslar was once again turning the sheets of the paper. This time he had less difficulty in finding what he was looking for. Almost at once his eye caught ominous headlines. With a sinking feeling he devoured the report, which was unusually detailed. It read:

"THE RICKMANSWORTH FATALITY
STARTLING DEVELOPMENT

"At an inquest yesterday afternoon at Rickmansworth on the body of Samuel Jamison, Gorsefield, Henniker Road, who died as the result of an explosion in his cottage on the previous evening, the possibility of foul play was suggested.

"James Richardson said that about six o'clock when walking close to the deceased's bungalow, he heard an explosion and saw a window blown out. He climbed in and found the deceased lying dead on the floor. The room was wrecked and bore traces of yellow powder. Witness telephoned for the police.

"Mrs. Martha Parrott, who worked for the deceased, deposed that he was between sixty and seventy and had lived in the neighbourhood for some three years. He was solitary in his habits and appeared to have no relatives. She was positive there was nothing in the house to account for the explosion.

"Thomas Kent, postman, said that on his evening delivery just before the explosion he had handed deceased a small brown-paper parcel. It was addressed in block letters and had a London postmark. He had remarked it particularly, as Mr. Jamison's correspondence was so small.

"Sergeant Allsopp stated that the police were of opinion that the explosive was contained in the parcel, which would suggest the possibility of foul play. The proceedings were adjourned for the police to make inquiries."

With a supreme effort Haslar recalled himself to his surroundings. Gina was speaking of the following week-end and he forced himself to discuss with her the arrangements they would make for the entertainment of their guests. But after breakfast he retired to the solitude of his study and gave himself over to considering the situation.

It really was more satisfactory than it had seemed at first sight. After all, though this idea of the police was unfortunate, he had expected it. An explosion of the kind could not possibly be considered an accident unless there were known explosives in the house. There were none at Blunt's. Moreover, that cursed picric acid had made yellow stains. For all Haslar knew to the contrary those stains could be analysed and shown to be picric. This would prove the explosive had been sent to the house, and the parcel was the obvious way. No, it was inherent in the scheme that the police should suspect foul play.

But that would do him, Haslar, no harm. It was one

thing to suspect the parcel was a bomb: it was quite another to find the sender. There was nothing by which the police could discover that "Jamison" was the Blunt who had disappeared from Edinburgh—he had never been through their hands. Therefore even if they knew that he, Haslar, was Matthews—which was extraordinarily unlikely—it would get them no further. Besides, even if a miracle happened and the police did suspect him, they couldn't prove anything. They couldn't connect him with the purchase of the chemicals or the construction of the bomb or show that he posted the parcel.

No, it was a dreadfully anxious time, of course, but he was safe. Haslar repeated the words over and over again to himself. He was safe! He was safe! No matter what the police tried to do, he was safe.

Ex-Supt. Cornish, C.I.D.

investigates freeman wills crofts' crime

THE MOTIVE
SHOWS THE MAN

IN MANY UNSOLVED murder mysteries, the true difficulty which has confronted the police is not that of finding the criminal, or the person who is most probably the criminal, but that of proving his guilt in a way which will convince a jury.

Mr. Freeman Wills Crofts, however, presents the Hertfordshire police with a problem in which, at the point where his narrative ends, there appears to be nothing to point to the identity of the murderer.

I congratulate Mr. Crofts on his ingenuity in devising what must, at first reading, appear to the ordinary man or woman to be a "perfect murder." But, in real life, although the detectives in charge of the case would certainly find it difficult, I am by no means convinced that they would be forced to abandon it as insoluble.

They begin their investigation with the knowledge of certain facts which suggests a definite line of inquiry.

The crime was committed by a person with some knowledge of chemistry.

That person had some very strong motive, which was not robbery, and must be explained by the relations between the murder and his victim. Therefore, the criminal was known to, or connected with, the dead man in some way. ›

The parcel had been posted in London. Possibly, though that was not stated in the report of the inquest, the postal district had been noted by the postman. Or the postmark might be reconstructed from the fragments of the box which remained.

These facts seem little enough, but they would be supplemented very quickly.

Suppose that I were the detective in charge of the case. I should first examine the body and note any scars or other distinguishing marks. Then I should go through the clothing very carefully. Probably I should first find nothing that was helpful. But either in his pockets, or somewhere in the cottage, which would be thoroughly searched, I should discover the balance of his last monthly payment.

This was at least £20 pounds and it had been made only a few days previously. The reason Haslar gave for sending the parcel by post had been that he was to be away for a few weeks. The conditions of the monthly rendezvous meant that this could only happen just after a payment. Otherwise, the blackmailer would immediately have demanded his next month's money.

I should therefore find quite a substantial sum in £1 notes—perhaps £15, almost certainly not less than £10. And I should learn, on making inquiries, that Jamison had no bank account, that he did no work, and that he paid for everything he bought in cash, but never with notes of a higher denomination than £1. Further, I would ascertain that he had had more money towards the end of his residence at Rickmansworth than at the beginning of it, and that he had recently purchased an expensive radiogram and an assortment of records, again paying in £1 notes.

Trying to discover the source of his income, I should find myself up against a blank wall. But the mystery surrounding this would itself tell me something. There had been something shady about Jamison and his money.

One of my main sources of information would naturally

be Mrs. Parrott. She would tell me all that she knew, and a good deal that she had guessed. Her guesses would probably be wrong, but if Jamison had had any visitors, or if there was any relative or friend with whom he was in touch, she might be able to assist me considerably. True, I would not get a line on Haslar in this way, because of the precautions he had taken, but I might uncover the secret of Jamison's identity, which would lead me, in the end, to Haslar.

In any case, I should discover that Jamison had gone up to town on the first Monday of each month. I might even learn that, on at least some of these occasions, he had gone to Victoria. And I should be inclined to associate these journeys to London with his source of income.

The possibility of blackmail would be present in my mind. But I would not rule out other forms of crime. In any case it would be useful to know if Jamison had a criminal record. I would have his fingerprints taken and sent to Scotland Yard.

Haslar had thought there was nothing by which Jamison could be identified by the police as Blunt, the Edinburgh bank clerk—he had never been through their hands. But Blunt had been down and out when he crossed Haslar's path for the second time, and he had already been a crook, though he had avoided arrest, when he was in Edinburgh. During the thirty-five years' interval between these two events, had he gone straight? It was hardly likely. And almost certainly, if he had been on the wrong side of the law, he had been found out and been punished.

In the cottage I should have looked carefully for any letters, diaries, notebooks—any scrap of writing that might help to throw light on Jamison's past. But even if I found nothing, even if Mrs. Parrott could tell me nothing, it is a hundred to one that, Jamison's character being what it was, his fingerprints would be in the records. And though he told Haslar that he had changed his name on leaving Edinburgh, he might have been convicted as Blunt, or his identity with Blunt might have been established.

If this were so, it would be only a matter of time before inquiries by the Edinburgh police would bring to light the story of Matthews and suggest a possible motive for the murder.

I should still have to trace Matthews and might find that a very difficult and laborious business. But was there no one—no relative or friend—who knew that Matthews had changed his name to Haslar and gone out to Australia? Had no one, before that meeting with Blunt, ever recognised him as Matthews?

It is at least possible that, even with no fortunate chance to help me, I should be able, in the end, to lay bare the whole story of Matthews' struggle and success as Haslar in Australia, and of his return to England.

But there might easily be a short cut to this—the fortunate chance to which I referred above.

I have so far assumed that, in my search of the cottage, I found no scrap of writing that could throw light on my problem. I have also ignored the possibility of Jamison having been in communication with some relative or friend. Let us say now, definitely, there there was no relative with whom he had been in touch—no one, except Haslar, who knew that Jamison and Blunt were one and the same. There was still one person with whom Jamison had communicated—Haslar himself. In a pocket diary, or on a scrap of paper, I might find Haslar's address, or—what would be just as good and perhaps more likely, his telephone number.

It was always by telephone that Jamison made appointments with Haslar. He would probably remember the number after asking for it once or twice, but he would naturally note it somewhere the first time he used it. And while Haslar had a powerful motive for destroying everything that might link him in any way with Jamison, the latter had no such motive where Haslar was concerned.

When planning the murder, Haslar wondered if, perhaps, the blackmailer had committed his secret to writing. He dismissed the idea because the document might be found by a third party, in which case Jamison would himself have been in an unpleasant position. But a telephone number would give nothing away while Jamison still lived—though it might take on significance after his murder.

That was a vital point Haslar had overlooked.

He had also failed to reckon with another possibility. After he had handed Jamison the money to buy his radiogram, we are told that the old man's demands increased till Haslar was parting with quite a considerable proportion of his income. It is not clear whether the monthly payments were larger or whether there were other and more frequent demands for lump sums, but, beyond the fact that he was drinking more heavily, there is no indication of any change in Jamison's mode of life, nor are we told of any other large purchase which he made.

Having regard to all the circumstances, it is possible that Jamison was accumulating a reserve. After all, Haslar, though his junior, was no longer young. He might die. He might be killed in an accident. And with his death Jamison would once more be thrown on his own resources.

The blackmailer would not keep this reserve in his cottage. He would know that this was too dangerous. He had no local bank account, Haslar was probably correct in thinking that he had no bank account at all. Banks usually want references from a new customer. But there was no reason why he should not rent a strongbox in a safe deposit. There he could place, not only his reserve, but also any papers he wanted to keep in readiness for possible emergencies.

He need not have written any account of his dealings with Haslar. But suppose he had obtained, from the offices of an Edinburgh newspaper, a photographic copy of the report of Matthews' trial and had placed that in the safe deposit. It might be useful to show to Haslar one day, if he was inclined to kick against the pricks.

Say, then, that in my search of the cottage, I found, in the pocket of an old suit, a scrap of paper with a telephone number. No name might be attached to it, but I would soon ascertain whose number it was and, as a matter of routine, Haslar would be interviewed, and asked if he had known Jamison.

Haslar has been living under an almost intolerable strain ever since his meeting with the blackmailer. His conduct at the time of the murder and immediately afterwards was that of a man who was near to breaking-point. Now, when he has got over his panic, when he thinks he is safe, he is suddenly confronted with a police officer, and realises that, in some way, a connection between himself and Jamison has been established.

He does not know exactly what the detectives have discovered. He probably thinks their researches are much further advanced than, in fact, they are. His reaction will almost inevitably arouse suspicion. He will betray agitation. Perhaps he will bluster.

But he will deny all knowledge of Jamison, and his family and servants, when questioned, will do the same.

Suppose that I have decided that this clue may be important and have gone to Oxshott myself. I have noted Haslar's agitation. Naturally, I accept what he says. But I tell him that I am anxious to learn who Jamison actually was—that I have reason to suspect that this wasn't his real name. Would Mr. Haslar come with me and see if he could identify the body?

This might conceivably result in the murderer going to pieces altogether, and the whole truth coming out. In any case, by the time that our next interview had finished, Haslar would again be in a state of panic, and I would know that he had something to conceal.

Now if, in addition to the telephone number, I had found a safe deposit key, and the strongbox contained particulars of Matthews' trial in addition to securities, I would be able to guess what the connection between Haslar and Jamison was, and have a very good idea of the motive of the murder.

I should therefore have some very interesting questions

to put to Haslar at our next interview. The answers would probably be lies, but that wouldn't matter. He would be definitely under suspicion, and police officers would be detailed to watch his movements. If he attempted to leave the country, he would be detained—and I would know definitely that he was the man I wanted.

Meantime, every fragment that I had been able to pick up of the box which had contained the explosive and the wrappings in which it had arrived, would have been examined by experts. However small these fragments, they might have a story to tell, and nothing of this would escape the trained scientists who did this part of the work.

There might be some link here that could be established, in spite of all his precautions, between Haslar and the crime. I know that "he was careful to see that nothing he had used in connection with the affair remained." Robinson, of the Charing Cross trunk crime, was careful to see that no trace was left in his office of the murder of Mrs. Bonati, but after all his labour a bloodstained match and a hairpin were found in his wastepaper basket and helped to hang him.

Haslar's workshop would certainly be searched. It might yield nothing. But even then it would still be possible that someone, himself unseen, had watched the murderer at his work of destroying the evidence and would come forward as soon as he realised that the incident which had puzzled him had a bearing on the crime.

Am I making things too easy for the detective by imagining all these possibilities? Even if none of my "fortunate chances" materialised, once it had been established that Jamison was really Blunt, ordinary police routine work would establish the connection with Matthews and trace the latter. It would take longer, but it would be done in the end.

But if Jamison had led a life of crime, there might be others besides Matthews who had a possible motive for desiring his death. They would all be traced and eliminated one by one. And with every suspect who satisfied the detectives that he could have had nothing to do with the crime, the unmasking of the real murderer would be brought a step nearer.

I have mentioned certain contingencies, however, in order to show that Haslar, when he thought he was planning the perfect murder, was very far indeed from doing so. There were too many unknown factors in Jamison's life for the crime to be safe.

And even now I have left out of account what was, perhaps, the most immediate danger of all—and one which Haslar must have realised, if he had thought intelligently about his problem at all.

He decided to kill Jamison, not because he was blackmailing him, but because he was a drunkard. ''In a certain stage of intoxication men of Blunt's type grew garrulous. Even if Blunt's intentions remained good, his action were no longer dependable.''

So the blackmailer was killed to prevent him blurting out his secret while under the influence of alcohol. But how could Haslar be sure that he hadn't done so already? How many times had he been drunk before Haslar saw him in that condition? How many times was he drunk between that incident and the murder?

Possibly he had thrown out hints, even mentioned names. No one might have paid any attention to what he said at the time, dismissing it as the maudlin raving of an inebriate. But the moment he was murdered it would assume a new and sinister significance. It would be recalled and repeated.

Those disguises, too, which Haslar put on to make his purchases, might actually have fixed the transactions in the minds of the chemists at whose shops he called. Nothing is so conspicuous as a disguise, when assumed by a person who is not accustomed to masquerade. And his altered appearance extended to a few details only—height, build and age were not affected.

The evidence of the shopkeepers, therefore, while it would not, of itself, lead to Haslar, would do nothing to destroy the case against him. On the contrary, it would add another link to the chain.

But suppose that, in the end, when every clue had been followed up, that chain was still one link short. I might know Haslar's history, I might be able to prove the blackmail and consequently the motive, but still be unable to show, to the satisfaction of a jury, that it was actually this man, and no other, who had prepared and posted the fatal parcel.

Even then I might still get him. I would go to him with the statements which he had made to me in the course of the investigation. I might be able to point to discrepancies between those he had made at different dates. I would undoubtedly be able to show that, in certain particulars, the story he had told me was at variance with facts which I had ascertained elsewhere. I would ask him for an explanation.

I think I would get the truth. I think that the long nervous strain which he had undergone would culminate, this his will would snap and that he would confess. The customary warning would make no difference—he would not realise that he was fastening the rope round his own neck. He would think it was there already.

But suppose he didn't confess. I might still arrest him, knowing that the news of the arrest might bring in fresh information.

One of my first facts was that the murderer had some knowledge of chemistry. So far I have been unable to discover that Haslar has such knowledge. But after his arrest his friend comes forward, as a matter of public duty, and says: "A week or two before the murder I lent Haslar this book. As you will see, it contains a description of the method which was followed in making the bomb that killed Jamison."

Another link in the chain.

Then, it may be, someone appears who has seen Haslar post the parcel. He remembers the incident and the date because it struck him afterwards, reading the newspaper reports, that it must have been just such a parcel which had caused Jamison's death. But he did not think it was *the* parcel until he saw Haslar's photograph in the newspaper.

And so the case is completed, goes before judge and jury. I think there is little doubt what the verdict will be.